LONG EXPOSURE

ARTS AND LOVERS

RACHEL CAREY

Cover design by Dar Albert at Wicked Smart Designs

Published by Oliver-Heber Books

0 9 8 7 6 5 4 3 2 1

PART ONE

1

KRISTIE'S PARTY, 2006

SARAH HAD ONLY BEEN asleep for a few minutes when she was awoken by a soft knock on the door. She could barely hear it over the distant bass music from the party. Clearly, Kristie was in charge of the iPod, because Kristie liked to play things at top volume, and her musical preference right now was for mystical trip-hop by sad Brits. Sarah could picture her roommate Kristie vividly, drifting around the living room in the silvery tank top she reserved for parties, her long black hair swaying as she topped off people's drinks from the monogrammed cocktail shaker that she had just received for her twenty-first birthday.

Sarah felt too tired for any of it, even though tonight's festivities had started out as a celebration in her honor. Officially, her roommates were hosting this soiree to toast the fact that, after almost two years, Sarah had finally broken up with her toxic boyfriend, Ivan. But no party at their apartment, even one celebrating Sarah's romantic liberation, felt like her own for very long. The pretty people had arrived, the hook-ups had started, and Sarah was alone in bed by midnight.

"Yes?" Sarah said as she awkwardly pushed herself up onto her elbows, her tank top falling slightly askew.

Ren stuck his head in the door, which was how Sarah discovered that she'd forgotten to lock it. The seductive bassline became temporarily louder. "Hey, Sarah?"

"Ren?" She blinked in the half-darkness. Her room was lit only by the thin slash of light from the doorway, some glow-in-the-dark stars, and her Miyazaki-themed nightlight. She had lived here for most of her time at university, first with her high school friend Ellen and now with her classmates Anya and Kristie, and her décor remained largely the same as it had when she arrived: a black and white poster of Paris, some CDs stacked in a pile, and a couple of film cameras lined up atop her dresser, their lenses flickering like cat eyes.

Ren slipped into the room. "Can we talk for a second?" His voice was unexpectedly tentative.

"Sure," she said warily.

She knew Rene Durand pretty well, so she didn't feel especially nervous that there was a young man in her bedroom. A couple of years ago, Sarah would have been thrilled to find him there. Ren was startlingly handsome. He had beautiful pale green eyes that he had inherited from his mother, an Afghani professor who taught feminist history at the nearby University of Montreal, and thick dark hair from his father, a handsome French-Tunisian man who taught philosophy at McGill. Ren's cheekbones had been gifted by some vengeful god who had it in for the young women of Montreal. In the half-light, his beauty looked a little unreal, like he was an elven prince from a fairy tale who had made a quick stop at the Levi's store.

"Were you sleeping?" he asked, closing the door behind him.

"Not really. What's up?"

She had first met Ren during their freshman year at McGill in an Intro to Photography class, and she had immediately become enamored with him, not only for his good looks but for his capacity to hold interesting debates about lens choice and the political underpinnings of documentary photography. Sarah had been a novice photographer, Ren a budding journalist, and their discussions had often continued long after class as they leaned against a wall and argued the merits of Stanley Kubrick's street photography or the CBC's coverage of the Iraq War. His recommendations for books and movies were solid, if sometimes irritatingly pretentious, and he seemed to enjoy taking polar opposite positions from hers on topics ranging from citizen journalism to the films of Gaspar Noé.

Sarah could admit that she had swooned over him for a good three months; he was exactly the sort of man that she had dreamed of meeting at university but didn't believe actually existed. It was like someone had ripped him from the pages of an existentialist novel, shoved a copy of Bukowski in his hands, and dropped him in front of earnest young women, custom-built to break their hearts.

Then a little over two years ago, as a gift to herself on her nineteenth birthday, Sarah had finally roused her courage to invite him to her birthday party. Ren had arrived with a bottle of cheap wine, chatted with her for twenty minutes about their philosophies of love, and then zeroed in on her willowy, blond friend Anya, flirting with Anya for the rest of the night and going home with her as soon as the wine ran out. Sarah had been devastated but unsurprised; she had always suspected that two people with unearthly cheekbones would gravitate inevitably toward each other's superior genetics. Sarah herself had a chesty figure that she feared made her look heavier than she was, with a round-as-a-moon face and ash-blond curly hair. She wasn't unattractive, but she had the kind of comfortable cuteness that men seemed to associate with girls who worked behind the counter at ice cream shops. Compared to Anya's ethereal beauty, Sarah felt thoroughly put in her place.

Somehow, Ren had insinuated his way into Sarah's friend group after that, seeing Anya for a few weeks and then hooking up with Sarah's friend Kristie when Anya went home for the holiday break. There didn't seem to be any hard feelings among the women involved when Ren shifted his attention; part of Ren's magic was that he found ways to irritate his romantic partners enough so that they were glad to be rid of him when he moved on. By the time Ren was sleeping with her high school friend Ellen a few months later, Sarah was deep into her fraught relationship with Ivan, a Polish international student with a history of depression, and she had learned to tolerate Ren as an intermittently amusing lothario who was best appreciated from the other end of the sofa. He was fun to debate about astrophysics or the problematic love lives of Byron or Rilke. But Ren was like a black hole; you could orbit him safely from a distance, but it wasn't wise to get pulled into his gravitational well of moody song quotes and indirect flattery.

She watched him now as he picked his way across her dark bedroom. "We're going to have to revoke Kristie's right to choose the music if she keeps playing her three favorite albums in rotation. You know that, right?" Ren had a tendency to announce his preferences as if they should become universal rules.

"Okay?" Sarah blinked in the darkness as he moved closer.

When he got to her bed, he turned and sat across it sideways with his back against the wall and his long legs stretched out so that Sarah had to bend her knees slightly to make room for him.

"So, question for you," he said briskly, "you know how you hate me?"

"I don't hate you. I tolerate you," Sarah replied in the world-weary voice that she had adopted with him years ago to cover her hurt feelings. Her cool detachment was more sincere now than it had been when she was nineteen and desperately in love with him.

"I'm just wondering if that tension might be because there's something going on between us." He waved a hand loosely between his chest and hers, clearly hoping she'd interpret the gesture without him needing to provide any specificity.

"Something like...?"

He shrugged. "I don't know. Sexual tension? I wasn't going to say anything while you were with Ivan, obviously."

"Good of you," Sarah said dryly.

Seriously? He was going to do this *now*?

He gave her a little smile, or what seemed like a smile in the near total darkness. "For the record, I'm glad you broke up with him. He wasn't good to you."

"Oh, thanks." Ivan had dumped her, but Sarah wasn't sharing that information widely. It made her look too pathetic. When Ivan had announced one day that they should break up before he headed to grad school in California, she had felt a shattering sense of loss and an equally deep sense of reprieve. She was hurt, of course, because she'd thrown so much effort into trying to please him, but she wouldn't miss the fights, the brooding, his constant insistence that Sarah would never love him enough.

"Didn't you ever wonder," Ren continued quietly, "about us? I feel like we have better conversations than we do with other people."

Did Sarah ever wonder about Ren? There hadn't been much else she had wondered about for a while. "Well, the fact that you hooked up with most of my friends means that I was pretty low on your priority list. So any wondering I may have done is in the past."

"But you know why I went out with them and not you, right?"

Her heart froze in place. She did not know, and she didn't know if she wanted to. "Why?"

He sighed, looking up at the plastic stars that were scattered on her ceiling, his elegant jawline lit blue from below. Her nightlight was a still frame from *Howl's Moving Castle* that she'd found at a street fair after falling in love with the film the year before. At the time, she had profoundly related to the lonely heroine and her passion for a handsome, emotionally unavailable blond sorcerer. It had seemed to represent her relationship with Ivan perfectly, which in retrospect was definitely a warning sign. Now the soft light made Ren's eyes look like they were filled with blue fire.

To her surprise, he shifted his entire body so that he was right next to her and then slid downwards, adjusting himself so that his head was near hers on the pillow. She was a little shocked but too bemused to be angry. She could always shove him onto the floor if he tried anything...which sounded fun, come to think of it.

When Ren spoke again, his eyes were on the ceiling. "I'm not good at relationships. And you're a relationships person. But I wanted to ask if you wanted to sleep with me. You were looking really sad tonight and that's one thing I'm good at. But we shouldn't do it if it will mess up our friendship."

Sarah could barely contain a burst of delirious laughter. "So you saw that I was sad and are nobly offering to cheer me up by giving me a good lay?"

He chuckled and leaned closer, his voice just audible above that stupid, sexy song that Kristie was playing. "Okay, first of all, there's nothing wrong with sex. It can be healing, especially after a break-up. That's one thing I know for sure."

"Oh, I'm sure you do."

He made a small sound, somewhere between amusement and frustration. Then she felt him shifting slightly lower on the bed, getting closer as he stretched beside her. She had always assumed that he got women into bed with a combination of witty flirtation and intense eye contact. Now she wondered if he did it by squirming into their blankets like a puppy.

Even more frustrating was that the tactic was working. Her heart was beating faster just being next to him; his body was warm through her thin sheets. She liked him, and she had always been attracted to him, and he was *right there*. She could pull him close and kiss him all night. He had given her permission to do it, and he smelled nice. He always smelled nice, like cloves and coffee and vanilla soap (mixed, admittedly, with hints of cigarettes and weed). Her nerves were humming like a struck chord and her cheeks felt hot; her body had clearly made the decision of 'all in favor' when it came to Ren. Her body had probably made that decision the first time she saw him in class, trying to reassemble a pen he had taken apart and getting a furious grimace on his face when the pieces wouldn't fit. She had been utterly lost for a while when it came to him.

"The thing is," he added quietly, "I really like you. And I know you don't want a relationship. But if we slept together, I mean as long as both people know it's casual and are sober enough to consent..."

"I had two glasses of wine and you had at least three of Kristie's martinis. Shouldn't I be the one worried about your sobriety?"

He grinned as he shook his head. "That was liquid courage so I'd have the guts to do this. Doesn't count."

"But why? I mean, why do this?" His face was dangerously close, so she pushed a little farther up in her bed to put a safe distance between them.

"Because I'm attracted to you?" His pale eyes looked

confused. "Because we get along? Even if you have total contempt for me?"

He was attracted to her? That was new. She stared at him in the half-light, her breathing shallow, then pushed up even further until she was fully sitting up.

"I mean, seriously, though, think about it, Ren," she said. "You've slept with both my roommates and now me? Do you just need the trifecta?"

"Is that what you think of me?" He sounded a little wounded.

"That's not what I think of you, Ren. It's what you do! First Anya, then Kristie, Suki, Ellen, Yelena, Paulette—"

"Yelena and I never hooked up. I took her home from the bar one time when she was too drunk to get home safely."

That was kind of him, but Sarah didn't let it stop her. "My point is," she said primly, "that I think this is an unhealthy habit for you."

She watched his mouth slowly crook in amusement. "You think what...I'm a sex addict?"

"No." She stared at the ceiling and searched for words. "Okay, so you know how if you go to a party and you announce that you're not drinking, most people will be cool with it, but there's always that one person who keeps pushing you to drink, and insisting you have a drink? And that's always the person who has the alcohol problem?"

His voice got quieter. "Yes?"

"Well, that's you with women. You're the person who can't be friends with a woman without taking her to bed, because you're the person with the intimacy problem."

She could tell that her remark had landed from the long silence that followed. "Well, if I'm a sex addict, you're a love addict."

"Ha."

"No, I'm serious. Look at you and Ivan." He slid up fully to face her now. "He wasn't nice to you. He didn't even remember your birthday. He didn't give you his coat that time it was snowing."

She remembered the day Ren was referring to: a late October weekend when they had gone to the movies as a big group and Sarah had naively chosen to wear a t-shirt, expecting the weather to be the same after nightfall as it had been four hours earlier. When they left the theater, the wind was up and it had started flurrying. After half a block of walking, Ren stopped and peeled off his sweatshirt under a streetlight, handing it to her without a word; it smelled faintly of coffee and weed, and she washed it carefully before returning it to him the next day.

Ivan had seen the sweatshirt exchange from a few feet away and had been furious with Sarah for not 'giving him a chance' to offer her his jacket. He had scolded her for not telling him she was cold and for not thinking about *how it would make him feel* to see her in Ren's sweatshirt. *Ren*, of all people. *Ren, the man-whore.* When they got home, Ivan and Sarah had one of their huge fights, the kind that ended with both of them in tears; it was the first time Ivan said he'd be suicidal if Sarah left him, and she had ended up apologizing for hours.

"I didn't want Ivan to give me his coat!" Sarah insisted now. "I wanted him to have it because I loved him."

"But that's my point. You're always giving more than people give you. That's... This is the whole problem with women."

Sarah's jaw fell open. "Did you just announce a whole problem with women? Right after admitting that you're incapable of relationships?"

He sighed, close enough to her shoulder that she could feel the warm puff of his breath.

"You know what you don't understand about love?" Sarah

went on. "It isn't about who gives more or less. It doesn't come with a calculator."

"Well, it should."

"Exactly. *You* think that way," Sarah said fiercely. "You're always focused on how many women you've slept with and how many orgasms everyone has had, but when you love someone—"

"I've given more orgasms than Ivan, I can tell you that much."

Her mouth dropped open. "You know nothing about that relationship." She could feel her face growing heated. Ivan wasn't Mister Orgasm, but he had gotten it right more often than not. Forty percent of the time, anyway.

"I didn't mean it like that."

Then another thought occurred to her. "So wait. If I wanted a relationship, let's say I wanted one with you, would that be something you were offering?"

There was a pause of several seconds before he looked away. "That's not the reality we're living in. Let's get back to the topic at hand."

By now, her emotions were tossing in an unpleasant swirl. This was likely to be her last chance to kiss the most beautiful man she had ever met, and she couldn't do it because they were friends, and because a small part of her was in love with him, and because a larger part was furious. "I can't," she said. "I'm sorry, but I'm not feeding into this weird fetish where you have to hook up with every girl within a fifty-meter radius."

"I don't see you like that," he said. "You're different."

She snorted. "And I'm sure you've said that to all the other women."

"No, I haven't!"

"You're like the boy who cried wolf, except instead of crying wolf, you're saying, 'You're not like the other girls.' But the only way I'm not like the other girls is that you haven't slept with me yet."

She heard the sharp intake of his breath as he pulled back to look at her. "You're important to me." His words grew faster now, more insistent. "Remember that night freshman year that I came to your birthday party? The only reason I hooked up with Anya instead of you was because we had that whole conversation about love. Remember? And you talked about how you were looking for something serious, and I wasn't, so it wouldn't have been fair to hook up with you. But I'm not *taking advantage* of people."

For a moment, Sarah believed him. She believed that he believed it, anyway. She suddenly felt vulnerable, like she'd admitted too much. She slid down again, deeper under the covers, twisting her face away from him. "Well, don't worry," she said with more sarcasm than she felt. "There is a whole party full of women out there, one of whom is sure to fall for your handsome, moody thing."

"You think I'm handsome?" She could hear a smile in his voice, which angered her enough to shove at him with her feet, just enough to push him slowly towards the edge of her bed.

"Goodnight, Ren," she said. "Go find someone else."

After a moment, she felt him heave himself up and take a step away from her. Then he paused. She could hear him in the darkness, stopping to look at her one last time. "There *is* no one else I like this much." The words gave her a strange sensation of vertigo, like she was getting everything wrong.

Then he turned and left, the music growing louder and quieter again as he shut her door.

Two days later, Ivan showed up on her doorstep begging for forgiveness, and Sarah reluctantly agreed to get back together with him. The next time she saw Ren, he waved at her once from across the street and she waved back. He had a strange expression on his face, almost like longing, and her heart did a flip at the sight of him, like she had lost something that she couldn't put a name to.

She didn't talk to Ren for another five years.

2

LIAM'S SOCCER GAME, APRIL 2011

IT WAS EARLY APRIL, and it was snowing in Toronto. Sarah didn't want to be outside at all, let alone hunched on a frosty wooden bench at one end of a soccer field, her hands tucked beneath her knees in inadequate handknit mittens, the lone observer of a casual soccer game that even the participants weren't taking too seriously. But Sarah had promised to cheer on her boyfriend Liam in his Friday night soccer game. Sarah had, in fact, enthusiastically gushed about how much she would enjoy watching him doing something sporty. As a young medical resident, Liam rarely had time to do anything athletic, and she wanted to prove that she could be a loyal, supportive girlfriend when he did.

So here she was, watching her boyfriend jogging back and forth through a light dusting of snow while Sarah shivered and wished that she had the courage to steal someone's thermos of coffee and curl up under her bench like an arctic ground squirrel.

Liam and Sarah had been together since shortly after she moved to Toronto; she had moved to the city from Montreal to share an apartment with her cousin Paul. Paul was a couple of years younger than her and had just finished getting a degree in theater; he needed someone to share his tiny, post-graduation apartment, and in exchange he had promised to hook her up with photography jobs shooting headshots for his actor friends. Shooting headshots had quickly become her bread-and-butter—or at least the artistic side of how she earned her bread. She also had a job doing graphic design at a small trade magazine targeted toward Canadian Mounties, which meant that Sarah worked from nine to five laying out articles about tactical negotiation techniques and then spent her weekends taking photos of hopeful young actors who earnestly sought her opinion on what color shirts to wear before staring moodily at the camera doing their best sexy glowers.

She was a little frustrated with her photography career so far. Her goal had always been to do fine arts photography, creating artistic visions that were interesting, edgy, and new. But she hadn't found a perspective that could gain any traction with the local galleries: neither her moodier, more personal work nor her attempts at tourist photos had found a place on any gift shop shelves or lined any gallery windows. Sarah was at risk of becoming a starving artist, exactly as her mother had once predicted.

During her first trip home from McGill, Sarah had announced her plans to become a photographer to her mother on their way home from church one Sunday, and her mother, Maureen, had fallen quiet for a good thirty seconds as they drove along the road in their small town.

"Does anyone actually make a living at that?" she had finally asked in a voice so gentle that Sarah dug her nails into her palms.

"You can if you're good enough," had been Sarah's fervent response at eighteen.

Now here Sarah was, almost ten years later, and it turned out that she wasn't good enough.

Paul was fun to live with, though. He was the cousin she had been closest with growing up, a de facto sibling since neither of them had any brothers or sisters. They grew up a little over an hour apart in a stark, underpopulated stretch of the Avalon peninsula in Newfoundland, and they had spent every family holiday tearing around the woods behind Sarah's house while her mother cooked a seafood casserole and Paul's mother, Delia, complained about the car ride. Sarah and Paul would play long, elaborate games together as treasure hunters or spies, searching for some valuable item that the bad guys were willing to kill to keep out of their hands. Paul was always the writer, shaping the dramatic stories of their games, while Sarah spent long hours designing them spy glasses and an arsenal of tree branch weapons.

Now Paul's optimism about his own creative career served as a dramatic contrast to her own. Paul still believed that he could make it as an actor, whereas Sarah had begun to accept that she was going to have to adjust her artistic dreams to align with cold, hard reality. That was one reason she was glad to be dating a doctor like Liam, someone whose path was predictable and well-paid. Her mother had literally burned a prayer candle in gratitude when Sarah started dating him. He was pleasant and polite, and he bought Sarah flowers on major holidays. He was the one part of Sarah's life that wasn't a total failure in her mother's eyes.

So Sarah had better not lose him. She shook her frozen mittens and slapped them together in applause as a cluster of soccer players wrestled for control of the ball near her. Her cousin Paul's face lit up with a grin as he passed it to his friend Ian; this was Paul and his actor friends' casual league, which he had been kind enough to invite Liam to join for the season.

Paul's wavy brown hair was damp in the wind, and he looked exhilarated and red-cheeked as he ran down the field.

Her eyes flicked back to Liam. He had dark blond hair and a lean body and wore the alert expression of a straight-A student, which was what had initially attracted her to him. Now he jogged back and forth in his defensive position, trying to track the action on the far end of the field.

There was another pass, a kick in her direction, and one of the players fell a few feet from her, his dark, curly hair startlingly familiar. She felt a wave of shock at the sight of beautiful, deep-set green eyes: Rene Durand was on the ground, five steps away from the tips of her frozen toes. He bounced up quickly to shake off a bruised ankle and started dusting off the light coating of snow from his elbow before his eyes met hers and widened in surprise. She must not have been recognizable in the woolen hat her mother had knitted for her last Christmas—she hadn't noticed Ren herself until then, too focused on pretending not to look miserable.

Sarah waved in acknowledgement, and Ren took two steps towards her as if to step out of the game before realizing what he was doing. He grinned quickly at her before turning to run back towards the other players.

He was here. Ren. A peculiar sense of elation rose inside her. She hadn't even known that he was living in Toronto.

The context of a soccer game made it even stranger. Ren had never been particularly athletic when she had known him. He had been wiry and lean at university, his physique shaped by lucky genetics, late nights, and the occasional cigarette. She remembered buying him ice cream or cooking him a frozen pizza a couple of times when he was seeing one of her roommates and admitted to having forgotten to eat for the entire day; back in school, she had mocked him for playacting 'the starving intellectual' and secretly envied that he could still look somewhat muscular without bothering to do anything. Now she watched him racing across the frosty field as if healthy physical activity was totally normal for him. She wondered if his personality had changed in some fundamental way.

It made her think about a rule she'd invented in high school with her best friend Marie: that whenever a guy was especially handsome, he would invariably be a brainless jock.

Marie had intoned it one day when they were fifteen: "The Lord distributes his gifts fairly. No boy shall be both gorgeous and interesting. If he looks like a model, then lo, he shall want to discuss his hockey games in painful detail and has never finished a book. So it was written and so it shall be."

Sarah had snorted out a laugh as they listed the various hot boys in their high school by which sports teams they were obsessed with—a casual dismissal of people who would never have been interested in them anyway, as Sarah was well aware at the time. She and Marie were the kind of social outcasts who dyed their hair bright colors and wore jewelry with skulls on it, and neither of them was turning down a lot of offers.

Ren had been the first guy Sarah met who had broken this pattern: he had striking cheekbones, gorgeous eyes, and a total lack of regard for organized sports. He didn't follow any professional teams and had never once announced that he had started lifting weights or was training for a marathon.

So what was he doing here?

Sarah had time to ponder the question as she watched him charging back and forth after the ball. The camaraderie between the players was obvious. Her cousin Paul seemed to be particularly friendly with Ren, but all of the players were tossing each other friendly insults as they demanded the ball or attempted another almost-goal. For the first time, she couldn't help but wonder if the 'handsome jock' trend that she had noticed in high school might be about something else. Women had always acted strange around Ren, pawing at his arm and laughing too loud when he made a joke, while men often acted jealous of him. Maybe getting knocked around on a sports field was the one place where his dark eyelashes and moody good looks didn't matter to people.

But why was she trying to guess at his innermost feelings? She didn't know him anymore. He had disappeared from her life without explanation.

As the game wrapped up, her cousin jogged toward her as Liam chatted with another player at the other end of the field.

"Hey!" Paul called. "I have to run to an audition. Liam will get you home, yeah?"

"Somehow I'll make it home alive."

Paul smiled at her tone and put his hands on her shoulders. "Be safe. Trust no one. Use whatever weapons you can find."

She nodded in mock agreement. "The mean streets of Toronto will try to break me, but I won't go down without a fight."

"You can make it," Paul said. "And I should get showered... They want me to come in tonight. It's a callback for a movie!"

"Go, go, go," Sarah replied, and Paul started running towards the nearest subway stop.

She saw Ren pulling a towel out of a bag and rubbing it over his hair. Then he turned and walked toward her, his expression filled with something she couldn't place. Affection? Puzzlement? After a few steps, he made a beeline to the container of coffee that his teammates had set up on the sidelines.

That made sense, Sarah thought. There was no reason she should get priority over coffee. She shivered in the brisk wind.

A moment later, he was standing in front of her, a paper cup in hand.

"Hey. What are you doing here?" he asked, a little breathless from the cold and exercise.

"Oh," she said, her voice sounding equally weightless, "I'm here to watch Liam." She waved one soggy mitten in her boyfriend's direction.

Ren's eyes flickered to Liam with a dubious look. "You're not cold?"

"Only from sitting still so long."

"Here." Ren handed her the cup. Of course it was meant for her; never underestimate Ren's ability to surprise you with kindness.

"So Rene Durand," she said, "playing sports. I thought I was hallucinating."

He laughed. "You may have been. I'm new to the team, and I guess they play inside in winter, which sounds a lot better." Ren grinned and gestured at the drifting flurries. "But it's good to be doing something active. I spend too much time at a computer these days."

"So what are you up to that keeps you chained to a desk?"

"Journalist. *Toronto Star*. I go out in the field for stories, but I'm at my desk more often than not. Right now I'm on the city beat, which means lots of waiting around for something interesting to happen and exaggerating the boring stuff to fill the page."

"Sorry that our criminal underworld is so disappointing."

He grinned. "Yeah. I thought being a reporter would be more like traveling the world by camel or interviewing biker gangs..."

"Like Hunter S. Thompson with fewer drugs."

"That's just what I put in my job application."

They smiled at each other. It felt like their old university banter: the nerdy references and dry teasing.

"And you? What are you up to?" he asked.

Sarah inwardly sighed at how boring her life was. "I do art direction at a magazine and take headshots. I haven't launched the dazzling career as a photographer that I envisioned for myself."

"And Liam is your boyfriend...?"

Again, a hint of doubt in her taste. She felt defensive, as she always had with Ren. "He's nice, actually. He's a doctor."

Ren nodded once, unsmiling.

"He's a good guy," she insisted. "Remember that time when you talked to me about Ivan not giving me his coat? You probably don't remember that."

"I remember." Ren's gaze was intense.

"What you said actually had an effect on me. I stopped dating jerks. Liam isn't the kind of person who wouldn't notice if I was cold." It occurred to her that Liam was literally keeping her out in the cold right then, but that was different; he never kept her awake crying all night. He was pleasant and affectionate when he was available, which wasn't always. "He works in emergency medicine."

"Are you going to marry him?"

The question surprised her. "It's still pretty new. We've only been together a couple of years."

Sarah could hear how that sounded as soon as the words left her lips. Liam had been very insistent that they not rush things. He was very busy, much too busy to discuss getting married, let alone planning for a wedding. Maybe his schedule would clear up some point. Just not this year. Probably not next year, either.

"I got married, actually," Ren said.

She tried to keep too much shock from her face. "Are you kidding? That's great!"

"Yeah." He looked abashed, one hand rubbing at the back of his neck. "She's an intellectual property lawyer. Grew up in Nevada. She does music licensing."

"She sounds brilliant."

Ren's smile widened. "Yeah. She has complete and total disdain for me."

"Well...smart woman," Sarah joked.

His eyes were warm. "You haven't changed."

"I'm more pessimistic than I used to be."

"You were always pretty pessimistic."

Sarah glanced over to see Liam approaching. "Well, I should..." Sarah started gathering her things. "It's great to see you! I'll come watch you guys again."

"Please don't," Ren said. "Don't sit out here in the cold. We should get coffee, catch up."

Sarah was certain that he didn't mean a word of it. "Yeah. My number is the same, if you still have it."

That strange expression was back in his eyes. "I still have it," he said.

"We should go to a museum or something. Let me know."

It seemed best to leave the planning in his court. He was married; she didn't want him to think she was hitting on him.

He nodded, watching her with the same unreadable expression. Friendliness? Pity?

"Hey," Liam said, breathing hard as he landed next to them. "What's going on?" He glanced between them.

"We were catching up," she explained. "We knew each other at McGill."

"Oh, okay," Liam said flatly. "Want to get going? It's freezing."

"Yeah." She met Ren's eyes, feeling a wave of genuine affection. "Good to see you."

Ren's eyes flicked between her and Liam as if he were deliberately hiding his thoughts. "Yes, definitely."

As they walked away, Liam slung an arm around her neck and kissed her on the side of her woolen hat. "I hope you weren't cold," he said. "I told you not to come."

"It was fun," she insisted.

"So you're going to hang out with Durand?"

"I think he was just being polite," she said quietly.

Liam nodded, glancing at her cup of coffee. "Is that warm?"

"Pretty warm. You should have it." She tried to hand him the cup, but he shook her off.

"I hate lukewarm coffee. Can we stop for an espresso or something? I'm freezing."

LIAM LEFT her in the coffee shop to head home for his early shift in the E.R., so she found herself curled up alone on her sofa by nine at night, her knees still chilly from the hours in the cold even now that they were tucked safely under a fleece blanket. She had decided to track down some of Ren's articles for the *Toronto Star* and had spent the last half hour reading his work on her laptop, using the heat from her aging laptop battery as an electric blanket. Ren's voice in his writing had the same biting perspective she remembered from school, even if his subjects were fairly mundane: bike theft, political grandstanding, new trends in cybercrime.

One article read, 'Even people unfamiliar with Mr. Sitka's politics are likely familiar with his eponymous restaurant chain, renowned for both its twenty-page menu and its even longer history of labor disputes.'

Or from another article: 'The compost bin serves as an apt metaphor for the fate of the community garden itself: it's hard to tell what will turn up next, but it may not be pretty.'

His photos were even better, sharp, and well-composed. Not all reporters took their own pictures, but Ren had an eye for framing and wasn't afraid to pick an angle and commit to it. She wondered why she'd never spotted his name in the paper and realized it was because she never read the local news. It was hard enough to think about the fate of the world, let alone restaurant fires and housing policies that she could do nothing about. Now the articles charmed her, full of his sharp perspective and dry wit. She thought of all the times he used to love making big, blanket statements back at school:

'All Polaroid photography looks pornographic. That's its entire appeal.'

'People who like Nietzsche are intelligent, but people who love him are bitter male virgins.'

'Dubbing films instead of subtitling them is an artistic crime.'

Some people found Ren's pronouncements annoying, but Sarah had always found his decisiveness amusing. And he never seemed to mind when she laughed at him, which was why they had gotten along.

She hadn't realized how much she missed him until he reappeared in her life again, but now she felt the loss of him as a pang. It would have been fun to have stayed in touch, in spite of everything that had passed between them. It would have been fun to have heard his takes on movies and books and society at large during the last few years. She always felt smarter after talking to him, especially when it was because she had proven him wrong.

A key turned in the lock. Paul entered, peeled off his coat, and walked into their tiny kitchen. He was wearing the nice black button-down that he considered his lucky charm at auditions.

"How'd it go?" she called.

"Booked it," he said.

"Yes!" She felt a rush of joy as she slid off her blanket to hug him. "That's great."

"No, no, I was kidding," he said, throwing open the refrigerator and grabbing a beer. "Their eyes glazed over in the middle of my first line. Usually people wait at least three lines before they start looking disappointed, but I guess this casting director was quicker than average."

"Oh, no." She struggled to find words to cheer him up that she hadn't used before; she'd given him a lot of pep talks.

"It's fine," he drawled. "I'll just have a beer and walk into traffic."

It bothered her to see Paul being pessimistic. She felt like one of the two of them ought to believe it was possible to make a career in the arts, and it certainly wasn't her at the moment.

"Are you committed to that beer," she asked, "or could I make you a cocoa? I made homemade whipped cream earlier for Liam but he didn't end up coming over."

He glanced at the beer. "I could have a cocoa. That's probably going to make me marginally less suicidal." He tossed the unopened beer back in the refrigerator and slumped against the wall.

As she pulled out the fancy cocoa powder she had gotten for Christmas, she spoke over her shoulder. "Want to watch an action movie? I was lusting after your *Speed* DVD."

"The DVD itself or Keanu in a buzz cut?"

"My lawyers have advised me not to answer that question."

"Fair enough. You make the cocoa and I'll put on the movie. But I'm stopping it if you lick the screen."

He walked to their small living room as Sarah spoke casually over her shoulder. "So how long has Ren been playing in your league?"

"Rene Durand? Just a week or two. You know him?"

"We were friends in school."

"That's right. I forgot he went to McGill." She could hear Paul setting up the DVD player. "Yeah, I met him on a shoot, and he was looking to do something active."

"Don't tell me he was acting in a film." She had a horrified vision of Ren booking 'handsome guy' roles with no effort while Paul, attractive but not dazzlingly so, struggled to get work. Paul was a wonderful actor; that was the frustrating part. He was naturally funny, great at improvisation, good-looking—a bit gangly but handsome, his light brown hair in a charmingly unruly wave on his head. He was the kind of guy you cast as the cute boyfriend or the relatable lead in a Neil Simon play.

"No, nothing like that. He was the stills photographer," Paul said. "He was friends with that chain-smoking director on the indie film... Remember when I played the schoolteacher ex-boyfriend who everyone thought was the killer but was actually just really socially awkward? Ren was shooting stuff for the press kit and we got to talking. He's a super nice guy. He looks like he's going to be a narcissistic asshole, but he's great."

"Yeah, he's a good guy," Sarah agreed.

Paul walked back into the kitchen and gave her a pointed look. "Do you have a history with him?" Paul's expression shifted to horror. "Oh, God, tell me you didn't sleep with him."

"No!" She shook her head quickly. "I was just surprised. He and I were friends for a while, and then we weren't."

Paul watched her from where he was leaning against the door frame. "What happened?"

"I don't know." She considered the question, stirring the cocoa. "I mean I do know. He asked me to sleep with him, and I said no."

Paul frowned. "And he pressured you, or..."

"No, no, no, nothing like that. I think he just philosophically believed in casual sex, and I didn't, so when I turned him down it became like this intellectual problem he had with me."

Paul considered this. "But if it was casual sex, he shouldn't have minded being turned down, right? I mean, if it was casual, why would he care one way or the other?"

"Huh. I don't know."

Sarah thought back to the time when Ren had pulled away from her group of friends. What had happened, exactly? He had simply stopped coming to their parties. And since she had rarely been the one who invited him—that was typically Kristie, who invited everybody—Sarah hadn't fully registered that he was gone at first, especially because she was busy getting back together with Ivan for what proved to be a last, doomed attempt to work things out.

Ren hadn't announced to her that they were no longer friends. He had still smiled when they passed each other on campus, still waved when they were in line for coffee near each other. But he had never approached her again, never come over, never chatted with her in the hallways about art or music. Had he been stung by her rejection? Was it the fact that she called him a sex addict?

At the time she had chalked it up, perhaps unfairly, to the fact that there was no chance of having sex with her and he had worked his way through all the other available women.

Now she found herself hoping he wouldn't disappear again. She hoped he wouldn't leave Paul's soccer league without a word, giving no reason why. But that was silly. He was married now. And he had chatted with her like everything was normal between them.

"I do like him," she said firmly. "He's a good guy. He's really decent and kind. He's just a little weird when it comes to women."

"Weird like..."

"Weird like he was a player. That's all."

Paul considered this. "He's probably grown up since then."

"I'm sure he has. He's married."

3

ART GALLERY OF ONTARIO, MAY 2011

TO HER SURPRISE, Ren's name appeared in her text notifications only two weeks after the soccer game.

it's ren if this is still sarah. want to go to AGO for yael bartana exhibit? haven't been

He was referring to a conceptual video show at the Art Gallery of Ontario, one of the city's larger museums for Canadian modern and contemporary art. Sarah felt a bright flash of excitement as she typed her response.

Would love to. Vaguely alienating political art and you haven't been yet? What's happened to you?

She wondered if she'd overstepped as soon as she sent it, whether they were still friends who could tease each other like that. She added a moment later: *Kidding of course. Mostly free for the next two weekends.*

He texted back less than a minute later: *next sunday works. you tell me when. i will explain in person how mortally offended i was by your earlier text.*

She laughed, and they made a plan.

. . .

The days before Sarah met up with Ren proved to be an unexpectedly difficult time for her. First, Paul announced that he was moving out of their apartment in order to move in with his girlfriend Trish, who had found a place with a patio garden and wanted to split the rent with him.

Sarah wasn't a huge fan of Patricia, the pretty blond actress whom Paul had met while they were doing a Sam Shepard play together, ripping each other's hearts out using wobbly regional American accents. In real life, Trish had an obsession with Kate Middleton and dressed in clothes that made her look like she'd always just arrived from playing polo. She spoke in a high, gentle voice and had adopted a weary tolerance toward Paul's jokes, which Sarah took as a warning sign of trouble ahead. Trish didn't seem as interested in the craft of acting as she did in how she looked while doing it...though maybe that was unfair. It wasn't like they'd discussed Stanislavsky technique together, but Trish seemed to spend a disproportionate quantity of time speculating about which outfits to wear to auditions versus what her characters' motivations were.

But Paul had every right to move in with his girlfriend; he should do whatever made him happy. The problem was that now Sarah needed a new roommate because she couldn't afford their place on her own. So she had invited Liam over and tentatively floated the issue with him, hoping that he might offer to move in himself.

"It's tricky," Liam replied when she had barely finished. "I still have four months left on my lease with Henry." Henry was a young orthopedist in Liam's hospital who collected Star Wars memorabilia, and Sarah had never gotten the impression that he and Liam were especially close.

"Okay," Sarah said gently. "So are you planning on renewing your lease with him? I mean, whatever you want is fine."

"I guess we'll see in four months," he said flatly.

"Okay." Her voice sounded small in her own ears, like she was speaking from the bottom of a staircase.

"Sorry, I've had a really stressful day." He sighed as his gaze turned to something out the window. "Someone died today."

Her face fell. "I am so sorry."

She felt horrible that a patient had died at his job. All the same, Sarah had a small, disloyal thought as she watched him pondering the trees outside her apartment window. She had noticed that people had a tendency to die in the E.R. on the days when she brought up important topics with Liam, like the status of their relationship, or how long he might want to live in Toronto, or whether he wanted kids. There seemed to be some mysterious, cosmic connection between Sarah saying, "What if we planned a trip next summer?" and the mortality rate in the emergency medicine department at Toronto General.

He was being clear in his own way, of course. She couldn't lie to herself anymore about his enthusiasm for her.

But all the same, he was a doctor. And her mother loved him. And fine, maybe he was still making up his mind about marrying her, but that was normal, right? Big decisions took time. Maybe she shouldn't be pressuring him, given how busy he was. Maybe the pressuring him was the very thing driving him away. Maybe if she just never mentioned their future, the engagement ring would appear on its own as a reward for her loyalty and patience.

Or maybe she had always been kidding herself that she was good enough for him.

By the time she was standing in the lobby of the Art Gallery of Ontario, she was deep in a multi-day spiral of sadness. Did she need to break up with Liam? Was she being too needy? Surely being with Liam was better than being alone. You didn't break up with your boyfriend just because he was acting distracted and tired. Everyone got tired.

The sight of Ren walking through the doors in one of his old leather jackets lifted her spirits a surprising amount. Here was a friend. A real, actual friend who could talk with her about photography, about books and ideas. She wouldn't need to think about the other aspects of her life for a few hours. It was a little annoying that Ren was wildly in love right now, but only a little. She was glad he was happy.

"The same leather jacket," she said. "Now that you're married, I was assuming you'd have switched to fleece vests."

"I see you're still dressing like the quirky lead in an indie film," he said, taking in her hair, now highlighted a sunny blond, her vintage dress and red ankle boots. His pale green eyes, up close, were such an unreal color that she had do the mental reset that she'd practiced when they would hang out in school: shaking off his stunning appearance so she could see her friend properly. He hadn't changed much: his black hair was a bit longer, his face less sharply boned. He looked healthier now, like he no longer forgot to eat for multiple days at a time.

"What do you mean? I mostly wore jeans when you knew me," she said.

"Sure, paired with a velvet jacket and a top hat."

"The top hat was one time. And your leather jacket was constant."

He shrugged, giving her one of his crooked grins. "Well, I couldn't exactly be a rebel without the approved rebel uniform."

They got into the line together to buy tickets. "So how have things been for you?" she asked. No point in talking about her own life.

"Not bad," he said, which she translated in Ren terms to mean they were fantastic. "Marriage is good. Work can be a bit dull."

"I'm trying not to tease you about being married, given your previous position on relationships."

He looked embarrassed. "Yeah, I know. I was young and stupid."

"Oh, I know," Sarah said with a laugh. She was tempted to admit that she had also been young and stupid, but she wasn't sure that she was any smarter now. She thought about Liam, whose cool rejection stung like a slap.

"Paola wants to meet you, by the way," Ren added. "She approves of anyone who puts me in my place."

Sarah raised her eyebrows. "Is that what you told her? That I put you in your place?"

"You were the only person who did back then," he said, his expression warm.

"Well, let's see a photo of your bride, then. I'm sure she's stunning."

Ren looked somewhere between abashed and excited as he took out his phone. His lock screen was a wedding photo, Sarah noticed, but he took the time to open up his full photo collection, picked one, and handed her the phone.

"Winter hiking in Banff a few weeks back."

His wife stood alone in the photo in front of a sweeping landscape, dressed in a slim white parka and tight-fitting grey leggings. She was even more stunning than Sarah had anticipated, with golden-brown skin and dark hair in a tight bun, her lips pouty and her cheekbones as sharp and narrow as ski slopes. Her faint smile was directed past the camera toward the stunning view.

Sarah felt a brief flash of worry for him: his wife didn't seem like she laughed very often, and she remembered him saying his wife had disdain for him.

"She's gorgeous," Sarah said.

His eyes lit up as he nodded, and she felt briefly guilty that she'd had any negative thoughts about this woman she hadn't met. It was jealousy, certainly. Just because his wife was beautiful didn't mean they were unhappy. Beautiful people could be just as happy as anyone else. It was one of the annoying things about life.

"Let me get your ticket, since I was the one who wanted to see this," he said as they got to the front of the line.

"You better. I paid for your ice cream at least four times back in school, and you never paid me back."

"I'll reimburse you right now...assuming, of course, that you brought the receipts from 2004."

"They're in a file with my accountant. You'll get an itemized list."

He bought them tickets and they headed towards the galleries, pausing in front of a large, bright photo collage that stood eight feet tall near the elevator banks.

"I'm not sure what I think of these. Photo collages made of smaller photos," Sarah said.

"They're the fast-food version of art," Ren replied. "They're a way to pretend you're saying something deep while having nothing to say."

Sarah smiled at his familiar decisiveness. Ren always gave you something to react to, even if he was usually overstating the case.

"Do you still do photography?" she asked him. "For fun, I mean."

"I do so much shooting and writing for my job that I don't have the time. I should get back into it."

They wandered the galleries together. It was nice talking to him like this, pointing out favorite images and artistic choices.

"Look at this. The tilt shift lens," she said, noting one photo of a mountain town. "I love that effect, where everything looks like a miniature toy."

"Tilt shift is gimmicky." There was a faint twinkle in his eye; he knew he was baiting her.

"It's a tool, like any other tool."

"A tool for being gimmicky."

"I have plenty of examples that it's not," Sarah said.

"Tilt shift and fish-eye lenses have no subtlety."

"Sit down, Durand. I'm pulling out my phone."

They sat down together on a bench in the middle of the gallery, and she pulled out her cell phone and did a quick image search until she found a photo of a rushing waterfall made with a tilt shift lens and long exposure. The lens and shutter choice made the waterfall look endless and dreamy, its rushing white foam like the ghostly train of a Victorian wedding dress.

"That's nice," Ren agreed. "But only because of the long exposure."

"All right. Hold on. I'm finding something else."

She could feel him smiling as she pulled up images of tilt shift lenses used in spooky, haunting photography of graveyards, with faint figures appearing in the mist.

"Okay, that's interesting," he agreed. "But I'm sort of done with black and white. It has become so self-serious. Nobody should be allowed to take black and white photos anymore."

"You make these broad pronouncements just to get me annoyed," she said. "Cartier-Bresson was not self-serious." Cartier-Bresson was one of the first artists that she and Ren agreed on back in school; his gorgeous shots of Paris were popular on postcards and dorm room posters, and Sarah had put up one of his prints as soon as she arrived at school.

"Cartier-Bresson was a sentimentalist," Ren said.

"Now you're deliberately being pretentious."

"Maybe," he conceded, smirking a little. "I should have said, people should earn the right to shoot black and white photography. It should be like a driver's license. You have to pass a test."

"I'll have all photographers submit their work to you for approval."

"Please do. If someone takes a self-portrait in profile, looking away moodily with half their face in shadow, they lose the right to shoot black and white photography for a year."

"There go half my headshots."

He laughed.

"You know, Paola hates museums," Ren said as they stood up. "She doesn't understand the point of art unless you're going to buy it. She'll only go to the museum gift shop."

"I suppose that's practical. What's the point of looking at art if you can't own it?"

He smiled. "She told me she only puts up with me because she can tolerate looking at me."

"Only wanted for your looks. Shocking."

"Well, I can't rely on my personality. Apparently, I'm pretentious."

An hour later, they were still talking about photography at the museum café, flipping through her website. She showed him the best headshots she had taken and talked about the challenges of the task: how it was hard to catch people's real personality, how actors would practice looks in a mirror and then look ridiculous doing them in front of the camera, how rarely people were aware of their best traits.

"None of us are aware of our best traits," Ren said lightly, looking through the images.

She allowed herself to drink in the sight of him in case this would be the last time they met up like this. His head was tilted down, his black curls tumbling across his forehead. He smiled when he glanced up.

Ren was *married*.

"These are really good, Sarah."

"Well, I studied photography. I'm supposed to be good at taking pictures."

He shook his head. "You do something special with your headshots, though," he said. "They have a narrative quality, like you're telling each person's story."

"Well, they pay the bills," she said at last. "Or some of the bills. I have a day job. When I first moved to Toronto, I used to come up with these creative ideas to try to get into galleries and nobody liked them, so I sort of gave up."

"I'm sure they were great."

"No. I think I have nothing to say right now," she said. "I'm twenty-six, and I no longer have any opinions on anything." Twenty-six felt terribly old to her, like the bitter end of youth.

He gestured towards the pictures. "Well, these say something. They say that you're fascinated by people."

"So are you," she said. "I read your articles in the *Star* and they reminded me of how observant you are. You always had this way of looking at people like you were missing nothing. I thought you could totally see through me back in school."

He looked genuinely surprised. "You were one of the smartest people I knew."

"Not about some parts of my life."

He frowned and looked down at the table, considering. "Well, I didn't have much insight into some things. I probably thought I did." He took a sip of his coffee. "So unrelated question," he added. "What happened between you and Ivan? I heard you two got back together and then I never heard anything else."

"Well, that's a long story, but the short version is, he broke up with me before that party of Kristie's, if you remember that night."

Ren nodded, his mouth a straight line. "I remember that night."

"He had gotten accepted to graduate school in California, and he knew I didn't want to go because I had this assistant photographer job in Montreal—which turned out to be a nightmare because the guy harassed me—but I didn't know that yet. So Ivan pre-emptively broke things off as a way to convince me to follow him. Like, 'You'll lose me if you don't come to California with me.' And when it didn't work, he begged to get back together. And I agreed, but once he was in California, I took the coward's way out and broke up with him by phone."

"Why not do it in person?"

"Because he used to say he might kill himself if I ever left him. Which I guess counts as emotional abuse. I didn't realize it at the time."

Ren's eyes widened. "Sarah..."

"Don't feel bad. It's over."

Ren's eyes were full of pity, and Sarah hated it. "Don't look at me like that," she said. "Someday I will be like you and happily married and dazzlingly optimistic. Wait and see."

He shook his head. "To be honest, I'm not feeling terribly optimistic either. I love my wife, but I think most people are profoundly screwed up. My job hasn't convinced me otherwise."

She nodded, then followed his gaze around the café. It was filled with young people adorned with nose piercings and corduroy jackets. University students, she thought, like she and Ren had once been. They looked so young to her now. It occurred to her that she and Ren had never hung out like this at school, just the two of them meeting over coffee. Instead, all their meetings had been incidental: chatting after class or when they ran into each other at a coffee shop or party. She wondered if he had never invited her on solo outings because it might have felt too much like a date. He had carefully made it clear that he had no interest in dating her.

It was a briefly mortifying thought, especially in the context of his gorgeous wife, but Sarah let it go. At least now she could hang out with him. Now that there was no risk of getting romantically involved, they could finally talk.

"So speaking of that night," he said. She had the rare experience of watching him struggling to find the right words. "My parents got divorced," he continued after a moment, surprising her. "I don't know if you knew that. Right around the time we stopped hanging out."

"I'm sorry," she said. "I didn't know that. I know you idealized them. Or maybe you didn't, but that was how it looked from the outside."

"No, I did," he said quietly. "They're both brilliant people. My mother seemed disappointed with me a lot of the time, but I wanted to impress her. And my father was incredibly intellectual and not always good at expressing his feelings. Anyway, right after they split, a lot came out about their marriage. Mostly from my mother. She told me they'd had an open marriage, which I didn't know. I mean, in theory, I knew they were in favor of that, because they were left-wing intellectuals who wrote about gender and so on, but I hadn't realized they were doing it themselves. But apparently my father was sleeping with former students who were twenty-two, twenty-three."

It struck Sarah that at the time Ren was learning that, his father was sleeping with people his own age.

"My mother said that after a while, it felt like they weren't married at all. Anyway, I think..." He shrugged. "I know you thought I was kind of an asshole back then. But before I found that out about my father, I used to see things differently."

"You thought sex was harmless," she offered.

He nodded. "You were the first person who told me I was being unhealthy who I actually *believed*. And after I found that out about my parents, I changed the way I was behaving."

"Because you didn't want to be like your father?"

He considered. "Yes. I think I didn't ever want to...I realized you can hurt people even if you're telling yourself that you're not."

She took a breath. "You know, that night..." Now it was her turn to struggle for the right words. "I didn't mean for us to stop being friends, I mean, if that's what happened, and you didn't just get too busy to come hang out. I don't regret not sleeping with you. But I do regret losing you as a friend."

He nodded, a wry smile on his lips. "You were just so brutally honest with me."

"Not my best trait."

"Not your easiest trait," Ren said. "But one of your best."

She watched him pick up a spoon and stir a coffee that didn't need stirring. He had the same restless quality he'd always had, and her old love for him woke in her chest like a sleeping giant, lumbering to awareness. She had to be careful to protect this friendship, if that's what this was. She had to protect herself, too...to not let herself feel too much.

"I'm glad we got to meet up," he said at last. That sounded like they wouldn't meet up again. She watched him put down the spoon and adjust his watch around his wrist, an old habit she remembered from school.

"Me, too," she said. "Maybe we can do this again next time there's a good art show."

"I'd like that."

When it came time to say goodbye, he kissed her on the cheek, looking serious for a moment. "You'll find something to say in your photography. You always do."

She watched him walk away and realized that he hadn't asked about Liam at all. That was fine. Better, maybe. She wasn't ready to talk about Liam. She wasn't sure what she wanted to do.

She went home and watched television alone, slipping an old 1940s movie into Paul's DVD player. Paul was staying at Trish's, though he hadn't moved his stuff out yet, and she realized she'd have to watch DVDs on her laptop soon.

When Liam texted her to ask if he could come over that night, she told him she was busy. But she wasn't. Not really.

No, she realized. Being alone wasn't so bad after all. She would just have to find a new roommate.

She broke up with Liam the next day. He was stunned by her announcement, which surprised her; she had convinced herself that he was disengaging as a way to push her away, to force her to break up with him so that he wouldn't have to. But that apparently hadn't been what was going on, because he started crying.

"What did I do wrong?"

"You just didn't seem excited about me," she said.

"I am excited. I've just been really busy."

"I know," she said quietly. "I'm sorry."

"I don't know what I'm going to do without you," he said, his voice breaking.

Three weeks later, she heard through a mutual friend that he was dating someone else.

4

PAUL'S HOUSEWARMING PARTY, JUNE 2011

PAUL'S FACE fell as he opened his door and spotted Sarah standing in his doorway. She was dressed in her favorite silk party shirt under a green corduroy jacket, clutching a bottle of wine, and she did a quick mental calculation of what could be wrong with her appearance that would bring that look to her cousin's face.

"Where's Liam?" Paul said at last.

"Oh." She realized that in the chaos of the last couple of weeks, she had forgotten to update Paul about her relationship status. "Liam and I broke up."

"Oh, no," Paul replied, his face falling. "I'm so sorry, Sarah." He gave her a warm hug, but he seemed distracted as he took the bottle of wine from her, placing her jacket on an overladen coat rack.

Was Paul more of a fan of Liam's than she'd realized? Sarah pondered his silence as she followed him into his new ground-floor apartment, taking in the carefully selected decor that must reflect Patricia's aspirational design sense: posters from the early 1900s for French wines, black and white photographs of Toronto landmarks, a charcoal grey accent wall. As Sarah glanced around the housewarming party, the source of Paul's discomfort came into focus: this was a couples party. Literally everyone except her was part of a couple—and not just a couple, but an elegant, attractive pair, legs crossed towards each other on white sofas as they chatted over brightly colored cocktails. She felt like she was trapped in a furniture advertisement.

"So what are you doing for a roommate?" Paul asked. "I thought Liam might move in if I got out of the way." Had Paul thought he was doing her a favor by leaving? It would be ironic if he had been trying to push her stalled relationship out of its stasis. He'd certainly achieved that goal.

"I found someone else to live with," Sarah said. "It's fine. She's an education student." Sarah had spent the week interviewing a handful of potential roommates before selecting a quiet young woman named Winnie who was in a teacher-prep program and barely had the courage to ask if she was allowed to put food in the refrigerator. A shy and self-doubting roommate felt like exactly Sarah's speed right then.

Sarah kept her smile plastered on as Paul led her past various tableaus of happy coupledom and into the kitchen, where one more couple awaited her like the punchline to a joke: Ren and his wife Paola, carefully arranging fancy cheeses on a large white platter.

Ren smiled at her as he looked up. "Hey!"

"Hey!" Sarah said brightly. "They've put you on cheese duty, I see."

"Unfortunately," Ren agreed, rearranging some cubes with a knife. "If there's an art to this I never learned it."

"The master's programs in snack arrangement are tough to get into," Sarah said.

"Very cut-throat. It's the knives."

Paola glanced between them. She was even more stunning in person, with large dark eyes and dark hair that artfully curled around her shoulders in long, loose waves. "Well, I had to give him something to do," she said. "Otherwise, he fidgets."

"Paola, this is my old friend Sarah," Ren said, gesturing with his non-knife-wielding hand. "She's Paul's cousin, but we knew each other at McGill. And Sarah, this is my lovely wife, Paola. Did your boyfriend come?"

"Liam and I broke up."

"Oh, no." Ren's eyes registered something that passed too quickly for her to track it. "I'm sorry to hear that."

"It was long overdue," Sarah said.

His expression settled into kindness. "Well, it gives you more time to shoot, right?"

She nodded. "I'll have to do a sad break-up photo series. Abandoned shoes on train tracks."

"Lonely pigeons in the park," Ren said.

"Empty plastic bags blowing in the wind."

Ren chuckled.

"Oh, right," Paola said. "You're the photographer."

"Yes." Sarah looked between them. "Well, one of them. There may be others."

Paola snorted. "I don't doubt it, knowing Ren."

"Oh..." Sarah struggled for words, unsure how to avoid the landmine that had appeared before her. "I just meant there are a lot of photographers...in the universe."

Paola's eyes shifted away from Sarah, a tiny dismissal; she seemed to have decided that Sarah was being boring, evasive, or both.

"Let's get you one of Trish's cocktails!" Paul cried with extra jollity. "They are shockingly strong, so brace yourself."

"Please yes," Trish said, emerging from the other room to join them. "Paola won't have any, and I prepared way too much."

Trish was in a white vest that she was wearing as a shirt and slim white pants, the kind of outfit that would have gotten stained within three minutes at an undergrad party but could remain pristine at a mid-twenties soiree. She prepared Sarah a martini glass of something bright orange, then twisted a lemon rind on top of it and handed it over, keenly watching for Sarah's reaction.

Sarah took a reluctant sip. It was overwhelmingly sweet and intense, a more obnoxious cousin of the cosmopolitan. "This is excellent, Trish," Sarah said, not caring whether it was true.

She pressed herself against the wall as the conversation ping-ponged around her in a non-linear tennis match about rental costs and new cell phones and what constituted charcuterie. As soon as she found a moment, Sarah slipped away and wandered out the back door into the garden, a deep, narrow space squished between seven-foot concrete walls on either side. The brick patio was crumbling around the edges but had been forcefully dragged into urban chic by the copious use of tiny lights and potted greenery. In one corner, a couple were having an intimate chat in the vicinity of a dwarf Japanese maple, and Sarah steered away from them to hide on a bench that was half-concealed behind a stretch of ornamental grasses. She took a breath, sipping at Trish's drink cautiously until someone appeared in her periphery: Ian, Paul's best friend and the taller half of one of the loving couples within. He saw her and approached with a friendly grin.

"Out here by yourself?"

"Communing with nature."

They spent the next few minutes gamely talking about gardening, though neither of them had a garden, and how nice it would be to enter the real estate market, though neither of them had the money to buy anything, until he finished his cigarette and she finished her cocktail.

Standing up too rapidly to follow him inside, she discovered that she was, embarrassingly, quite drunk. She had apparently become a lightweight in her mid-twenties. Her drinking habits typically involved some red wine a couple of times a week, but that had declined even further now that Paul wasn't around to have people over and Liam wasn't there to take her to fancy meals. In the past two weeks, she had consumed exactly one drink when she went to Anya's house for a Sunday brunch. It had seemed too maudlin to drink alone, mourning the break-up that she had asked for.

Now she carefully made her way into the kitchen to find water to sober herself up and found herself in the middle of an intense conversation between Paola and Trish about the toothpaste campaign that Trish had just booked.

"It's still crazy to me that that's where the money is," Paola was saying.

"Well, television and movies, too," Trish said. "But think about it. During a sports game, millions of people see an advertisement. In television, the viewership is so spread around now that ads reach way more people than TV shows."

"So unless you're in a huge movie..."

"And indie films pay nothing," Trish said forcefully. "Nothing. You might as well be in a play."

Sarah spoke gently. "I was looking for water?"

"Seltzer is in the fridge," Trish said. As Sarah attempted to slip past them, Paola stopped her with one fine-boned hand on Sarah's upper arm.

"Hold on a minute. I am dying to ask you something."

Sarah paused, deer-in-the-headlights. "Yes?"

"What was Ren actually like in college?" Paola asked. "Did he hook up with tons of women? Because he will neither confirm nor deny."

Sarah hesitated. "Oh, well...I guess you could say he got a lot of female attention, understandably, but—"

"Why understandably?" Paola's expression was sharp.

Shit. Sarah was drunk. She was usually more careful than that. "He's attractive, I guess I meant, but—"

"That's true," Trish interrupted. "He could do modeling. I was just telling him this."

"No, I mean, but he wasn't..." Sarah searched in the echoing cavern of her drunk brain for the correct words. "It wasn't like he was constantly sleeping around. It was more like he had a few things with different women. I don't remember anyone he dated seriously, but there may have been someone." There. She felt proud of herself. That was well-stated for a drunk person, surely. "Not me, of course!" she added quickly, just in case that was Paola's worry.

"Why not you?"

Paola was a lawyer, Sarah remembered too late, and she was being cross-examined. "Um, well..." Sarah's bright tone was harder to maintain when the question poked at old wounds, but she did her best. "Well, I suppose we were better as friends. Or I wasn't hot enough for him," she added.

Whoops. That last part wasn't supposed to leave her mouth. She had been scrambling for something that would make Paola realize that Sarah wasn't a threat, but not that. Paola was staring at her.

"Sarah's leaving out the part where I hit on her and she turned me down cold," Ren said, entering the kitchen. So he must have heard everything. Excellent.

"Why did you turn him down?" Paola asked, her eyes back on Sarah.

"Because she thought I was an asshole," Ren filled in.

"An interesting, well-read asshole," Sarah added with what she hoped was a light smile.

"Well, some things don't change," Paola replied dryly, and Ren walked up to his wife and kissed her on the cheek.

Sarah found a can of seltzer and hurried outside again, this time finding the back patio mercifully empty. The evening had grown cool and quiet, settling down into the lush peace that the city sometimes found in the season between spring and summer. Sitting among Trish's tiny lights, she felt like she was floating in a sea of stars. She felt like she was drowning.

She took a big sip from the can of seltzer water. If she could have had Liam back by her side, just for the next hour, she would have been tempted. She had been an outcast in high school, and the feeling always came back to her at moments like this, whenever she felt like she was a puzzle piece that had ended up in the wrong box, epically unsuited for the environment where she found herself.

But this was fine. She was fine. She would just wait out her drunkenness outside. She'd give herself ten minutes and then she'd be stable enough to make some polite goodbyes. That should be enough time for Paola to forget she existed, hopefully.

The night sky was cloudless, though nearly without stars because of the light pollution from the city. The ornamental grasses in front of her shuddered left and right like a line of inebriated soldiers. Paul hadn't come over to talk to her, she realized. Not once, even though he threw her concerned looks from time to time. She could see him inside the house now through a slice of window, circling around Trish, following her orders as he prepared more ice.

He looked happy.

He was no longer part of Sarah's life, she thought, feeling some of her old teenage melancholy. He wasn't her reliable person anymore. Not the way he had been. He belonged to Trish now. Trish was lucky to get Paul's kind, trustworthy, hilarious perspective whenever she had a bad day or temporarily hated the world. And Sarah didn't have that anymore. She missed him.

She thought about how it had been for them as kids: Aunt Delia, Paul's mother, arriving like a storm cloud at Sarah's tiny house and immediately complaining about everything: the food, the portions, the state of disrepair of their yard. Paul making jokes to lighten the mood, even when he was only eight or nine years old. Sarah's mother patiently apologizing for everything in her small voice, trying to ride out the tempest. Paul's father trying to calm down everyone so his wife and his sister could get along...without ever acknowledging that all the friction was caused by his wife.

Sarah's mother Maureen had always been good at making herself small. Her father had been killed by a drunk driver when Sarah was eight, and after the funeral, her mother had slowly collapsed into herself until sometimes it felt like there was nothing left of her but fear. Fear of driving at night. Fear of men, hurricanes, and health problems, three things she found equally confounding and unpredictable. When Sarah hit puberty a year earlier than everyone else and started getting bullied because she was too chubby, too weird, her breasts too big, her hair too curly, Maureen had suggested that Sarah simply try to blend in.

But Sarah had defied her. She had gone the other way. She had worn fishnet stockings and dyed her hair blue, had listened to weird music and written dark poetry. She had left the province for a prestigious university, something that almost no one from her high school did.

But she didn't feel brave now. She didn't feel like she fit in with the beautiful people in the beautiful apartment with its ridiculously boring wall art.

She missed all her old friends: her sarcastic friend Marie who had stayed in Newfoundland to work as a nurse; her cool friend Kristie, who had moved to Los Angeles to work in costume design; her best friend Anya, who lived just outside

Toronto but was busy with an unexpected pregnancy that had turned into an unexpected marriage; her steady, feminist friend Ellen, who had moved to a suburb outside Ottawa to work in a women's bookstore. Sarah had no close friends in the city anymore, and Paul's presence in her life had kept her from noticing. She had been able to cling to Paul's friends, to Paul's and Liam's social lives.

Now her reality was coming into sharp focus, and loneliness was at the center of the frame.

The wind picked up just as Ren came out and sat on the bench next to her.

"I'm very drunk," she warned him.

"Are you?" He smiled. "It may be because Trish has been serving us lighter fluid."

"I only had one. But I never drink like that. Not strong alcohol. Never, ever. I've grown so *boring*."

His smile grew. "I forgot how chatty you get when you drink."

"Chatty?"

"You pontificate," he said. "You politely pontificate. It's like hearing your stream of consciousness."

"Oh God."

"No, it's amazing. Because some people are hiding nasty thoughts beneath the surface that come out when they're drunk, but you're just hiding more of you."

She frowned, thinking that her real thoughts were not very nice at the moment. They were about how much she disliked his wife and resented all the happy couples inside the house. She forced herself to look skyward. She could feel Ren leaning back against the wall next to her as he looked up.

"Not many stars," he observed.

"It's one thing I miss about Newfoundland. The Milky Way was always visible when I was growing up."

"I used to go camping outside Montreal as a kid, and the stars were amazing."

"It's like missing a piece of your soul when you can't see them." She was definitely very drunk to say something like that.

She could feel him watching her. She glanced at him and saw his eyes on her lips, not with intention but like he was lost in thought. Then his gaze went back toward the party, and the moment drifted by like a leaf on the wind, another thing she couldn't figure out about Ren.

"You know, I didn't think you were an asshole," she said, "back in school."

"But you had contempt for me," he replied.

"I didn't have contempt for you."

His eyes returned to the sky above them. "What happened with Liam?"

"It was when Paul moved out. I asked Liam if he wanted to move in. And it would have been fine if he said no. Except he didn't. He said that his lease lasted four more months, and he couldn't make a decision that far ahead."

"Jesus."

"And I had such a perfect record with men until then, too," she said with mock seriousness.

He gave her an amused look like he wanted to say something but was consciously holding back. Something strange was passing between them, and she didn't know what it was, but she knew it wasn't safe. Not for either of them. She carefully rose to her feet and looked at him unsteadily. "I'm having that drunk feeling where my head seems to be moving very slightly faster than my feet. You know that feeling?" She took another sip of her seltzer water. "I'm going to go get a taxi."

"You're okay to get home?"

"Definitely," she said. "I'm very good at pretending to be

more sober than I am. I just act extremely calm. That's what I did at all of Kristie's parties."

"I was completely fooled."

"I have skills, Monsieur Durand. Hidden skills."

He stood up and walked inside with her, his hands in his pockets.

"Five months! Are you serious?" Trish's voice carried from the living room as Sarah entered. Paola wore a contented smile as she stood at the center of the charcoal accent wall, the whole room buzzing around her with excitement.

"Five months until what?" Sarah asked, looking at Paola, then Paul, then Trish.

"Until the baby!" Trish cried.

Sarah almost asked, "Whose baby?" But she stopped herself.

"Me and this ridiculous man," Paolo announced to Sarah, waving a hand at Ren, "are having a child."

Sarah turned to Ren, who looked a bit stunned by the public announcement. "You didn't tell me," she chided.

"We're not announcing it too widely. Although I guess now we are." He met her eyes and then looked at the floor.

"You're going to be a great father," she said with drunken fervor, hoping he could sense that she meant it.

"Let's hope he is, because I will be working all the time," Paola said, "so he'll be home with the baby more than I will."

There was something wrenching in Ren's expression as he watched her, and she willed it not to be pity. She didn't want pity. She didn't want him thinking of her as the lonely single woman watching everyone else's life move past her.

She excused herself a few minutes later and wrangled into her jacket, lying to Paul about having a headache. Paul gave her another big hug at the door.

"I'll call you," he said. "I want to have a real talk about Liam and roommates and everything else."

He wanted to have a 'real talk' about her break-up, and he hadn't been able to do it in front of Trish. That felt significant. She'd been around him all night and he hadn't even attempted a meaningful conversation. Maybe he just didn't want her crying in front of strangers...or maybe it wasn't safe for anyone to be a mess in front of Patricia.

Still, Paul looked at home in his new apartment, with the new posters and the new furniture and the new friends. She hoped that he and Trish wouldn't get any ideas about imminent babies, though. Their relationship didn't seem headed for long-term happiness, but what did she know? Ren and Paola seemed happy, and she hadn't gotten a great first impression of Paola, either.

"Goodnight!" Sarah called from the doorway. She saw Ren wave at her from across the room, his eyes full of something. Definitely pity. She closed the door and left them all to their coupledom.

That night, Sarah pulled out her DSLR camera and set up a series of silly photos of herself in various awkward positions, lying upside-down and sideways on her bed. She shot herself slumped on her comforter, her fancy party clothes looking lumpy, her legs askew. At first, the photos represented how useless and unattractive she felt, but eventually, she began to exaggerate them even further—flopping herself like a rag doll over the whole bed. Taking up space.

She got a precise mental image of a possible photo and gathered the materials: half-wilted flowers from an old bouquet. Scented candles. Silky scarves. Romance novels. All her jewelry. She staged it all around her bed, piling things high, scattering blankets, taping fabrics to the wall, lighting candles. She put on six different necklaces at once. Then she put on her ugliest, least sexy pajamas, lay across the entire bed, and flopped her head backwards over the edge of the bed towards her camera, her hair almost touching the floor. With one hand tucked beneath a romance novel, she tripped a remote trigger to open and close the shutter on her camera lens over and over as she adjusted her pose.

She would call this photo *The Single Life*, she decided. When she looked at the image, she loved it. It felt like the beginning of a series.

5

THE KRISTMAN GALLERY, NOVEMBER 2011

SARAH STOOD in front of one of the bright white walls of the gallery, feeling like she herself was another piece of art on display. There should be a label under her saying: ***Young Photographer Acting Nervous*, Mixed media: cotton-blend fabric and flesh.**

It was Sarah's first gallery opening in Toronto. She was part of a group show of six up-and-coming young photographers, painters, and video artists, and she had an entire wall set aside for her *Single Life* series in one of the city's smaller, edgier downtown art galleries. Now she hovered in uncomfortable heels and a sheath dress at the opening, occasionally meeting eyes with the other young artists who all seemed inexpressibly cooler than she was. They were standing in their assigned corners as potential buyers circulated in a meandering orbit of cheap wine and stilted conversation.

"This is yours?" A woman in her sixties with a silvery bob of hair leaned close to one of the photos, peering at a detail in the upper corner.

"It is," Sarah agreed. The question felt superfluous; all the photos were self-portraits.

The woman stepped over to examine another photo, then chuckled and moved on to the next artist without even glancing at the rest of her work. Sarah needed to get used to that: the inconsistent attention, the casual dismissal in people's eyes. This was part of the game, she supposed: developing a thick skin, selling herself as much as her work, acting charming in the face of rich people's knowing looks.

Her friend Anya had stopped by earlier, apologizing for having to run but giving her an assertive hug and a long stream of enthusiastic gushing. Her roommate Winnie had come by as well and had quietly eaten a single piece of cheese on a napkin before giving a half-whispered compliment and slipping out the door. How Winnie managed to function as a student-teacher in a room full of Toronto public school students was beyond Sarah's imagination; given Winnie's general disposition, Sarah suspected that they were eating her alive.

Just as Sarah began to consider helping herself to her own glass of wine and then hiding in the back hallway to down it, she saw Paul entering the door and peeling off a black and white checked scarf as he looked around to find her. Trish had purchased a peacoat for him, and Sarah could concede that it made him looked appealingly dashing, if amusingly British. Someone else had entered behind him, too—surely not Trish herself. No, it was Ren. Sarah's stomach flipped at the sight of him. Were Paul and Ren good friends, now? The idea made her sad—that Ren was now accepted as part of Paul's social circle but she herself was not.

"There she is!" Paul called when he saw her. He stepped forward and gave her a casual hug, his wool coat exuding the chilly fall air. "This is so exciting!" His eyes flicked to the photos and back again. "Your first show in the city!"

Ren stood back, smiling at her in one of his scuffed leather jackets. "Hey," he said warmly. She gave him a hug and smelled a whiff of a stolen cigarette on him.

"Aren't you supposed to be having a baby right now?" she asked.

"Five days 'til deadline," Ren said. "But I wouldn't have missed this. Why didn't you tell me you had a gallery show?"

"You'll know why when you see the work," she said with a self-deprecating laugh.

Ren immediately went to examine her photos as Paul followed behind. Her heart pounded from nerves, watching him pause at the first one. At least there was no gratuitous nudity, but in every other way the photos made her feel completely exposed. Her *Single Life* portraits made Sarah seem by turns comical, confident, and absurdly lonely.

"Inspired by the break-up with Liam, I take it?" Paul asked over his shoulder.

"And your housewarming party," Sarah replied to Paul. She saw Ren register this with a frown. "When I was the only single person there," she reminded them.

"That was entirely an accident," said Paul, waving a hand in protest, and Sarah repressed the desire to point out that in spite of his denials, Trish hadn't invited her over again. Sarah and Paul had had coffee a few times and he had been warmly supportive of her break-up and her new artistic goals. But she and Paul never did anything involving Trish, nothing that meant Sarah was going to be part of their core friend group. Fair enough, Sarah supposed; she didn't like Trish either and shouldn't expect unreciprocated affection. It still made her sad.

She watched Ren taking in the photos in order: *The Picnic*, which depicted Sarah lying on a checkered blanket alone in a park surrounded by empty bottles of wine, her legs clad in rainbow tights, smears of blinding white sunscreen on her cheeks; then *The Sunbather*, a portrait of her alone at a beach, wrapped in a sandy towel and reading a smutty novel under a neon pink umbrella as the legs of an attractive young lifeguard walked past. Ren stepped in front of a photo of her in a bubbly bathtub, then moved on quickly.

She noticed a few women registering Ren from across the room. That must happen to him everywhere. She realized it had been a while since she'd even remembered how beautiful he was. She was too busy missing him. He hadn't called her again since the museum day. She hadn't reached out, either, of course. His wife was having a baby; she felt like he needed to be the one to maintain the outlines of their friendship.

"These have so much of your personality," Ren said when he returned to her side.

"Sassy and self-absorbed?"

"Sunny but with a razor-sharp wit," Ren offered. "No, I just mean they have a perspective. An opinion. It's a really cool direction for you."

"It's like you're a theater director," Paul agreed. "Designing costumes, staging sets."

"Well, we'll see if any of them sell. They may be a little too pointed to hang in people's living rooms."

"I would buy one," Paul insisted.

Sarah almost snorted. "Can you imagine a photo of me with my legs akimbo between Trish's black-and-white photos of Toronto tourist attractions?"

Paul winced a little, while Ren looked like he was suppressing a laugh.

"I'm sorry!" Sarah cried. "That came out snarkier than I intended. Your place is lovely. Very...clean."

"We're engaged, actually," Paul said. Sarah stood frozen in shock for a half-second before her smile returned.

"Wow! Congratulations! Look at you two." She waved her hand between them. "You're engaged, and you're having a baby.

Checking off all the big ones. I might be forced to call you adults soon."

"We probably won't get married for a couple of years," Paul added, "to save up for the wedding Trish wants. But that's the plan."

"Well, that makes sense. Let Trish plan what she wants! And you," Sarah added, turning to Ren, "need to send me a photo of your gorgeous baby as soon as it arrives."

"Any day now," Ren said. "Paola warned me that I better not freeze up when the day comes."

"We're actually meeting them for dinner soon," Paul said. "So we should get going. Hopefully, she doesn't go into labor before the food is on the table."

The fact that neither of the women had stopped by Sarah's opening felt like a statement; Ren caught Sarah's hurt expression before she could hide it.

"Sorry I haven't been free to hang out much," Ren said gently. "Paola's had a tough pregnancy."

"Well, she's in the home stretch." Sarah upped her good cheer in the face of his kindness. "I should let you both get to the restaurant so you'll be ready to whisk her away to a hospital if required."

"As long as I don't have to do the delivery," Ren said. "That's my nightmare. Having the baby come in the taxi."

Sarah smiled. "You can handle anything. You once stayed up for thirty-six hours straight to finish a paper on Thomas Pynchon."

"I'll remind myself of that when changing diapers at 2 a.m."

"*The Crying of Baby 49*," Sarah joked.

"I think diapers are more like *Gravity's Rainbow*," Paul replied. He took a breath. "Well, I'm glad we made it. This is tremendous work, Sarah."

She held her chin even higher. "I have suffered for my art by having solo wine parties and reading trashy paperbacks."

Paul gave her a kiss on the cheek, then Ren gave her a light hug.

"I want to hear about all your shows," Ren said quietly. "I mean it. You promise?"

"I promise."

And she watched her two favorite men in the world leave together to return to their partners and their bright, hopeful lives.

She glanced at her photo entitled *Bathtub*. In the image, she was dangling one leg over the edge of a tub, the rest of her mostly covered in mounds of frothy bubble bath except for a bit of her collarbone peeking through the foam. One confident hand with purple nail polish raised a beer can in victory. She had used a pop flash, 1970s style, like she had been caught by paparazzi. Sarah loved the image, even if Ren hadn't.

The photo made her look exactly like she felt. Ridiculous. Messy. A little hopeful in spite of everything.

6

TORONTO OUTDOOR ART FAIR, JULY 2012

REN TEXTED her a week after the arrival of his new baby.

Alejandro Omar Durand De Leon. Born November 8th, 2011. Baby and mama are perfect.

The image he sent had clearly been taken by Paola: Ren sat in front of a large, curtained window looking thrilled and exhausted, his face unshaven, clutching a miniscule bundle that squinted up from an adorably fashionable blanket. Their baby had been given a small, black cap for the occasion and squinted up like an ancient Italian man about to play bocce.

She wrote him back appropriately gushing replies and he asked her how her art show had gone.

Four sales! She wrote. *Paid my rent for the month and got a fisheye lens.*

Congratulations. Tell me you're kidding about the fisheye, he replied.

Just trying to get you worked up. It was a regular wide-angle, she wrote back.

He responded kindly about her talent, but she felt sad. They didn't feel like friends anymore, and she realized in retrospect that maybe he had only been allowed to hang out with her when she had a boyfriend. Once she didn't, Paola had drawn a line in the sand. Breaking things off with Liam had caused Sarah to lose her friendship with Ren as well.

OF COURSE *they picked the name Alejandro*, Anya wrote when Sarah shared the name with Anya and Kristie in their group text. *Couldn't pick something with one or two syllables. Wouldn't be Sophisticated and European.*

It's a badass name, Kristie texted. *I bet Ren's wife is impossibly hot and classy. Signed, Krishnakali.*

LOLOL, Anya wrote. *Everyone knows you are impossibly hot and classy, K.*

Ren's wife is definitely a hot, smart lawyer, Sarah replied. *But she hates me for some reason. She looked at me like I'm either a threat to their marriage or boring as toast. Not sure which.*

It's because Ren was in love with you at uni, Kristie wrote back.

Ha ha ha ha ha, Sarah replied.

TO HER SURPRISE, three weeks later, she heard from Ren again.

sarah, Ren wrote, *home on paternity leave and lack of sleep is pushing me into deep moral crisis about the ethics of watching reality tv. how are you doing? hopefully another photo series in the works.*

Sarah took a moment to enjoy the visual of an exhausted Ren breaking down and watching the Real Housewives of Anywhere before she texted back. *Glad you're having ethical crisis about reality tv. Fortunately the ethics of your field of journalism are above reproach.*

stabbed through the heart when I was looking for support, he replied.

Sorry. I shouldn't mock you when you're sleep deprived. I'm working on photos but not yet a series. Maybe I will watch reality tv to get inspired.

a Sarah Drakenberg reality tv photo series sounds either horrifying or brilliant, he wrote back.

aiming for horrifying AND brilliant, she replied.

He responded quickly. *Like your hummus-flavored cookie recipe from sophomore year.*

For the months that followed, Ren and Sarah would text every three or four weeks, usually about local art shows or occasionally because one of them had read a book or seen a film that the other one might enjoy. He would send photos of the baby occasionally, but only when she requested them. She would send slightly ridiculous ideas for her next photo series.

Going on a Dorothy Lange kick, she wrote to Ren at one point. *But feels exploitative to shoot poor people. Can I shoot people who only THINK they are poor, like college students without enough money to buy newest video games?*

Shoot them looking longingly into the middle distance, Ren replied, *clutching a crumpled Starbucks gift card.*

She grinned. *Is black and white allowed in this circumstance?*

Ren texted back: *You have my permission. Sepia-tone preferred, though. Gallery show should play fiddle music from the 1930s to set the tragic atmosphere.*

A couple of weeks after that, Ren texted her again.

On a horror film kick. Let the Right One In was brilliant. Have you seen?

Sarah was at her desk when she got the message. *Not yet. Are you watching horror movies when Jandro is awake or asleep?*

Asleep. But maybe he's subconsciously being trained to think that quiet screaming from the other room is normal, Ren replied.

And you were worried about being a good father.

A FEW WEEKS LATER, Sarah wrote to him.

I think I just saw your dad being interviewed on television about artificial intelligence and the nature of human consciousness.

Ren wrote back: *that was him.*

He looks so much like you.

Ren's response took a long moment. *Yes.*

I think I understood about one word out of ten.

Ren wrote back: *Then it was definitely my dad.*

SARAH HAD NOTICED that all their exchanges ended carefully after four or five texts. Sometimes she ended the text exchange, sometimes Ren did, but it felt like they were carefully setting the boundaries of their friendship, making sure that if Paola read the texts, she would have nothing to worry about. They never got personal in their messages; it was all gentle teasing about which character from *Breaking Bad* Ren related to the most, or how Sarah could possibly enjoy books by both Jonathan Franzen and Nicholas Sparks.

She didn't mind. It was better than not having him in her life at all. In fact, her commitment to the 'single life' in her art had coincided with a rapid development of her life as a single person in general.

Winnie, her roommate, was actually pleasant to live with most of the time, even if she seemed to be in the wrong profession. They would get together on Friday nights and watch romantic movies together, which had proven to be almost as much fun as watching action films with Paul. Winnie would bring home a bottle of wine, Sarah would make cookies and popcorn, and they would pause the movie at key moments to critique the unhealthy relationships on screen or to sigh about a particularly beautiful actor.

Anya was also fully back in Sarah's life: she was finally starting to emerge from the shock of new parenthood now that her baby was old enough to go to daycare. She'd gotten a job doing marketing at a downtown Toronto children's theater, and once every week or two, she had time to emerge from her maternal existence to meet up and say snarky things over coffee or brunch.

Equally fun was the fact that their old roommate Kristie had moved back to Canada from Los Angeles and now lived in Toronto, too; she had spent a few years working as a costume assistant on feature films and wanted to launch her career as a costume designer in the Toronto film and theater scene. Within two weeks of her return, Kristie was once again throwing elaborate parties, now held in a massive, edgy loft space that she shared with four roommates in a renovated factory building. Kristie had streaked her black hair with a single line of silver and had adopted a faint Southern California lilt, in which her pitch would shift octaves within a sentence to make an important point.

Sarah found that she was less lonely as a single person than she'd been when dating Liam, which felt like an important lesson. Paul, by contrast, seemed to be growing more pessimistic about his acting career. She secretly wished he would follow Kristie's path to Los Angeles, which had many more acting opportunities than Toronto. Instead, he talked vaguely about his upcoming wedding plans and grumbled about how he should have gone into comedy writing, but it was 'too late' for that. It didn't help that Trish's career was going comparatively better, at least in terms of booking modeling jobs for outdoor clothing catalogues. Sarah worried for him.

One day in early July, nine months after her *Single Life* gallery opening, Ren finally texted Sarah about having an in-person meet-up.

toronto outdoor art fair? he wrote. *meet me sunday? i will have jandro.*

She agreed at once.

THE ART FAIR was an annual event in the city in which visual artists gathered to sell their work in dozens of booths in a central outdoor plaza. Sarah had briefly considered renting a booth herself, but hadn't been able to justify the expense of getting a tent and table and making dozens of prints in the hopes of selling a few of her weird photographs. It was an ideal outing for meeting up with Ren, though. The weather was hot and still as she stood near the middle of the city square, right near the letter T in a giant three-dimensional Toronto sign near a reflecting pool. She was wearing a bright sundress with yellow flowers on it and carrying her photography gear in her backpack in preparation for taking some headshots later that day.

She spotted Ren a few minutes after the hour, walking towards her in a black t-shirt and dark blue jeans, wearing an alert baby strapped to the center of his chest like a bomb. Little Jandro was looking directly towards her and Sarah laughed at the infant's expression: bewildered, curious, his legs flung out both ways.

"Hold on!" she said. "Stop right there."

She pulled out her camera as Ren stopped in place against

the backdrop of milling people. He threw out both hands in a helpless gesture as she took a photo of him and the baby.

"What did you see?" he asked when he approached.

She swung the camera around to show him the LCD screen image of him and Jandro, echoing each other, their arms flung out wide.

"It was your son's expression," she explained with a grin. "Like he was having an existential crisis about his place in the universe."

Ren grinned. "I think that's what babies do all the time."

"I'm going to do a photo series about existential babies," Sarah announced. Ren smiled at her affectionately. "I'll show them in various settings, puzzling over the state of humanity."

"I'd love to see it." He looked down at his son. "Yeah, he's supposed to face towards me in this carrier, but he insists on facing out."

"He's a budding journalist," Sarah said. "Wants to know what's going on. Shall we introduce him to some high culture?" Sarah gestured to a booth where someone was selling cutesy landscapes of wide-eyed deer and rabbits.

"Jandro and I do nothing but high culture," Ren said with a smile, "also known as watching fish tanks in the pet store."

"So how have you been doing with fatherhood?" she asked as they threaded through the crowds together.

"I love it. Not getting much sleep, but...he's a good one. Good-natured. Easily distracted, but so am I. I've scaled back on work to keep an eye on him. I'm mostly freelancing these days."

"What language are you speaking with him?" she asked. "You grew up with French, right?"

Ren nodded. "We're planning on raising him with French from me and Spanish from Paola and then letting him pick up English in daycare. He'll probably hate us for a while, but it seems worthwhile in the end."

"He's your son, so he'll probably be reading Camus novels by kindergarten."

"Please, Sarah," Ren drawled. "Camus is preschool. He'll be reading Proust."

"The proper age for *Remembrance of Things Past.*"

"*Remembrance of Things Yesterday.*" Ren grinned. "They say he'll learn to speak later because he'll have to sort out all the languages. But there are worse things."

"And are you getting any help? Childcare, grandparents? I know Anya had trouble when her daughter Ilona was born because her whole family are up north."

He looked away. "Paola's parents recently moved back to the States, and mine are in Montreal, so it's just me right now."

"Your parents don't make it down much?"

He shook his head. "My mother is against having children on principle. Did I tell you that? You would appreciate this, Sarah. My mother wrote an article in a feminist magazine about how no women should have kids, ever. She argued that the only births should be accidental because no woman was ever truly happier after having a child. And she published it when I was sixteen."

Sarah felt startled by the story. She knew she was supposed to be amused, but there was something in Ren's tone that made her wonder if he felt as casual about it as he was pretending to. "How did you find out about that? She didn't show it to you..."

"No, but they interviewed her for a Montreal newspaper about it and it got back to me through a classmate. So that was fun," he said.

"That sounds hurtful."

"No, I mean, I got it," he said, shrugging. "She and my dad both came from really repressive backgrounds in terms of sexuality and gender and all of that, so they went the other way. My mom's parents were Christian refugees, my dad's mother is a conservative Muslim. When my parents met at the Sorbonne, I think they decided to become the exact opposite of everything their parents had been. So they doubled down on sexual freedom, personal freedom, stuff like that. The more progressive, the better."

"Like how Ayn Rand was raised in Soviet Russia so she fought for people's right to be selfish?"

"Did you just compare my radical feminist mother to Ayn Rand?"

Sarah laughed. "I'm sorry. I was extrapolating. Unfairly."

"No, you're right in a way. My parents are classic left-wing academics, and they took some extreme positions. Which is fine, you know, but at sixteen, that wasn't my favorite thing to hear. I felt like I ruined her life."

They were silent for a moment. Ren was unconsciously moving Jandro's hands up and down, keeping the baby in motion. "But yeah, it means...most people's parents get excited when there's a grandchild. But my mother...she's fine with Jandro. She's not unexcited. But she's a little skeptical. She doesn't understand why I'm doing this when I could be working on my journalism career. Why would I want to stay at home with a baby?"

Sarah considered Ren's choice to mostly stay at home in light of his own parents' attitudes about children. "Well, he's beautiful, so I'm glad you and Paola had him."

Ren grinned. "Yeah. He looks more like Paola than me, which is good."

She wondered if he subconsciously attributed everything good about his son to his wife. That might be chivalry, but it might be a self-doubt that Sarah had never noticed in him before.

They stopped and looked at the work of artists and painters from all over Canada. Some of the pieces were blandly pretty but others were wildly creative and new. On impulse, Sarah spent one hundred dollars on a tiny painting that was done in the style of the Mughal Empire, all detail work and dotted gold, but instead of depicting medieval warriors on horseback, it represented a group of tattooed young hipsters reclining on motorbikes and staring at their cell phones. Ren bought a photo print of the Northern Lights reflected in a lake in Iceland and carefully placed it in his backpack between some spare diapers.

"Travel goals," he said as he carefully tucked it away.

"That's a beautiful baby," a passing woman said with a smile as Sarah rocked Jandro in her arms while Ren rearranged his bag.

"Oh, he's not mine," Sarah replied, startled. "It's his baby."

The woman turned her gaze to Ren as he stood up. "That's a beautiful..." The woman trailed off, caught in Ren's eyes like she was hypnotized. "You have a beautiful baby," she said in a rush, then turned abruptly and walked away, blushing.

"Oh my God." Sarah was laughing. "How do you deal with that?"

"Deal with what?" Ren asked, adjusting Jandro back into place in his carrier.

She would never have been able to say this at university, but something about having a baby strapped to Ren's chest made it feel possible. "How do you deal with being so handsome that people stop talking in the middle of their sentences when they see you?"

"That is not what just happened," Ren said. Seeing her skeptical glance, he shrugged. "Okay, so..." He paused again.

"Go on." Sarah felt brief delight at his discomposure.

"So I have girls' eyes, right?" Ren began.

"You do?" Ren's beauty wasn't just about his eyes, but Sarah wasn't going to say so.

"It's the lashes. I get them from my father, and boys used to make fun of me in school. They said I looked like a girl, that I was gay, all that stuff. And I was no good at sports, which didn't help. And I was named Rene, which sounded like a girl's name to my English-speaking classmates."

"Wait a minute. Is that why you went by Ren?"

He shrugged, hiding a smile. It was funny to find that out about him after all these years.

"Anyway, when I got into my later teens, it turned out that girls found my eyes attractive, and it felt like getting something back for all the teasing I got. But...it's not real, right? I mean, I understand my looks catch people's attention, but I always preferred people who didn't notice them much at all." Ren met her gaze warmly.

Did he mean her? She felt a little ashamed. She had definitely noticed his looks when they first met.

She tried for a light tone. "Well, I'm glad you have a healthy philosophy to deal with that terrible cross you have to bear."

"It's been hard," he agreed with a grin as they walked.

"I guess your wife is equally gorgeous, so you've provided people with a useful distraction when she's next to you."

He paused in his stride. "Yeah. Paola's um... Listen."

Sarah stopped to face him. His expression was strange.

"I'm moving. I told you that Paola's parents moved back to the States. Her father manages hotels, and he came to Toronto to launch a boutique hotel line, but that's done, and he got a job offer in Las Vegas and moved back there last year. So Paola wants to move there to be closer to her parents. In Nevada."

"And you're all going." Stupid Sarah. Of course they were all going.

"I'm going to have to find something to do for work down there, but it's really important to her, so... She always talked about going back to the States or Mexico where her grandparents are, but it was going to be a few years from now, when

Jandro was a bit older. But now she wants to do it right away. Her mother has health issues, and she wants to be closer to her, make sure that Jandro's grandparents get to spend time with him."

"Can Paola work as a lawyer down there?"

"She's going to study for the Nevada bar. It might take a year or two, but she can do the coursework online. She'll be working for her father's business in the meantime, doing contracts. And I'll figure something out."

She tried to put on a cheerful smile. "Well, you've covered people behaving badly in Toronto, so I'm sure there are plenty of people behaving badly in Las Vegas that you could write about."

He looked uncertain. "Yeah. If someone will hire me. It's not a good time for newspapers right now. Initially, I'll probably stay home with Jandro. We're going to live with Paola's parents for a while to save some money."

"Ren..." It sounded potentially nightmarish, living with his in-laws as an unemployed stay-at-home dad while his wife worked for his father-in-law. She didn't want to say so, but she couldn't force her usual cheerful attitude. "That sounds really hard."

He looked unexpectedly defensive. "I can handle it."

"Of course you can. That wasn't what I meant." Sadness was hitting her in a rising wave. It felt like they had just recovered their friendship in the last year, and now it was being washed away again. "When are you leaving?"

"Three weeks."

Her heart dropped. "That's soon."

"Yeah. Paola's going down next weekend, taking Jandro with her. I'll follow her once I sort stuff out here. We're getting someone to take over our lease."

"I'll miss you," she said at last, her voice more emotional than she meant for it to be.

"I'll miss you, too." His tone was carefully neutral.

He was watching her closely. She had to act calm enough that he didn't give her that look filled with pity again.

"Well, don't stop texting me," she said, managing a little bit of cheer. "I'd miss getting to mock your depressing taste in movies."

"I won't."

She wanted to give him a hug, but his son was between them, a solid wall of baby, utterly consequential. Jandro would be the most important thing to Ren from now on. She didn't mind coming after his wife and son, but she did mind not mattering to him at all. And that would happen, surely, if they weren't in the same city anymore. They would drift apart. It had happened before.

"Your baby series," he said. "I want to see it, Sarah."

She smiled, feeling tearful. Before he left, he gave her a kiss on the side of her forehead that lasted a few seconds longer than she expected. She tried very hard not to think too much about it.

7

PAUL AND TRISH'S WEDDING, OCTOBER 2016

SARAH DIDN'T THINK she liked Las Vegas. It was true that she had only been there for an hour or so, having taken a taxi from the airport directly to the hotel where everyone was staying for the wedding. So it was possible that there were parts of the city that felt earth-bound and real, but she hadn't found them yet. Her hotel lobby had a faint minty smell and was teaming with half-drunk businessmen, foreign tourists, and women in animal print fabrics. It was the last place on earth she would have expected to find herself for Paul and Trish's wedding. But here she was.

The wedding had gone through its own journey of twists and turns over the last few years. Paul's father had gotten cancer a few months after Paul got engaged, and Paul had ended up moving back to Newfoundland to care for his dad in what was supposed to be a three-month stay while Trish remained in Toronto finishing up her four-episode arc as a social climbing trophy wife on a television series. After it became clear that Paul wasn't coming back anytime soon, they had officially split up.

Sarah should have felt relieved that Paul had escaped Trish, a woman defined by her impatience for emotional mess and love of beige home décor, but instead Sarah felt a deepening concern for her cousin. She suspected his decision to stay home had less to do with his father's health and more to do with his mother's tendency to be the drama queen, the needy center of every problem. Sarah worried that sweet, hilarious Paul had traded one controlling woman for another, playing the role of peacemaker between his ailing father and his verbally abusive mom.

She herself rarely went home to Newfoundland except for an obligatory visit with her mother at Christmas, but she made a point of flying back more often when Paul returned, partly just to check on him. He always seemed profoundly grateful to see her, but it saddened her to realize that he had given up on acting entirely.

"I didn't have the It Factor," he told her one day over coffee in downtown St. John's. "The It Factor being money, connections, and insane amounts of luck. I have to find something else to do that won't make me want to kill myself."

"What about teaching?" she suggested. "You'd have a captive audience."

"Can you imagine?" he said. "My poor students."

"You're nerdy enough, that's all I'm saying."

Strangely, Sarah had experienced exactly the opposite of Paul when it came to her own artistic career: her *Existential Innocence* baby series—the one that she had half-jokingly announced to Ren—had turned into a massive, runaway success.

It had begun with that initial photo of Alejandro that she had snapped on her last day with Ren. She later re-staged the photo with a different baby, only this time with a plan for a photo-edited collage. At the center of the photo was a curious, awkward baby, arms spread wide in confusion, dressed in a pale cream onesie...and around him, Sarah had added a spiraling image of the Milky Way, trails of light representing shifts in time and space: a baby as a representation of existential doubt, the inner lost child within. Then she had taken photos of Anya's toddler daughter pondering a mountain range like a romantic poet, and photos of her roommate Winnie's nephew staring into a fish tank where the large, murky eye of some strange leviathan creature stared back.

Her *Existential Innocence* series became a minor hit at the Kristman Gallery, but it had led to an even more unexpected outcome: commissions. Various wealthy people got in contact with her after her show to ask if she would do portraits of their own babies and toddlers against strange, moody backgrounds. Surprised by the request but needing the money, she agreed, with the caveat that she retained artistic control over each photo. So she had spent the last couple of years creating photo collages of people's babies: babies who appeared to be lost in the forest; babies sitting on bales of hay contemplating broken farm equipment; babies who perched in old-fashioned, rusty baby carriages in abandoned factories, their eyes wide. The photos were faintly pessimistic but never depressing, lightly ironic but never unkind, and they had become a must-have for nurseries among some of the wealthier families in Toronto, and then Ottawa, and then New York City.

After her first year of photo commissions, she had been able to quit her magazine job, and now she only booked the occasional headshot session as a favor to a friend. Instead, Sarah was doing exactly what her mother had once deemed impossible: making a living entirely as a photographer, doing art she enjoyed, and earning enough to live well. She could even take the occasional trip to Europe.

The money had changed other things for her, too. She had gotten into better shape and had made peace with her looks, finally realizing that her appearance was workable and attractive, if not dazzling. She wore red lipstick and put her curly ringlets, highlighted a pale blond, into messy up-dos. The inner doubt that had haunted her from years of childhood bullying felt less constant now. Another boyfriend came and went, and she felt fine with it.

So when Paul called her one August to announce that he was back with Trish and getting married in Las Vegas, she was surprised, but the cost of a last-minute trip would not be a burden.

"How did this happen?" He hadn't even mentioned that they were back together.

"Trish came to visit a friend who was offering her a job in St. John's, and we realized we had never gotten over each other. So we decided to go to Vegas and just do it."

"Why Las Vegas?"

"It's somewhere we can do it quickly. We don't want a big thing. We just want to be together."

The words made her heart melt into a soft little puddle, and she didn't even like Trish.

"I've always liked the American Southwest," he continued, "although I won't have time to explore it on this trip."

"So you're moving back to Toronto?" Sarah tried not to sound like a hopeful little kid.

"No. She's living in St. John's right now, helping her friend start a media company. She's always wanted to travel, so she's excited about Newfoundland."

Sarah didn't bother to tell Paul that Newfoundland was the last place you should go if you wanted to travel. The island province was not without its charms, but it was emphatically the end of the line, the last stop on the travel train. You could fly from St. John's to Toronto, Montreal, or Halifax, but that was about it. It was a terminal destination.

But he sounded happy, and Sarah tried to sound happy for

him. "This is wonderful news," she said, doing her best to mean it.

"Will you be there? Will you come celebrate with us?"

"Of course."

"It's going to be small. Probably fifteen people and Trish's parents. Ren's still out there so he can come, too."

Sarah's breath caught, but she managed to control her voice. "That's good to hear. I miss Ren."

That part was true. When Ren had first moved to New Mexico, he had done as promised: sending her a friendly text every few weeks, almost as often as when they were living in Toronto. She had replied in kind, sending him updates on her baby photo series.

Then one day, two years after he moved to Nevada, he had sent her a quick text with a photo of the desert at night with an astonishing Milky Way arcing above: *Desert outside Vegas.*

Stunning, Sarah wrote back.

He replied: *Everyone who comes to Vegas should be required to go out in the desert to experience nature.*

Sarah had replied: *If you keep making these strict rules for people, you're setting yourself up for disappointment.*

He hadn't written her back.

A few weeks later, she sent him a joke about rewatching *Howl's Moving Castle* and realizing she had become less like the earnest heroine Sophie and more like the grumpy fire demon Calcifer, and he never answered. Fair enough, she thought. Maybe he hadn't seen the film.

A month later, she sent him a text about the opening of her babies show in New York City, where it was having a brief run at a sister gallery of the Kristman.

That's great. Congratulations.

Thanks, she replied.

Then nothing. She realized he had stopped writing her entirely. It was always her reaching out to him.

She asked Paul whether Ren was okay, and he replied, "I think so. He's having some family stuff. Why?" She mentioned that he had stopped texting her, and Paul said that he was probably very busy.

"It's tricky for him," Paul told her. "Living with the in-laws. I think he's working part-time, too."

Sarah wondered a little if Paola had told him not to text her...if Paola had told him not to text any women. Would Ren admit it if that were so?

A week later, perhaps after talking to Paul, Ren had texted back: *hope you're well.*

You too, she wrote. *Everything okay?*

Then nothing.

Sometime later, she wrote him on his birthday. *Happy birthday, Ren.*

Thanks, he answered.

It was so flat and polite compared to the way he used to write her that she felt embarrassed, like she was being sent a message. Had she crossed a line somewhere? Flirted without meaning to? She went through their old texts for a smoking gun where she had messed up. Nothing seemed too bad, but almost anything could be read as flirtatious if you squinted your eyes and stared long enough at it.

So Sarah waited for him to write her again. She would let him make the first move this time. She didn't want to do anything that would threaten his wife or his marriage. So she waited, and waited, and waited.

He wrote her a brief, perfunctory note on her birthday, but that was it.

After a year had passed with nothing more than birthday exchanges, she stopped asking Paul for updates about Ren. It hurt to know that he was staying in touch with Paul and not her. But now, arriving in this strange hotel in Las Vegas for Paul and Trish's wedding festivities, Sarah knew she would finally see Ren again. She wondered how he was doing, how his marriage was going, why he had stopped texting with no explanation. She was hurt but had no right to be, which was the most mortifying form of sadness.

As if on cue, just as she was walking down the hallway to her hotel room, awkwardly juggling her key card, dress bag and wheeled luggage, Ren Durand stepped out of a room immediately in front of her, closing the door softly behind him.

His appearance was unusually unkempt, his hair mussed and clothes wrinkled.

"Ren?"

He spun to look at her, his expression going flat. "Sarah. Hi." His voice was low.

"What's up?"

Then the door swung open behind him and a pretty redheaded woman was standing there in a t-shirt and silky pajama shorts, her hair in a chaotic tangle. "Weren't you going to leave me your number?" she asked.

Ren's eyes shot to the woman. "Uh...Right. Yes. Sure."

Sarah watched him do a pat-down of his outfit as he searched around for his cell phone.

"Well, I'll just..." Sarah said, waving vaguely, and kept walking. Her room was only two doors away, and she could practically feel Ren's mortification radiating toward her as he spoke to the woman in low tones.

"Here. And what's yours?"

"I mean, I don't have to call you," came the young woman's irritated reply before Sarah managed to unlock the door to her room. "But I do come to town a lot." Sarah slipped inside and shut the door as quickly as she could.

Everything about the scene felt unreal and sordid. Wasn't Ren married? She stood inside her hotel room door and sent a quick text to Paul.

Hey. Ren and Paola are coming to your wedding, right?

That should be vague enough to fish out the details.

Her phone buzzed a moment later. *Not Paola. It would get awkward after the divorce.*

Sarah heard footsteps outside her door that she knew were Ren's. He was standing there deciding whether to knock. She waited, frozen in place, then heard a quiet sigh before the footsteps kept going.

She wondered what to text Paul, whether to mention what she'd seen. Instead, she wrote, *When was he divorced?*

Paul replied: *Finalized a couple of weeks ago but separated a year. You guys should catch up. He may be slow getting going today because my bachelor party went late but he'll be at the rehearsal dinner.*

Bachelor party. That explained the bad Vegas cliché that she had stumbled upon. It still seemed so out of character for Ren. At school, he had hooked up with young women he liked talking to, not ones whom he wasn't interested in giving his phone number to...at least, none that she knew of. Maybe he had a whole other life she'd never known about.

She stood there, pressing her back against the wall and shutting her eyes tight. Something else hit her, a delayed reaction. He was still gorgeous. Startlingly so. Of course he was.

Everywhere she visited in Las Vegas seemed to have some kind of gimmick: flamingos, fountains, shiny red décor. At the Thai restaurant that Paul and Trish had picked for dinner the night before the wedding, the gimmick was massive fish tanks on the walls lit by glowing blue light. Everywhere in the city sounded like a dance party and smelled like cigarettes, and this place was no exception, Sarah thought. But it did look cool.

As she entered the private room reserved for their event, she paused to give a quick hug to Trish, who looked as slim and elegant as ever in a navy-blue cocktail dress, and then turned and threw her arms around Paul.

"Guess what! I got a teaching job!" Paul half-shouted in her ear over the aggressively loud music.

"Are you serious?"

"I'm going to be a history teacher. For twelve-year-olds."

"Poor little bastards."

"I know! And I'm doing acting again. I've started an improv group."

"That's fantastic. Send me a video of you doing improv!"

"Absolutely no fucking way," he said with a laugh.

As she released Paul from her hug, she noticed Ren standing behind him, dressed in his usual dark colors as if he wanted to recede into the wall.

"Hey!" she said as she approached, acting like they hadn't seen each other earlier.

"Hey, Sarah." He was frowning.

Everything about him felt overwhelming suddenly: that he was here, and close, and staring at her. She took another step towards him. "How are you?"

"Fine."

"And the boy? How old is he now?"

"He's almost five. He's in pre-school."

"The famous Camus years."

He finally broke into a grin. "Right. Picking up English has not been as easy as we'd hoped."

"Well, I'd love to see photos of him," she said. "If you want to share any." There, she was being normal, right?

"Sure." He stared at her for a long moment. "Can I talk to you for a minute?"

Weren't they already talking? "Of course."

"Over there, maybe?"

He led her to the quietest corner of the room, where they could stand in the half-darkness just beyond the edge of the biggest fish tank. He leaned close to her and she thought again that he was almost stupidly attractive.

"So that woman you saw me with before..." he said just loudly enough to be heard above the music.

"Mmm?"

"Paul's bachelor party last night, we all got pretty drunk. And she's very nice, I mean I had a nice talk with her, but I don't make a habit...since my divorce, I don't make a habit..."

"Ren, it's fine. You didn't do anything you have to justify."

"I know, I just..." He took a breath.

"I just didn't know you were divorced."

His mouth opened in shock. "Paul didn't tell you?"

"I didn't ask him. I guess I was waiting for you to tell me."

Ren looked down again. "Right."

"Why'd you stop texting me?" There. That was what she really wanted to say. "You stopped completely. At first I thought you had gotten busy, but...maybe you did get busy, but..."

He let out a long, slow breath. "Yeah."

"I thought we were friends, and then it felt like..." She couldn't finish. She didn't know what it had felt like. Like she was a seductress he had to cut out of his life? Like he just didn't like her anymore?

"No. We are friends," he said now. "I hope we are."

Sarah had a strange feeling of suspense. Half of her—more than half—had expected him to say that he hadn't even realized he'd stopped texting her, that he had just gotten so busy that he had largely forgotten she existed. But his expression suggested that there was an explanation after all.

"Did I do something?" she asked.

"No!" He looked surprised.

She wondered again about Paola. Had there been a prohibition against talking to her? But if so, why hadn't that ended when he separated from his wife?

He met her eyes. "I just...my marriage was not...good. It was falling apart. And I know you predicted that."

"No, Ren." Was that what he'd thought? During that last conversation at the art fair, that she'd been insinuating he would get a divorce?

"I felt... It felt weird writing you and not telling you I was having trouble. But explaining it...I thought...I guess I didn't want you to..." He stopped.

Oh God. Did Ren think she was going to hit on him? Did Ren think that if she heard his marriage was on the rocks, she would make a move? What an utterly mortifying thought.

"You didn't want me to what?" she asked, trying not sound defensive and failing. She had been dating someone, she thought angrily. She wasn't going to throw herself at him at the first opportunity. In the middle of his divorce.

"I didn't want you to say you agreed with her," he said at last. "I didn't want you to tell me that you'd never expected my marriage to work because I was kind of a fuck-up."

She stared at him. "You thought...have I ever said anything about...?" She frowned. "I mean, I teased you about getting married, but only because..."

He frowned. There was a long silence. Ren tilted his head to one side, watching her as if he was trying to figure something out. Then he sighed slowly. "I guess...Paola made me feel like you made me feel at university sometimes, like she thought I was an idiot. And after a while, there was nothing left about me that she liked." Sarah watched Ren's pained expression. She'd never seen him like this. It was like the divorce had ripped him open, brought out some new level of honesty she had never witnessed before.

"No," Sarah said gently. "I think you do a great job of taking care of people, and I'm sure you do a good job taking care of your son. You were nice to me in school. Always, even when we were arguing. Even when I turned you down. And if Paola didn't respect you, and didn't see that about you, that means she never understood you in the first place."

He stared at her for a moment. There was the flash of a self-deprecating smile. "Well, if I'd known you were going to say that, I would have reached out earlier."

She smiled briefly. "I just missed you."

"I know, I just...and I didn't want to hear that you were dating another one of your jerks."

"I'm not dating one of my jerks," she said. "I'm not dating anybody."

His eyes were warm as he looked at her, and she felt a wave of nerves. It hit her then that they were both single. He was looking at her like he wanted to kiss her, and for once, she felt sure that he did. Her insecurity had blinded her to the possibility he might like her back in undergrad, but now she thought she could understand him better. He glanced at her hair, her tight wrap dress.

"Me neither," he said. They stared at each other.

"Hey you two!" Trish called. "We're telling everyone to eat."

"Come on," Sarah said gently, nudging his arm. "Let's check out this Vegas buffet. Although I guess you get those all the time."

"My Vegas buffets usually involve Jandro's leftover bags of Cheerios in my car."

"Thai food!" Trish said to everyone, waving at the trays. "It's amazing. Trust me."

Trish seemed unexpectedly calm for someone who had seemed poised to be a full Bridezilla in her mid-twenties. That was a healthy sign, Sarah thought. She glanced at Trish's parents standing nearby in fancy clothes, chatting with Ian, who was serving as best man. It was good, also, that Paul had told his parents not to come. The official reason was that he and Trish were returning to Newfoundland to celebrate with Paul's parents, but Sarah suspected that he also didn't want his mother to create any drama.

It was going to be a good night, Sarah decided. In all sorts of unexpected ways. She and Ren sat next to each other at the table and slowly filled in the details of the last few years. Ren had never gotten a solid journalism job in the States, but instead had been going out to shoot photos in the desert and had a couple of his photos in galleries. She told him that her *Existential Innocence* series was still going strong and showed him some of her favorite commissions.

As the meal wrapped up, she covered a yawn, tired from her long travel day.

"You're tired," he said gently.

"I should probably turn in before I nod off into my Tom Kha Gai."

"I wish I could head to bed myself, but I need to go see what errands Paul wants me to run in the morning." It was like Ren to be kind and helpful. She always forgot that about him.

"Are you staying at the hotel? I guess not."

He shook his head. "No, but Jandro is at Paola's for the whole weekend."

"Sure," she said. "Hey, I have tickets tomorrow to that James Turrell art installation called Akhob. Want to come? I reserved them weeks ago on Kristie's recommendation. She was on a film shoot here and told me it was the thing to do. I got two tickets in case I could drag Paul, but it sounds like he'll be busy, so you could come instead. If you haven't been."

"That sounds amazing," Ren said. "I've heard about it and wanted to see it."

"Then it's a plan. We'll go be art snobs together."

"I thought I was the art snob and you were the voice of pop culture."

"Either or. I could switch roles for a day."

He gave her a warm look. "Text me the details."

As Sarah took a taxi back to the hotel, she wondered whether Ren was going to call the redhead from that morning and meet up again. But she wouldn't let it worry her.

Sarah and Ren were having a moment, weren't they? Just maybe not the kind that sent you to bed with someone.

THE ART INSTALLATION by the renowned visual artist James Turrell required ticket reservations weeks in advance, and was improbably hidden within a Louis Vuitton store in the mall. Ren was waiting for her outside at the pre-arranged time, looking much more put-together than the previous morning in jeans and a black button-down shirt. He gave her a hug when he saw her, and she let herself smell him: the same nice smell of spice and coffee, with a lot less weed.

They were part of a group of only four people allowed to visit the space for the next half hour. They got a brief introduction to the installation, put on cloth booties over their shoes to keep from tracking in dirt, and then entered the installation via a row of black stairs, stepping inside a round portal. The space itself was a large hollow room shaped like a giant white egg, perhaps twenty-five feet across, with a distant wall lit up by hidden light sources. Once they were inside, the whole space began to slowly shift color, the walls slowly gliding into radiant shades of scarlet, then lavender, then blue.

They stood there in silence, watching as everything around them glowed more brightly by the second. Sarah thought of making a joking remark, but it was too beautiful for her to want to spoil it: the silence, the color, the slow shift of the light. It began to feel like they were floating in space, with no clear demarcation between the smooth floor and the curved walls. After a while, Sarah lost track of time entirely. The other two people were silent as well, staring around them in awe.

She glanced at Ren and saw that he was looking at her intensely. She smiled and he stepped closer, so that he was just beyond her reach, gazing right into her eyes. For a moment, they were the only people in the universe.

She was now even more tempted to make a joke to escape the intimacy of that look, but she stopped herself. The wall behind him slowly shifted to a cooler blue, endless as the heavens. The light felt as pure and simple as a prayer. When it grew to be too much to keep gazing at him, she shifted her eyes back to the walls, and so did he. Everything was a radiant purple, now.

"Thank you for inviting me," Ren whispered.

She reached over and took one of his hands, and he squeezed her hand and held it for a full minute before he gently let it go. She felt herself glowing with joy. They were together. Maybe not forever, but for today. This felt like a date, only better. It felt like a date where they didn't have to speak at all.

When they exited back into the upscale mall again, the sense of beauty and quiet lingered in the spaces between their words. She had taken a taxi to the exhibit while he ran errands for Paul all morning, but now he offered to drive her back to the hotel. His car was small and practical, a toddler's car seat locked permanently into place.

She looked out the window, knowing that this time tomorrow she would be on a plane back home. The music on his car radio was a series of sad, lingering songs by singer-songwriters; it wasn't at all the kind of music that Ren had listened to in college. Back then, he had been all about Serge Gainsbourg, Air, and Stereolab: elegant, hip music with a layer of emotional remove. Now his preference for heartfelt songwriters like Ray LaMontagne and Lord Huron felt startling.

Ren was sitting in his feelings, now. This was new.

An hour later, as she slipped into her wedding-day party dress alone in her hotel room, she took a moment to consider what her sense of connection with Ren really meant. He lived in Las Vegas and couldn't move because of his son. Her work was in Toronto. But at least they were friends again. At least they could have that. The important thing was that she knew that he cared about her. She mattered to him.

Had he really believed that she would agree with his wife during his divorce? The idea nagged at her. She had always thought he knew her, could guess at her thoughts, but he had gotten that so wrong.

LAS VEGAS HAD dozens of wedding chapels, and Trish had selected one with a garden theme, filled with garlands of fake roses and a white arbor decorated with cloth lilies. Sarah couldn't fault Trish's taste; if you had to pick a Vegas chapel, this one was the closest you could get to an elegant countryside wedding with zero Elvis involved. If Trish was this laid-back, Sarah thought again, if she was relaxed enough to do a Vegas wedding, then maybe Trish and Paul had a chance to work out as a couple. Maybe Trish could scale her expectations down to what Newfoundland had to offer.

Trish appeared a few minutes later in a lovely white

wedding dress that was silky and loose, minimalist to the point of being almost a slip-dress, her blond hair delicately pinned in a low bun. She looked radiantly gorgeous walking down the aisle, and in spite of herself, Sarah got emotional as she watched Paul's expression melt at the sight of her.

This was love, Sarah thought. No need for anything fancy. Trish and Paul had learned to bend and adjust for each other. Maybe she could find someone who would do that for her, too.

Sarah tried not to make eye contact with Ren during the ceremony, but she caught him looking at her once, and he smiled before they both looked away. The event itself was over quickly; the chapel had another ceremony starting in a little over an hour. They all headed to the rented party room that Trish and Paul had reserved back at their hotel, the same hotel where Sarah was staying.

Ren caught up with her again and offered to drive her to the reception, and again she was happy to accept the ride; she wanted more time listening to sad music with him, regretting what they couldn't have.

"You look beautiful," he said quietly when they were alone in his car. "That's a great dress."

"Thank you," she replied, smoothing down the rich green fabric. "It's a thrift store find. I know those are your favorites."

"I always liked your clothes," he said. "I liked that nobody but you would have them." She looked away, unsure what to do with his compliments.

"Trish looked stunning."

"She did," he agreed. She watched his fingers drumming on the steering wheel. The old, restless energy was still there. Why was he nervous? It occurred to her that maybe Ren was wondering if they might sleep together tonight. Or was he worried that was what she wanted and he wasn't sure how to tell her no?

They couldn't have a relationship, she thought, but they could have a one-night stand. One night where they showed that they cared about each other, one night where they could touch each other the way she had wanted to touch him since forever. She could picture kissing his face, running her hands through his hair, laughing in bed together. That would still be meaningful even if nothing else followed, wouldn't it?

Now that she was more experienced, she found that her feelings about casual sex had shifted dramatically. When she was twenty-one, hooking up with Ren would have been a devastating mistake, and she had been right to avoid it. But this felt different. They lived a thousand miles away. They couldn't make commitments. They were just two friends seizing a little time together, exorcising the hurts of the past. She could hold him, kiss him over and over, and go home knowing that they had shared something special with each other. She thought about the redhead from the day before. If Ren could sleep with a stranger, surely he could sleep with Sarah. Surely Sarah would be judged worthy for one night of passion, especially if she was leaving the next day.

Sex could be healing. Ren had said it himself, all those years ago. Maybe he had been right.

The thought made her feel shy around him. It made her feel shy when they entered a small party room with a sparkling view of the Las Vegas sunset. It made her feel shy when he brought her a glass of champagne. All the single women's eyes were on him, of course, and that made it feel even more strange that he was so focused on her. There were Trish's actress and model friends, long-legged and artfully coiffed, but Ren didn't leave her side.

The speeches came after the meal, fast and funny. Paul's buddy Ian, who knew the bride and groom from a play they'd all been in, told amusingly pointed stories about meeting them both

—stories that made Trish sound finicky and Paul sound prone to self-sabotage. Trish's sister Eleanor spoke about how marvelous Paul was, gushing over him in a way that Sarah found wonderfully accurate. Then there was music from a DJ, and Sarah tried to focus on dancing with the whole crowd, scared to find out what it would be like to dance just with Ren. Finally, he came close to her, moving in that understated way that she had found sexy at Kristie's parties back in undergrad, and it was almost too much.

A slow song came on, and she wrapped her arms around his shoulders. He slipped his hands around her waist, his fingers warm, his breath against her shoulder. The music filled the air around them like a thick blanket. She rested against his shoulder and shook her head.

"What is it?" Ren asked in her ear.

"It's just..." She hesitated. "Being around you again. It's strange. It's a nice strange."

"It is," he agreed, looking into her eyes. He really was looking at her like he was going to kiss her and she looked up at him until the tension grew almost unbearable.

The music grew faster then, and they slowly parted, returning to their chairs. He brought her a drink of water when she said she was worried about a hangover on her flight, and when he handed it to her, his fingertips touched hers like a promise.

It finally grew late, so she said goodnight to Paul and Trish, then told Ren that she was going to bed. Ren followed her out. If this raised any eyebrows, Sarah couldn't find it within herself to care. Her heart was beating faster, her breath shallow.

They stood inside the hotel elevator in silence as it went down from the penthouse floor where they had held the small reception down to the floor where she was staying. Ren was parked in the basement somewhere, and she waited to see what he would do.

"Wait. What time are you leaving tomorrow?" Ren asked at last as the elevator arrived at her floor. He stepped out of the elevator and stood with her there.

"Noon tomorrow. I should probably leave for the airport around ten."

He nodded. "Right."

This was it. She waited for him to hurt her, to say that he wasn't interested. And that would be okay, she told herself. She was tougher than she once had been. "I want to keep hanging out with you," he said. "I know you're tired, but if you're willing to stay up for a bit, I'd like that."

"Do you want to come and sit on my bed and we'll find a terrible movie or something?"

He nodded silently and followed her down the hall.

Had she been too obvious? The strange part was that she really would be content just to watch a movie with him, as long as it meant that he stayed. Sitting together until dawn watching movies and chatting would still be better than nothing. Kissing would be preferable, but she would take whatever he was offering.

When she entered her room, she let the door slide shut with a soft click behind them. Only one light was on, just at the doorway, and she didn't turn on the others yet. She just stood still, gazing at him, trying to read the moment, nervous from trying not to ruin things. Her whole body was aware of his presence as he watched her from a foot away. They hadn't moved. He gave a little half-smile and then raised one warm hand to her cheek, caressing her, then leaned forward and kissed her.

Her heart was already racing. The kiss was tender and lingering, and it felt absurdly, shockingly good. She had always assumed that he would be decent at kissing, but this felt perfect enough to make her giddy...like jumping off the edge of a cliff and discovering that you could fly. She leaned into the kiss, sliding her hand around his neck, pulling him towards her as he slid his fingers around her lower back, pressing their bodies together.

He ended the kiss slowly, then stared at her for a moment. That did not feel like a one-night stand kiss, Sarah thought hazily. Her cheeks grew flushed and she felt close to tears.

"Sarah," he whispered tenderly, pressing his nose against her cheek, resting there.

She tilted her head to kiss him again fervently, wrapping both arms around his shoulders, trying to tell him everything she didn't dare to say: that she cared about him, that his ex-wife was wrong about him, that he was wonderful, that even though they couldn't have a relationship, they could have this. A night together. Just this once.

He responded with as much intensity, backing her up against the wall with his whole body, pinning her with his warmth as if to make sure she didn't go anywhere. One of his arms braced against the wall, the other pulling her waist toward him, and she felt breathless with how good it felt. This was so much better than she could have imagined, so extraordinarily good that it made her want to laugh. Of course it was incredible. Of course it always would have been. He slid one of the straps of her dress away from her shoulder to kiss her there, and she felt like swooning in his arms.

"Sarah," he whispered against her neck. "I've wanted you for so long."

"Ren." Her voice sounded faint and breathless. She ran a hand through his curls the way she'd wanted to do since her freshman year. They were thick and soft, lush between her fingers. She stroked her hands along the sides of his head tenderly. "Ren," she said again, spoiling herself with the sound of his name in her mouth. She loved him. She had to be careful not to say that.

"Since freshman year, you've been in my head," he whispered, kissing her shoulder, her neck, the bottom of her chin.

"God, I was so in love with you back then," she said.

He paused, then went completely still against her. "What?"

She blinked as he pulled back to look at her.

"I don't mean now," she said hurriedly. "I know we can't... we can't be anything, that you have to stay here."

"You were in love with me?" he repeated slowly, as if she had confessed to murder. "Back at university?"

"I..." She trailed off as she tried to read his gaze. "Yes?"

"That whole time you acted like you hated me."

"I didn't hate you," she said.

He carefully stepped away, still staring at her. "So then," he said, "so when I was hooking up with Anya...you loved me?"

"It was a long time ago."

She watched him take a breath. Naked shock. That's what his expression was. Surely he must have guessed at this, but he didn't seem to have suspected at all.

"Jesus." He leaned back against the wall a couple of feet away from her, his eyes focused just above her head.

"What?"

"It's just...you would date these assholes. And meanwhile, I was hooking up with your friends and you... And it's...was it because I was an asshole? Is that why you liked me?"

She wasn't sure whether to be angry or embarrassed. "No!"

"Why did you like me back then?" She wasn't sure why he was so upset.

"I don't know. I just did. I liked the way we joked, and I liked talking to you. I wasn't dramatic about it. I didn't expect you to date me."

"But I dated your roommates."

"But I wasn't mad at you for it."

"You never said you liked me." His voice was frustrated.

"When would I have told you?"

"I don't know. Any of those nights that we spent talking to each other?"

"If I'd told you I liked you, you'd have run away because you would have assumed I was asking for a relationship. I preferred having you as a friend to not seeing you at all."

"And when you were with Ivan?"

"That made my feelings less intense, but they didn't go away."

He rubbed his face. "Okay." He was speaking almost to himself now. He shifted a little farther from her. "Okay."

Sarah tried to pull herself together, to slow her racing heart. "Why is this so bad?"

He looked down as if he were replaying his memories. "So okay."

"Ren," she said gently, "I'm not expecting *anything* from you."

"No, it's not that," he muttered, but he wouldn't meet her eyes.

"I don't understand what's wrong."

He took another deep breath. He still wouldn't meet her eyes, but his voice was steady. "I am so sorry. I don't think I can do this."

"Okay..."

"I am so, so sorry."

He opened his mouth to say something else, closed it, then walked to the door, opened it, and was gone.

She didn't hear from Ren again that night. After a few moments of standing stunned in the doorway of her hotel room, she went to bed and stared up at the hotel room ceiling, a murky grey expanse in the darkness, listening to the air conditioning unit turning on and off in a meaningless pattern until dawn.

When she came down to breakfast in the hotel restaurant the next morning, she found Paul there alone, though he had a plate ready for Trish's arrival. Sarah had a quick breakfast with him and a few other guests who slowly surrounded them. Then she hugged him goodbye and promised to come to St. John's at Christmas. Trish was still nowhere to be found, and neither was Ren, of course, which felt both predictable and horrible.

Sarah stopped by the hotel's lobby restroom with her luggage on her way out. Soon after she had entered a stall, she overheard Trish talking to her sister Eleanor as the women stood by the mirrors.

"Like, at a certain point, you have to be realistic, you know?" Trish said.

"Yeah, I get that," Eleanor replied.

Sarah stayed quiet, listening.

"He adores me. And that's...I mean, I could marry someone with more money, but I think it's important to marry someone who's madly in love with you, you know?"

"And you're madly in love with him, too, right?"

"Yes." Trish's voice had just a touch of hesitation. Or was Sarah imagining that? "And I'm thirty. At a certain point, you have to give up on the fantasy and pick a guy who's healthy for you."

Sarah waited until they'd left the restroom before she slipped out, quietly rolling her wheeled luggage through the lobby with her eyes on the ground so she could avoid speaking to anyone. She walked straight to the taxi stand in front of their hotel. She was furious on Paul's behalf, but her boiling outrage slowly subsided on the taxi ride to the airport.

Was what Trish had said really so wrong? Was her attitude that bad? Hadn't Sarah herself pursued a fantasy the night before, only to be smacked in the face with reality? What was wrong with Trish deciding to pick a husband who liked her?

When she got off the plane in Toronto, there was a text from Ren. Her heart squeezed in her chest when she saw his name.

I'm sorry about last night. I want to talk but I need some time to think first.

She wrote back: *Okay.* And then like a fool, she hoped to hear from him for the rest of the day.

And the next day, too.

And the next.

And then she knew. She should have known right away, maybe. A week passed, and then another. He didn't write, and Sarah picked herself up and kept working.

8

ANYA'S PARTY, OCTOBER 2016

TWO WEEKS after Paul and Trish got married, Sarah went to a barbecue at Anya's house, which was located in a cool little neighborhood in Toronto filled with small, cute houses from the 1940s. Sarah had promised to arrive early so she could help Anya set up while Anya heard all the entertaining details about Paul's wedding. Sarah arrived with her arms full of bags of assorted party items Anya had forgotten to buy, then followed her friend around the kitchen of their small rental house. She had to dodge around Anya's daughter Ilona as the girl raced past them and disappeared into the backyard in search of her father. Sarah liked Anya's husband Jeremy. He was a quiet computer programmer who handled Anya's roller coaster of moods with a deadpan, gentle calm, and he had remained remarkably stable throughout Anya's accidental pregnancy, a fast-tracked wedding, and sudden fatherhood. He popped inside to greet Sarah cheerfully before returning to the yard to start up their grill, and she and Anya quickly fell back into their roommate pattern: working together as a team to line up food on trays and pour chips into colored bowls. Kristie was coming, too, though she was following her typical schedule of running two hours late; she would be bringing a new boyfriend who was an actor in Bollywood films.

"Let's hope we don't lose Kristie to Mumbai next," Sarah said as she opened a packet of colorful party napkins. "I feel like we just got her back from L.A."

"Well, I can't fault her taste in men. The new guy is gorgeous and has three hundred thousand followers on Instagram. And speaking of, Ren is as beautiful as ever, I assume?" Anya ran a hand through her long blond hair. Her fashion sense had turned more practical since becoming a mother: she had moved from flowing white dresses to flowing embroidered shirts over jeans.

"Oh yes, still stunning. And he..." Sarah took a breath. "He kissed me and then announced that we should definitely not sleep together and left."

Anya paused in the middle of pouring a bowl of chips to stare at her.

"Or maybe, more accurately, I threw myself at Ren and he turned me down." Sarah busied herself with the napkins.

"Oh my God." Anya blinked. "Oh my *God*, Sarah."

Sarah shrugged. "It's fine."

"Is it?" A long moment passed.

"Here's what bothers me," Sarah admitted at last. "I saw him leaving the hotel room of some redhead the morning I arrived. He met her during Paul's bachelor party and slept with her, apparently, but then somehow he couldn't possibly bring himself to sleep with me."

"Well, he's always been weird about you."

"But why? I mean, he literally went through my whole friend group...I don't mean...I don't mean, like, he went *through* you all."

Anya laughed. "God, he was so hot and so uninterested in an actual relationship. You know what he told me to get me into bed? That philosophically, I owed it to myself to explore my sexuality. Like sleeping with him was something I should do for myself, like treating myself to a manicure."

Sarah gave a weak smile.

"Okay so..." Anya considered her. "What exactly happened?"

"Well, we were flirting, I guess. I mean his divorce had just been finalized, which I hadn't even known about until I got there. But we seemed to be flirting. And then he came to my hotel room, and we were kissing, and I admitted to having been kind of in love with him at university and he said we had to stop."

"Oh," Anya said. "Okay. That makes sense."

"And just to be clear, I didn't say I loved him or expected a relationship. He lives in Nevada."

"No, but that makes sense. I mean, I haven't seen him in years, but at McGill he was...you know, he was Ren. The hot intellectual who had a two-week shelf life as a boyfriend. But with you, he was this other person."

"Because he wasn't attracted to me."

"No. That's a very you thing to say, Sarah, but no. You may not realize this, but Ren used to talk about you when you weren't there. Like, 'Sarah would hate that.' Or 'Sarah loves that book.' It drove Kristie crazy."

"He just thought I was a big nerd."

"It wasn't just about nerdy stuff. It was everything. Like, 'Hey, what movie should we put on?' 'Let's ask Sarah when she gets back.' Kristie was convinced he was in love with you, which is one reason she split with him. She thought you were going to get together. She never told you this?"

"No."

Anya shrugged. "She probably didn't want to get your hopes up. And then he didn't ask you, and you started dating Ivan like three weeks later. But my point is... He wasn't necessarily in love with you, but it was like you were the only person whose opinion mattered." Anya shrugged. "So maybe when he found out you liked him, he realized he could have had a real relationship the whole time and it freaked him out."

"He said that I was only attracted to assholes, so I must have liked him because he was one."

Anya raised her eyebrows. "I mean..."

"It's not true, though. I didn't know Ivan was an asshole when I started dating him. I thought he was a sensitive guy who was in touch with his feelings."

"Oh, he was," Anya agreed with a grin. "It was everybody else's feelings that he struggled with."

Sarah sighed, feeling an overwhelming sense of sadness. "It just hurt."

"Men that handsome are nightmares," Anya said. "Because they can get away with it. But you know what? I'm going to introduce you to some nice, normal guys at this party. There are at least two single men coming."

"Oh, no. No way."

"Just meet them," Anya said. "Have a normal date with a normal human being. It's the best way to get over what happened. Trust me."

Anya was as good as her word. As soon as the guests arrived, Anya introduced Sarah to Danny, a personable actor in his early thirties who was a puppeteer and had just been hired to run the weekend programming at Anya's theater.

Danny explained that he had agreed to perform a free puppet show for the children at Anya's party in exchange for a six-pack of his favorite beer.

"I take the big offers where I can get them," he joked.

"So does your agent get ten percent of the beer?" Sarah asked.

"That's the problem with an acting career. Once you pay your agent and manager, there's not much left of the six-pack."

Danny wasn't precisely handsome, but he had the kind of face that you liked immediately: soft brown eyes, round nose, freckled cheeks. He asked for her number at the end of the night, and within three weeks, they had been on six dates and already felt like a couple.

Everything about Danny felt safe. The biggest difference between him and her previous boyfriends was that he so clearly wanted to be with her. Sarah had never been with anyone so eager for things to work out, so eager to get married. He talked about having kids within weeks of dating her—not as a definite thing, but as a hypothetical that he was excited about. He loved her baby photo series, he admitted, because he loved babies.

Having a guy who was serious about their future changed the whole dynamic of the relationship, Sarah discovered. It meant that they were both willing to make compromises. It meant that he listened to her concerns and apologized more often. By November, they were already making plans for him to come home for Christmas to meet her mother. Danny's mother had died when he was a teenager and his father wasn't in the picture, so he was eager to experience Christmas morning in Sarah's tiny house in the woods.

On Sarah's birthday in November, three days after she and Danny had booked their flights to Newfoundland, she received a text from Ren.

Happy birthday Sarah. I am sorry I went silent. I know I owe you a huge apology. Jandro will be visiting his grandparents in Mexico City for Christmas and I was planning a short trip to Toronto then. I wondered if I could meet up with you while I'm in town. I want to talk to you and apologize in person.

I'm really sorry, she wrote back. *I will be in Newfoundland for Christmas. My boyfriend Danny and I are visiting my mother. I am sorry to miss you in Toronto. Maybe we can talk by phone.*

Half an hour later, he replied. *Good to hear that things are going well for you.*

Thanks. I hope they are going well for you, too, she said.

He didn't text her again, not about Christmas or anything else.

She texted him to wish him a happy birthday the following summer, and he wrote back a polite '*Thank you, Sarah. I hope you are well.*' She was already married.

THE WEDDING CEREMONY with Danny happened in the spring of 2017 near Sarah's hometown in Newfoundland. It was a simple affair: Sarah and Danny didn't have much money, and they were both in their thirties and ready to start trying for kids. They booked a restaurant overlooking the water in St. John's, and Anya, Winnie, and Kristie made the trip out. Sarah's high school friend Marie got drunk and gave an amusing impromptu speech about their escapades in high school theater and why everyone should have known that Sarah would marry a puppeteer, and Paul made a cheerful speech about how Sarah had always been there for other people and it was nice to have someone who would be there for her. Paul's father had recently passed away, so Paul got a little emotional during the speech. He was still doing improv but dealing with his mother's escalating emotional demands, exactly as Sarah had feared. Trish didn't make the wedding because she was on some kind of a documentary shoot.

When Sarah and Danny flew home to Toronto, Sarah felt like her real life was finally starting. She had the career she had always wanted as a photographer and was still paying her rent with the continued success of her *Existential Innocence* series.

She had good friends, went to fun parties, and had a lifetime commitment from a man who adored her and wanted to start a family.

And that should have been her happy ending.

And it almost was.

It almost wasn't a disaster.

PART TWO
SUMMER 2025

9

FRIDAY

"CAN you pick up some New Yorkers this afternoon?" Paul asked Sarah. She was at her mother's house, having arrived in Newfoundland only the day before to visit with her mother before attending Paul's second wedding.

"So many demands," Sarah teased. "First you want me to be your photographer, then your chauffeur?"

"I'm desperate here. Abby's got two friends flying in from New York who didn't rent a car because they don't have a driver's license."

"How is that possible? Are they fifteen?"

"They take the subway, babe," Paul drawled. "It's so much faster."

"Okay, okay." Sarah sighed. "How will I recognize them?"

"Trust me, you'll recognize them," Paul replied.

And surprisingly, she did.

As she stood in the small airport in St. John's, a man and woman walked towards her among the scattered people disembarking from the Montreal flight. The woman was tall and gorgeous, with brown skin and wearing a bright orange angora sweater, long skirt, and slinky suede brown boots. The man was compact, handsome, and dark-haired, wheeling a pristine white carry-on and holding a suit bag.

"No, it won't calm me down," the man was saying. "My life will be flashing before my eyes for the whole weekend. I literally almost died."

"You said the exact same thing about our SoulCycle class."

"It's these tiny planes," the man continued. "Now I know how Amelia Earhart felt."

"We were on a 727, not a Cessna," the woman said.

"I can't be expected to know what either of those terms means."

"Excuse me," Sarah said at last. "Are you here for Paul and Abby's wedding?"

They stopped and looked her over. "Are you the famous Cousin Sarah?" said the woman.

Sarah nodded. "Are you Jasmine and Lucas?"

"Were we that recognizable?" the man named Lucas asked.

"You gave off strong New York City vibes," Sarah said.

"It's because *you* look helpless," Jasmine said to the man. "And *I* look amazing." She smiled at Sarah. "I thought Cousin Sarah would be fifty years old and wearing a checkered apron."

"That's my wedding day outfit," Sarah replied, and Jasmine laughed.

"God, this place is so cute." Lucas glanced around. "Can I say that? Is that offensive? Just smack me if I say something offensive."

"It's fine. I grew up here, but I've been living in Toronto and Montreal for the last twenty years. You can think this is cute."

They headed together towards luggage claim.

"So what are the men like," Jasmine asked, "if you grew up here? We were debating on the plane. Are they like, hot farmers, or hot lumberjacks, or hot fishermen?"

"Yeah, what's the vibe?" Lucas asked.

"So you two aren't..." Sarah waved between them.

"Oh God, no," Jasmine said. "He's like my—gay life partner? I would have brought an actual date but my boyfriend decided he needed to move back to Puerto Rico."

"I can be your gay life partner, but you're not mine," Lucas replied to Jasmine. "My gay life partner is Matt Bomer."

"Someone has to know you exist to be your life partner," Jasmine said.

"Lies," said Lucas. "I know what's in my heart."

"Since my divorce," Sarah said, "I think I am my own life partner."

"I love that for you," Jasmine replied, waving a manicured hand up and down at Sarah. "I don't even know you and I love that for you."

Sarah smiled. "I guess the answer is that Newfoundland men are hot fisherman and hot miners. Offshore drilling is big up here."

Lucas smiled. "I'm going to translate that into everyone looking like Ben Affleck's character in *Armageddon*."

"Be my guest."

They watched as the luggage started to arrive. "So you're completely over romance?" Lucas asked Sarah. "See, I aspire to that level of serenity."

"It's not that I don't approve of it for other people," Sarah said. "I'm happy for Paul."

"Didn't Abby say you're shooting the wedding?" Jasmine asked.

"I offered. I don't usually shoot weddings but I'm making an exception for Paul," Sarah conceded.

Jasmine looked thoughtful. "You know I've barely met Paul. Is he like Gilbert Blythe?"

Sarah almost snorted. "Way more sarcastic than Gilbert Blythe. And I haven't met Abby yet because she was visiting her niece last time I came through," Sarah admitted. "But I am really glad Paul's ex Trish is out of the picture."

"Yeah, what happened with his ex-wife?" Lucas asked. "Tell us the gossip."

Sarah thought about how to sum up Trish and that whole saga. "They were together for a long time," she said. "Trish came up here, married him, and then a couple of years later, cheated on him and ran off with this documentary guy who worked for the CBC. But to be fair, Trish had to deal with Paul's mom, who can be pretty toxic."

"Abby said they're not inviting Paul's mother to the wedding," Jasmine said.

"Thank God," Sarah said fervently. "That woman ruined every holiday for my first eighteen years."

"There!" Lucas called, pointed to a fancy suitcase. "That's yours, Jasmine. And my zebra bag."

Sarah helped them collect their luggage. She was struck by how much it already felt like she was friends with them. She wondered if it had to do with them being chatty New Yorkers or just that they all lived in cities, were single, and were around the same age. She had refrained from asking Paul how old his new fiancée was, but she felt relieved that it seemed likely—based on these two—that Abby must be in her late thirties or older.

After what had happened in her own marriage, Sarah had privately hoped that Paul wasn't marrying someone much younger. That would have been a little too depressing.

Sarah walked out to her mother's borrowed car with Jasmine and Lucas, pondering Jasmine's question. What were the men like in Newfoundland?

It didn't matter, she told herself. She had decided that she was going to be single for the rest of her life.

. . .

"Oh my God," Jasmine said, stopping Sarah with an iron grip on her elbow. "Who is *that*?"

The hotel that was hosting the wedding was a white-clapboard structure with rolling lawns that tumbled towards the sea. When they walked inside the main lobby, several guests were already chatting in armchairs or looking at the view, so Sarah followed Jasmine's gaze and then froze at the sight of a handsome, dark-haired man standing a few feet away. He was talking in Quebecois French to a much larger, blond man she didn't know who stood well over six feet tall. The dark-haired man was Ren.

It had been over eight years since she'd seen him, but he still had his lovely, curly hair, though it was now touched with grey. He still had those alarmingly pretty green eyes, slightly crinkled at the edges. He was still beautiful.

Sarah couldn't move for a moment.

"Are we talking about the one who looks like a lost Hemsworth brother or the one who looks like Alain Delon?" Lucas asked.

"I can have both. Why not both?" Jasmine said.

Right then, Ren turned his eyes toward Sarah. His gaze locked with hers and for a moment he looked as frozen as she felt. He didn't smile, just stared for so long that he lost track of his conversation, and she watched him blink and then ask the blond man to repeat what he'd been saying.

She should have known Ren would be here. She should have asked Paul about it, but for some reason it had never crossed her mind that he would come. In her head, Ren was forever in Las Vegas, raising a child, sleeping with redheads. She hadn't known that he and Paul even kept in touch. She hadn't asked.

"Looks like the hot guy only speaks French," Lucas said with a sad sigh to Jasmine. "Just my luck."

"That's Ren," Sarah finally said. "He speaks English." She took a step forward, just as a dark-haired woman stepped into her path to greet them.

"You made it to the ends of the earth!" cried the woman, looking between Lucas and Jasmine. This must be Abby, Paul's bride. She turned to Sarah with a grin. "Are you Sarah? Thank you so much for rescuing these two. I had to run around all day finding tiny items with white flowers on them."

"Happy to help," Sarah said.

"I'm Abby. Did I say that? If not, blame it on bride brain. I don't think I've formed a coherent sentence in the last forty-eight hours."

"Babe, you look so radiant that I hate you a little," Jasmine told Abby.

"It's the sea air. I look exactly the same, but the air is making you drunk and confused."

"Is that what Newfoundlanders get to blame things on?" Sarah asked. "That would explain my entire high school experience."

Abby laughed, and Sarah saw how radically different Paul's new bride was from Patricia. This woman seemed warm and funny but utterly grounded, the kind of person who would never put pristine white sofas in an apartment where she planned to serve bright orange cocktails. She was definitely closer to forty than thirty, which also felt like a small relief.

"And you're okay taking pictures of the wedding?" Abby asked Sarah. "Because Paul said you offered to do that as your gift. But we have two guests willing to take photos, so if you want to relax, please tell me and I'll shift it to our other volunteer."

"I offered to help out as well," came a male voice. It was Ren, standing at her elbow, smiling at her.

Sarah turned to him. "Take photos?" Her brain seemed to be working slower than usual.

Abby looked between them. "Is that okay? Since you're both professional photographers, Paul thought you could both give us that as your wedding gift, but seriously, if one of you wants to bow out..."

"A professional photographer?" Sarah asked.

Ren nodded. "That's what I do now, yeah."

"Oh." She stared at him, confused. She vaguely remembered him having a few photos in a gallery, but that had been years ago.

"I'm going to let you guys get settled, put your bags down," Abby said. "And then a few of us have to do the ceremony rehearsal out back, and dinner is a five-minute walk from here. All the information is in the welcome bags in your rooms."

Sarah stood back so Abby could throw her arms around her New York friends for an extra hug. She turned to Ren, finding it difficult to meet his eyes now that it was just the two of them.

"We'll talk later maybe?" Sarah said to him.

"Yeah, of course," he said softly, looking her over. Sarah knew she looked different now. Her hair had gone from ash blond to bubbly blond to its current warm honey color, and she tended to iron it out into carefully constrained waves. But she knew her face looked older. Of course it did.

When Sarah stayed out late when she was in her early twenties, she would sometimes wake up with a weary, colorless pallor, light-brown smudges beneath her eyes and faint wrinkles across her forehead. Now Sarah had discovered that this was the normal face she saw every morning before putting make-up on. Forty looked to her like twenty-five after going on a bad bender. Maybe that's what her last fifteen years had been: one long, rough night. She wished he weren't still so gorgeous. It was a little offensive, frankly.

She forced another smile before she turned to walk towards the check-in desk at the hotel, reminding herself that Ren had hurt her. Seeing him again had made her briefly forget. She always did this when it came to him. She was too ready to forgive. But this was Paul's second wedding and she had no plans of repeating the mistakes from his first one.

And also...Ren was a professional photographer?

As soon as she got to her hotel room, she looked him up on her cell phone: 'Rene Durand photographer.' She didn't know what to expect, but a website came up right away: 'Durand Night Photography.' The page was filled with artistic, gorgeous nature photos taken in the hours between dusk and dawn. There were shots of the Milky Way over the desert, the Northern Lights over a snowy tundra, snow-capped mountains with shooting stars raining down above them, swirling star trails spinning through the sky in a two-hour-long exposure.

The story of his business was summed up on his website in large, high-contrast prose. It had begun with him bringing clients on photography workshops to Zion National Park outside of Las Vegas. Then his workshops had expanded: to the Grand Canyon, then Joshua Tree, then to Banff, to Iceland, to Norway and New Zealand. He taught people how to do astrophotography and night photography, shooting the Milky Way and the Northern Lights in far-flung places for eye-popping prices. He could easily be making a living entirely as a photographer, now—she could live quite comfortably on what he must be making from workshops alone.

How had Paul never told her this?

He had never told her because she had never asked, she realized. And because Paul had known it might be a sensitive topic, given that Sarah herself had quit photography entirely.

It made sense that Ren was successful, she thought bitterly, looking through the photos. Who wouldn't want to travel to the farthest regions of the world with a stunning man who would show you the stars? He probably knew every constellation, could predict the next meteor shower, could plan whole trips around the phases of the moon.

He must be so happy, she thought. There he was, living in the States, raising a son while jetting around the world shooting the stars over mountains and deserts. He was probably even married again.

Gorgeous people had a right to be happy, she thought, feeling petulant. They had a right to be successful and talented and profoundly content down to the depths their souls.

Because life wasn't fair.

She jumped a little when someone knocked on her door a few minutes later as she was taming her hair for the rehearsal dinner. She was keeping her look simple because it was a 'working weekend' for her—or that's what she was telling herself to keep from focusing too much on the wedding itself, the marriage and joy and romantic hopes. She had offered her services to Paul as a gift primarily as an act of avoidance, so she wouldn't have to feel quite so alone while watching the happy couple celebrating their union. So her outfits were elegant but practical, and her hair would be up in a bun most of the time. Her heart felt wrapped up just as tightly, knotted up and tucked away so it wouldn't make a mess.

It was Paul at her door, and her breathing calmed a little.

"Hey, gorgeous," he said, giving her a hug. She could tell from his mood that he would think anyone looked gorgeous. He was practically bubbling over with joy.

"Hey!" she cried, taking a step back. "It's lovely to see you so happy. I met Abby and she's wonderful."

"Finally, I got it right," Paul replied, another irrepressible grin emerging.

"And I'll suppress any snarky comments about Trish," Sarah replied.

He frowned as he nodded. "I hope Trish is happy. I'm just really glad she's not trying to be happy around me anymore. You know what the lesson is, here, right? You'll find your person. It just takes time."

"Yeah, I know," she lied. She was tempted to tell him that she'd sworn off romance, but she didn't want him to try to talk her out of it. Blissfully happy people tended to do that; it was like they were drunk and wanted everyone around them to share in the collective delusion.

"You saw Ren?"

"Yeah," she said. "You double-booked photographers."

He looked serious again. "Is that okay? You both offered. I'd said yes to him first, but...I should have hired somebody, but I thought this way you didn't have to get me a present, and it's such a simple wedding..."

"It's fine. I'm sure Ren and I will be able to divide up the work. I was just surprised to see him. It's been a long time."

"It has," he said, looking thoughtful. "You should talk to him. Maybe one of you can shoot tonight and the other can do tomorrow, or one of you does the ceremony and the other does the reception."

"Sure."

"All right, I need to get to the rehearsal," Paul said, grinning. "You can come if you like. Or skip it and we'll see you at dinner."

"Get out of here. You are annoyingly happy."

"Feel free to slap me. I won't even feel it." He grinned and then headed back towards the lobby and his bride.

Sarah followed him outside a few minutes later so she could watch the rehearsal for the ceremony, since it would help her plan out her shooting the next day. The hotel was shaped like an oversized, three-story barn, but it was fairly elegant by Newfoundland standards—spacious and quiet, with great views and a friendly staff. The ceremony itself would be on the sloping lawn between the hotel and the sea, where a few chairs were already set up as place-markers.

The rehearsal began, and Sarah watched it to keep track of who was who: Abby's sister Laura was the maid of honor, dark-haired and gorgeous as she walked down the aisle with Paul's buddy Ian, who was doing an encore of his 'best man' duties. Abby's niece Hannah, who looked about nine years old, was joking like a young stand-up comedian as she walked down the aisle practicing her moves as flower girl.

"Petals for you, petals for you, no petals for you!" she said to a pretend audience, miming the tossing of flowers.

The hotel's manager, doubling as the wedding planner, told everyone where to stand as Abby and Paul laughed and joked with each other.

They all seemed so comfortable. It all seemed so *nice.* Why did that hurt? She had told herself that she could be happy for Paul, but the sight of two people who were obviously in love kept clawing at her heart.

She would have to regroup. She couldn't melt down at the first sight of people in love. She glanced over at Ren, who had arrived a couple of minutes after she had and was looking around at the sky and the ocean as if evaluating the most spectacular parts of the scenery for potential photos.

He had grown more solid over the last decade, though not in a bad way; he seemed less like a dreamy, ethereal fairy prince and more like a handsome adult man. Still, he remained so attractive that it seemed strange she knew him personally. His cheekbones and dark eyes made him look like some moody, brooding romantic poet, especially with a light wind whipping at his hair. He looked over at her and smiled. She tried to wipe her sadness away and smile back, and he frowned at her expression, as if he could register the effort that was going into her halfhearted cheer.

She wondered again if he had gotten remarried and swatted the thought away like a pesky insect. Some deep part of her knew exactly why she had never asked Paul about Ren. She didn't want to hear that he was married again. She didn't want to think about why that would hurt.

ABBY HADN'T LIED about the close distance between the hotel and the restaurant where they were having a rehearsal dinner; Sarah followed a group of scattered guests on the short walk along the curve of the two-lane road to a restaurant a half a kilometer away, her camera bag slung heavily over her shoulder, feeling grateful for her practical shoes.

The road hugged close to the sea, and she was soon surrounded by the quiet wash of sound from the pounding surf, interrupted only by the occasional call of gulls or the hum of a rare passing car. The smell of tangled seaweed brought her back to childhood: the isolation and poverty of her home province, its insularity and quiet beauty. She had spent her teenage years driving the short trip from her town to the coast with her two best friends. They would climb on the rocks and throw pebbles into the waves, talking about their plans to escape. She had first kissed a boy on a rocky beach like this one, their lives feeling achingly full of potential.

She paused and swung her camera out to capture the guests drifting like scattered seabirds in the last light of sunset, her heart heavy with a feeling she couldn't place.

Grief, she thought. She was grieving.

After she took the photo, she registered someone standing close to her. Ren was behind her, only a couple of steps away, dressed in his usual charcoals and greys, a fancy camera bag on his shoulder.

"Nice capture," he said quietly, and the phrase infuriated her. He did photography for a living, now. And she hadn't even known.

"We should talk about how we want to handle this," she said briskly. "Do you want to shoot the rehearsal dinner and I'll do the wedding? I don't want them to feel overwhelmed by too much camera presence. There are only about twenty guests, so we should keep a light touch."

"True," he said, smiling at her professional tone. "How about you do the rehearsal dinner and I do the wedding?"

She shot him a look. This seemed vaguely insulting, especially given that he only seemed to shoot stars and mountains. "Have you shot a wedding before?"

"Well, no..."

"Have you shot people?"

"I was a journalist." He smiled even more.

Of course. He was perfectly qualified for this, just as much as she was. Still, she had shot her friend Anya's wedding years before. "I've shot a wedding, so I think I can handle the ceremony and reception."

"Do you not want me to shoot?" He was giving her an odd look. "I just wanted you to be able to relax and enjoy yourself."

"Well, I'm not doing that either way, so it doesn't matter."

His frowned. "Why not? Do you not like Abby?" His green eyes regarded her keenly.

"No! No, not at all. I like her. I'm honestly just..." She sighed. "I'm not terribly optimistic about weddings these days."

"Ah." He nodded.

They had arrived at the restaurant and paused, stepping to one side.

"Okay, we can both shoot," she said, her eyes fixed on the

ground so she didn't have to see his thoughtful expression. "You decide how to divide things up."

He nodded. "Sure. I would like to talk to you at some point, too. Maybe after dinner?"

Oh, no.

Was he going to make the apology that she had been owed all these years? She didn't want it anymore. She didn't want to feel anything else right now. What she was feeling already was more than enough.

"Ren," she said, "you don't owe me an explanation for... Everything that happened was a long time ago."

His eyes were full of something she couldn't read. Mischief? Pity? It was frustrating sometimes, trying to get a lock on him. "I'd like to talk to you all the same," he said.

We're not friends anymore, she wanted to shout, but she couldn't get the words out. That would be a little too unkind. She was a grown-up, so she was going to have to let him hurt her one more time.

"Okay," she said quietly. "We can talk later." He smiled at her with more affection than he had a right to, so she turned away and walked into the building.

The restaurant was small and unfussy, the kind of place that sold fried clam platters and lobster rolls, though the separate dining room reserved for the event had been nicely decorated with flowers for the occasion. The evening seemed relaxed: there were around fifteen people at dinner, a few bottles of wine on a table in the corner, and trays of food arranged to one side: lobster rolls, pasta, and steamed mussels. Quiet pop music played. She got out her camera and stood to one side, taking some establishing pictures of the space, the room, the view.

One good thing could be said for photography: it took your attention away from yourself. For the next few minutes, she was framing shots, checking focus, and adjusting her exposure.

Everyone in her shots was laughing and happy. Everyone was a portrait of joy.

Then her lens found Ren chatting with a petite blond woman with punk rock hair and a lace dress. Sarah recognized the woman vaguely as Lisette, a friend of Paul's from his improv comedy group in St. John's. She had met Lisette at Christmas a couple of years ago and knew her to be a close friend of Paul's. An old jealousy rose up—an ancient hostility towards any other woman talking to Ren—and Sarah shook it off. He could sleep with Lisette if he wanted to. He had been willing to sleep with anyone but Sarah, so she should be used to it by now.

"Do you need help?" came a small voice. Sarah glanced down and saw Abby's niece looking up at her. The little girl had seemed half-asleep a few moments earlier, but she had apparently revived.

"Sure," Sarah said. "Remind me your name?"

"Hannah."

"Hannah, tell me if there are any important people I should take photos of."

"Hmm." The girl considered the room. "You should get Paul and Abby."

"True," Sarah agreed. Sarah picked up her camera and took a quick shot of the bride and groom.

"Get them looking silly," the girl added.

"Excellent idea. Can you get them to do something silly for me?"

"I think so," the girl agreed, then ran off.

Kids got along with Sarah. That was on the great ironies of her life, Sarah thought. Kids loved her. Sarah watched as Hannah ran up to Paul and covered his eyes, making him laugh. Sarah took a few shots.

A moment later, the girl returned. "Can I tell you a secret?"

the child said. "Ollie is going to ask my mom to marry him. I gave him permission."

Sarah smiled. "He's the red-haired man?"

"Yeah, over there," Hannah said. Sarah had noticed Abby's sister Laura standing on the tiny balcony with her boyfriend Ollie, leaning out towards the water and looking up at the stars. Laura was a striking dark-haired beauty with a delicate chin, and her boyfriend looked dapper in a perfectly tailored suit.

"I'll see if he's doing it now," Hannah said.

The girl ran toward her mother, and Sarah readied her lens, but then Ren stepped right in front of her and took the picture. Ren had patiently waited all night, not shooting, but as Ollie leaned over to talk to Laura in front of a glorious emerald-blue sky, Ren had opened his shutter once and gotten the perfect shot. Stupid Ren with his journalist's eye.

Ollie and Laura began to dance to the music, laughing, and they looked perfect doing that, too. Ren took more shots while Sarah leaned back against the wall, motionless, watching him. Why did he have to be good at everything? It made her feel so much worse.

As the dinner wrapped up and the cheerful guests gathered their jackets and hugged the bride and groom good-night, Sarah carefully packed up her camera, taking her time. If Ren wanted to talk to her, she might as well wait for him so they could talk on the way back to the hotel. Best to get it out of the way early, because she didn't want to spend all weekend worrying about what he might say. Sure enough, he smiled at her and put up one finger as he finished up a conversation with Paul.

Sarah sighed and waited by the door.

Ren caught up with her as the last of the guests were leaving and fell into step with her on the crunchy gravel of the parking lot. The night air was cool and the small fir trees across the street stirred gently like they were sharing secrets.

"I've never been to Newfoundland," he said. "It's pretty spectacular." She glanced up at the Milky Way arching above, the stars radiant against the last quarter of a waning moon.

"It's definitely remote," she said. Beauty didn't affect her like it once had. Sunsets, rainbows, sudden storms...she felt nothing about them these days. Not for the last three years, maybe four. She had wondered for a while if that was what had killed her impulse to do photography: a deadening inside, a lack of hope that tracked with the slow decline of her marriage. When she was young, she could look at the sky and believe all that beauty was meant for her, like a message from the universe. Now each sunset and starry night seemed profoundly indifferent to her, so she had become indifferent as well. Seeing beauty now felt like stepping inside the temple of a religion that she no longer practiced or believed in.

"So what are you doing for work now? Paul said you stopped doing photography," Ren said, shoving his hands in his pockets as they began to walk back to their hotel along the small coastal road.

"I work in marketing at a bank. I do corporate headshots and events photography along with some graphic design."

"And you like it?"

Sarah took a breath. "It's steady."

He watched her intently. "Steady can be good."

"It can." It wasn't. Sarah's manager at the bank was a fussy, difficult man named Owen, who was possibly the worst human being on earth.

Technically not the *worst*, she supposed. Owen was several years younger than her but he had graduated from a fancy business management program, and he had a malicious streak that he considered a 'management style.' He particularly liked setting people up to fail in order to win small arguments or find reasons to fire them. Maybe he was the worst person on earth who had never done anything illegal.

Ren said nothing, watching her face. A gust of wind blew in from the water, making her shiver.

"Cold? You can borrow my jacket."

She shook her head quickly. That was the last thing on earth that she wanted, to find out that Ren still smelled the same. She held her arms tightly around her.

"I looked up your photography website," she said. "It's pretty amazing."

"It's the places I've been that are amazing." At least he wasn't showing off, she thought. But Ren had never been one to brag. She hadn't loved him for no reason; he could be thoughtful and self-effacing when he wasn't breaking hearts. "So how has the rest of your life been going?" Ren asked. "You split up from your husband, Paul said?"

"Our divorce was finalized a couple of months ago but we've been separated for almost a year."

He nodded. "And no kids, right?" he asked. "The two of you didn't..."

Sarah winced fractionally at the words. "No. No kids. How about you?" She was desperate to change the subject. "Any more kids for you? How is Jandro doing?"

She watched him twist his watch in a circle as he considered his answer. The familiar sight brought a painful echo of her old affection for him rising sharply in her chest. "Jandro is okay. He's turning fourteen soon, and he'll be starting eighth grade in the fall. He has ADHD, so that's been tricky. Paola wants him to apply to private boarding schools for high school. She doesn't like any of the schools near us and she thinks the atmosphere around Las Vegas encourages him to slack off. But I've taken him out on some photo workshops with me recently and that has been good. I think he's one of those kids who needs to get away from the computer screen, do stuff with his hands."

"You were a little like that," Sarah said. "Restless."

Ren nodded. "Yeah, he definitely got it from me, but I managed it better. I think there are too many distractions now. Video games and stuff. But he's young. He can definitely turn things around."

"Of course he can," Sarah said kindly. She sometimes forgot that people with kids still had challenges: it didn't mean their lives were perfect or that their kids were doing perfectly. "And did you get married again?"

"No." His eyes fell to the ground in front of him. "Nothing serious for me in that department. I've dated a little, but I haven't lived with anyone."

"It's hard to find someone," Sarah said, though she felt sure that Ren would never find it hard to find someone.

He nodded. "I fell in love once, and that was it. No one else has measured up."

"She didn't appreciate you, though."

A distant smile came to his face. "I think she did appreciate me but I didn't know how to open up to her."

Sarah took a breath. "Well, I can say that my decision to remain single after my divorce has been surprisingly relaxing. Once I removed the possibility of dating, my life has gotten a lot calmer."

He gave her a curious look. "So no dating since the divorce?"

"No dating for me ever again."

"Ah." He looked out at the ocean and said nothing. Was that skepticism in his tone? The possibility annoyed her; surely Ren of all people could understand being cynical about relationships.

"I mean, not ever-ever," she said, in the hopes of avoiding a debate. "But I can't see it. Who knew that I would embrace the Rene Durand philosophy of no relationships ever? I've turned into you freshman year."

"Not exactly." He gave her a strange look. "Actually, I had a question for you."

Something in Sarah's chest started racing like a mouse on a wheel. Was he going to...? Surely not. Definitely not that, surely?

"I have a workshop coming up next week," Ren said. "I scheduled it when I found out about Paul's wedding. It's a one-week night photography workshop in Gros Morne National Park."

"That sounds beautiful." The park was famous in Newfoundland—a spectacular region on the west coast with fjord-like bays and rolling hills. It was a seven-hour drive from her hometown, but she had gone there on an overnight camping trip in her teens.

"I'm taking ten people out to shoot there; we're focusing on the Milky Way. New moon conditions. It should be pretty great if the weather holds. But I haven't found an assistant to help out. I was wondering if you would be willing to do it."

She was almost too surprised to answer. "Be your assistant?"

"For the workshop, yeah. I know you're overqualified for assistant work, but I could really use a second person who knows what they're doing."

She felt at once relieved and devastated that he wasn't asking something more personal, a feeling that she had no interest in examining. "So when is this?"

"The week right after the wedding. Monday through Friday. You'd have to take the week off work, but I could pay you for it. I was thinking ten thousand for the week, if you're interested."

The sum was a bit stunning. She had some debt left over

from her divorce, and that would clear it entirely...if she could convince her horrible manager to let her take the time off. "You must be making good money from those workshops."

He shrugged. "I get a lot of Silicon Valley tech guys who want to learn photography. They're high maintenance but they can afford to pay well. But that's why I like to bring help. Some of the folks who come are experienced photographers who just use the workshops as an excuse to go shoot in new places, but I always get a few who don't even know how to use their cameras. So the teaching part is pretty hands-on, and it helps a lot to have a second person. Gros Morne is remote, too. There'd be some hiking in, maybe an overnight at a fjord. My concern is that if anything comes up, like someone gets injured, I need someone who can keep the workshop running while I take the person to the hospital. Not that it's likely, but I know from experience that it's not wise to do this alone."

"I know nothing about night photography."

"Fair enough. So have you heard of these things called f-stop and ISO?"

"Very funny."

"That's my point. You're a great photographer. The rest are just tricks and details that I could explain to you on the way. Everyone in the workshop is flying in to Deer Lake on Monday, and I was going to drive out there Sunday after the wedding. I could show you the basics on Sunday night."

For a moment, she considered it. She could really use the money, and the workshop sounded fun. But going would also mean being with Ren for an entire week, hiking trails and wandering forests by his side.

"I don't know," she began. "I don't know if I can get time off."

"You have a day or so decide," he said. "But it would be a

huge help." He smiled that heartbreaking smile, and she hated him for a moment.

"I think I have to say no. I'm not sure if my work would even—"

"Take a day to think about it. Please."

She sighed. "I'll think about it."

When she got back to her hotel room, Sarah lay in her bed for a long time. It was painful to see him again, painful to contemplate a whole week with him, painful to say no. She got up and walked to her window and looked at the stars scattered across the night sky, stunning and endless in the clear night. There was a small plush armchair in her hotel room, so she pulled it close to the window and looked outside for a long time, waiting for the stars to give her answers that they didn't have.

10
SATURDAY

SARAH SPENT Saturday morning driving the long route home to pick up her mother for the wedding festivities later that day. Her mother had insisted she didn't want to spend more than one night at a hotel because she couldn't 'abandon her birds' for any longer; Maureen had inherited two small parakeets from an elderly neighbor, and they provided a constant focal point for her general anxiety about leaving her house. This meant that Sarah would be driving an hour and a half round-trip on Saturday morning to pick up her mother for the wedding and then would do the same on Sunday to take her mother home again. She had agreed to this plan because she knew that her mother would otherwise skip the wedding entirely and sit at home for the weekend, fretting and second-guessing her decision not to attend.

When Sarah pulled up to the small driveway of her childhood home and knocked on the door, she found her mother already waiting in her small kitchen, dressed in a silvery peach church dress.

"Lovely dress!" Sarah had developed her 'bright and cheerful' voice in her teen years when dealing with the freight train of her mother's anxiety, and she still pulled it out every time they began a conversation.

"Well, I just don't know," Maureen said, smoothing the skirt down.

"It's perfect."

"I haven't been to a wedding in so long. My last wedding was your wedding."

"It's going to be a lot of fun. Paul loves you."

"Is this a formal wedding? The invitation didn't say. You know, some people have very informal weddings now."

"I think the dress is just right."

"Well, it's the only one I have."

"And it's perfect." Sarah loaded up her mother's small overnight bag in her car as her mother spoke to the birds.

"You'll be okay," Maureen cooed to the parakeets, who responded with a bored sideways shuffle on their perches. "I'll be back before you know it."

Her mother had to check on a few more things she may have forgotten to turn off, and then they finally pulled away from the house and headed down the small two-lane road that curved through her town.

"So Danny is still living with that girl?" her mother began when they had finally gotten going. It was a strange question. Did her mother think something significant had changed in the living situation of her ex-husband in the last few weeks?

"As far as I know, yes."

"And they're having a baby?"

"They had the baby," Sarah confirmed.

"I still can't believe he would do that to you," Maureen said, for the fiftieth or the hundred time. "Men reach a certain age and they lose their minds. I think he'll be back once he realizes what a mistake he made."

"I think I'm better off without him," Sarah replied firmly.

"Of course. Of course you are." Her mother was silent for a moment, watching the familiar local landmarks drift past her window: the fire station, the playground named after a dead fisherman, the primary school named after a dead politician. "All the same, though, it's hard to be alone. Especially in your forties and fifties."

"You didn't date anyone after Dad died."

"Well, no one would have wanted me at that age."

"You were younger than me," Sarah replied.

"Well, true." Her mother smoothed down her skirt again. "You can't just bring a strange man into the house when you have a daughter."

"I've been out of the house for twenty years, Mom."

"I know. I should have done something twenty years ago. But now I'm too old."

"You could date."

"Oh, no. Not at my age."

"And for the record, I'm fine. I'm happy."

"Of course you are. Of course you are."

The worst part of her mother's gentle prodding was that none of it was malicious; she just floated along on a stream of anxiety that circled back to where it started in an endless loop, like a slow-moving ride at the world's most depressing amusement park.

"Would I want to see a therapist? Oh, no, not at my age," her mother would say whenever Sarah brought up the subject of her mental health. "I don't even know what I'd talk about."

Sarah had given up trying to convince her mother to seek treatment for anxiety and depression; she tried to tell herself that her mother was happy being unhappy, but it never felt quite accurate.

Over the next hour, Maureen fretted about potential traffic from road construction, even though they were scheduled to get to the hotel two hours before the wedding. She fretted about whether Sarah would have time to put her dress on and do her hair before the event. She fretted about whether her nephew Paul even wanted Maureen to come to his wedding, and whether it had been too much of a bother to come get her, now that it was too late *not* to come get her, and whether the money she had put in the envelope for Paul's wedding gift was sufficient, even though it was all she could afford.

"Paul just wants to see you," Sarah said. "He would be happy if you gave nothing."

"Well, I wouldn't give *nothing*. You can't just give *nothing*."

"You're almost the only family Paul has left. I'm sure he's just thrilled you're coming."

"Don't you think he should talk to his mother?" she added. "I can't believe that he stopped talking to her."

"Aunt Delia was horrible. You know this. She was always mean to you."

"Well, I'm sure she's sorry if it means her son stopped talking to her. I can't imagine never talking to your mother."

"Please don't bring up Delia to Paul," Sarah pleaded. "Not today."

"I just keep thinking about how sad Paul must be not to have his mother there. And his father passed. You lose people so unexpectedly, and then you regret not making up with them when you had the chance."

"Just don't bring her up today," Sarah said again. "Some other time, maybe. But not today."

"Oh, well, okay. I won't say anything if you think it's better not to."

"I think it's better not to."

When they arrived at the hotel, they spotted Paul waiting outside, looking dashing in a dark suit. Paul approached their parking spot and helped her mother out of the car, a warm smile on his face.

"You look amazing, Aunt Maureen," Paul said.

"I keep thinking how sad it is that your mother isn't here," she replied. Sarah caught Paul's look and rolled her eyes skyward.

"Well," said Paul, "I think we're going to have a pretty good day."

"I know," her mother said. "I won't bring it up. Sarah told me not to bring it up. I just keep thinking that anything could happen to people at any time, you know? And then you never a got a chance to make up with them."

From what Sarah understood, Delia had been banned from Paul's life after drunkenly storming into one of Paul's improv shows and insulting him and his girlfriend while they were on stage. It sounded like an ugly scene all around, the end of Delia's long downhill slide into increasingly malevolent behavior.

"Thanks for coming," Paul said cheerfully, giving her a kiss on the cheek as he released her hand, then holding the hotel door open for her.

"I don't know if this dress is fancy enough."

"It's perfect," Paul told her.

"Well, I just don't know," she replied as Sarah shot Paul an expressive look and then steered her mother inside. She led her mother straight to their hotel room, where Sarah quickly slipped into an elegant wine-colored jumpsuit and wine-colored flats and then slid a couple of extra camera batteries into her camera case.

"You're not wearing a dress?"

"It'll be inconvenient if I have to squat to take a photo."

"Well, I guess that makes sense." Sarah felt a wave of relief that there was something—one small thing—that her mother was okay with. "That's nice of you to take photos."

"I volunteered. It'll keep me busy."

"Well, that's true. Do you think my birds will be okay until tomorrow?"

"Your parakeets are fine. I'm sure they're sleeping."

"Well, I suppose." Maureen looked out the window anxiously. "It's awfully windy out there, isn't it? Do you think they can have the wedding outside if it's like that?"

For once, her mother's anxious observation had a basis in truth. The weather for the wedding was beautiful but gusty, and the ceremony arrangement next to the sea looked both stunningly dramatic and dangerously close to being blown away.

"Well," Sarah said with a sigh, "the photos won't be boring, at any rate."

After heading outside and helping her mother find a seat among the white chairs set up on the lawn, Sarah stood to the side, the warm gusts of wind tossing lone strands of her hair into her face, her eyes meeting Ren's across the aisle. His camera was already out and ready, and he grinned and took her picture before walking toward her. She felt angry at him again, though this time it was for no clear reason.

"So I was thinking I'll get the bride's entrance and exit," he said. "You focus on Paul's face when she comes in. I can do the ceremony and kiss, you do the processional, that way we're not clicking like paparazzi the whole time."

"Sounds good."

"Is that your mother?" he asked. "She looks like you."

"She drives me crazy."

"They all do. It's their job."

Just then, one of Paul's improv friends hopped in front of the chairs with a guitar.

"Hey, I'm Amber, I'm the live music," she said. She started playing a stripped-down version of a Vivaldi tune on her guitar as Abby's niece Hannah, dressed in an elaborately flowing flower girl dress, tossed rose petals that were instantly carried skyward by the wind. Abby's sister Laura came next, walking down the grassy aisle with Paul's friend Ian. Sarah glanced toward Laura's boyfriend Ollie, who was watching from his seat, his face quietly awestruck. Sarah snapped a picture of him before returning her camera to Paul.

Abby came out of the hotel next, looking radiant in a flowing white dress, but immediately her long veil began to blow around her face like an attacking seagull that she had to fend off. She started laughing, and Sarah turned her camera to Paul to catch him laughing, too. As soon as Abby made it down the aisle, Abby's sister Laura ran over to remove the aggressively swirling veil, and the sisters laughed together as it wrapped around them both. Sarah got a perfect shot of the two of them, the veil raised around them like a fingering mist, smiling at each other. The image made her emotional even as she took it; sometimes you knew when you had a perfect shot.

Then the vows began and Sarah stepped back to let Ren take over. He was subtle about it, she noticed. She only heard his camera click every twenty or thirty seconds, but at perfectly chosen moments: right when Paul and Abby exchanged rings, right when they gazed lovingly at each other, right when they kissed. His journalism training must be kicking in. He knew how to capture the key moments in a story.

As the ceremony ended, Sarah slipped to the back of the aisle to grab a few last shots of the newlyweds grinning and walking towards her. Then she hurried back to her mother's side; her mother was talking to an elderly woman who was a former neighbor of Abby's about the likelihood of a storm blowing in. Sarah helped both women across the grass as they walked towards the hotel.

"You know there's another photographer," Maureen observed as Sarah walked between them.

"Yes, I know," Sarah said.

"He's very handsome," said her mother.

"True," Sarah agreed.

"I never trust handsome men," said the elderly woman who was walking with them.

"They aren't reliable," Maureen replied decisively, as if she had a long history of being disappointed by dashing playboys.

Sarah glanced back to where Ren had paused to take a photo of a sash of white fabric that was drifting dramatically from the altar towards the sea. As she watched, the cloth detached from the altar and whipped upwards towards the sky. Ren kept shooting.

She felt a pang of regret that she had missed the shot, and another thimbleful of anger that Ren had gotten it. It made her want to kick her shoe against the wall like a toddler. Ren wasn't supposed to be here. And he kept smiling at her.

He approached her a couple of minutes later in the hotel's lobby, which was already set up for a cocktail hour.

"I can cover this if you want a break," he said quietly.

Sarah glanced around. Paul and Abby were standing in a corner, having decided to skip over the formal photos because of the wind and instead chatting and laughing with friends.

"I'm okay," Sarah said. "Shooting gives me an excuse to take a break from my mother. She's very anxious."

"In that case," he said, "you shoot for a while and I'll get you a drink."

He gave her another of his charming smiles and walked over to the bartender who was standing in one corner of the lobby pouring wine.

She remembered the last time he'd brought her a drink, the last time he had treated her like a date. A part of her wondered what the explanation would have been for that night—the explanation he had tried to give months later—but she also desperately didn't want to know. She had no interest in kissing him now. That felt like a relief.

Paul walked past her and glanced at her camera. "Hey! You're off the hook for the night."

"No need," Sarah said. "I'm having fun taking pictures."

"Well, if you get tired, please feel free to stop."

Ren returned with a glass of red wine—of course he remembered what she liked—and leaned against the wall next to her as she took a sip.

"Beautiful spot," he said as the first rays of sunset stretched through the windows. "I may step out and get some shots of the location."

"Be my guest," Sarah agreed. "I'll stay here in case anyone starts dancing on tables."

"Or doing complicated pre-choreographed dances."

"Drunkenly fist-fighting," she added.

"Confessing their decades-long crush on the bride."

"I'll get video for that one," Sarah agreed.

He headed outside and she glared at his back. He was still so *fun*. She took a large sip of wine and then raised her camera again.

The evening continued without a hitch: a low-key cocktail hour transitioning into a sit-down meal, the bride and groom coming around to chat with guests. Ren and Sarah took turns shooting and circling the room. Ren spoke French with Lisette's brother for a while and then chatted with Jasmine and Lucas. Sarah kept her mother occupied, then got some candid shots of Paul's Newfoundland improv friends as they laughed with Paul's Toronto acting friends.

Watching Abby and her sister Laura from across the room, Sarah tried to identify why she was having such an intense set of feelings. One part of the answer was simple, she realized. Abby and Laura were more or less her age. And they were in love. She had almost forgotten that such a thing was possible. Love seemed so out of reach after her divorce, but watching the two sisters, she couldn't help but be swept up in a small wave of hope.

When it came time for toasts at the end of the meal, Paul toasted his lovely bride for helping him to laugh again. Then Abby stood up to join him.

"And folks, we have something shocking to confess to you," Abby said. Sarah raised her camera, ready for something big. Were Laura and Ollie going to announce their engagement?

"For those of you who don't know, Abby and I actually got married some time ago at City Hall," Paul said. "This whole ceremony is a lie."

A few people jokingly booed.

"We did it for green card purposes," Paul added. "So take it up with the government."

"But," said Abby, "I think that is important to say because we also wanted to share that we are expecting a baby. And it will not be a shotgun wedding because we were technically married. So this is a celebration of our life together but also the fact that we have a baby due in October."

The room erupted with cheers, and Sarah took photos. She took photos of the joy and laughter on Abby's and Paul's faces. She took photos of the little girl Hannah jumping up and down and then hugging her mother. She took photos of Laura and her boyfriend Ollie applauding.

When the applause finally ended, Sarah lowered her camera. She felt unable to move for a moment. As soon as she could slip away without drawing attention, she slid outside the doors into the gusty evening and walked out of sight, where she leaned against the side of the hotel, her back pressed against the shingles, her eyes on the soft green haze of the horizon.

Her chest hurt like someone had kicked it with a boot.

There was a sound of a door opening and closing. She didn't dare to look up and see who it was, but a moment later, Ren was beside her, leaning next to her against the wall, blocking the gusty summer wind. His presence felt like the thing she most desperately wanted and exactly what she didn't need right then.

"Hey," he said, "everything okay?"

Sarah nodded, carefully composing herself so her voice wouldn't shake. "Yes."

He let out a slow breath, looking out at the indigo blue of night. "Can I ask a personal question?" His eyes were serious.

Oh God. What had Paul told Ren? She hadn't even told the whole story of her divorce to Paul, too afraid of upsetting him. "Go ahead," she said, feeling suddenly bone tired.

"You and your husband," he said gently, and her heart was throbbing like it was trapped in a vise, "did you have different perspectives on having kids?"

"No." Her voice sounded empty. "We had the same perspective."

"Okay."

She wanted him to leave, but he wasn't leaving.

"We had fertility issues," she said finally.

"Ah." Ren nodded. "I'm sorry."

She looked away into the darkness. She had a sudden, horrible sense that she might throw up right there in front of him.

A look came into Ren's eyes. She saw exactly the moment he put it together. "So your photo series with the babies..."

She nodded. "That was where all my work was. That was my entire income."

"Shit," he said quietly.

She was glad he could see the implications without her needing to spell it out. He understood, but he hadn't been there. He hadn't lived it.

All day, every day, shooting photos of people's babies. All night, every night, editing photos of babies on her computer. Babies floating in space. Babies surrounded by fields of wheat. Babies drifting down rivers with the flow of the current. Babies in factories, in old cars, in deserts and swamps and abandoned steamships.

All of her money had come from that one photo series, and all her money went into her attempts to get pregnant, then into a possible adoption that fell through. And there were miscarriages. One and then another, until Danny came home one day with a heartbreaking look in his eyes and said, "Something has happened."

And like a fool, Sarah saw his face and assumed that someone was hurt. "Is everyone okay?" she asked him, not yet realizing that the injured party was her.

Ren could guess at it, but he didn't know.

"I'm so sorry," he said.

She felt sick all over again. "Please stop. The one thing I have never wanted from you is pity, and that is what you always seem to give me."

"I don't pity you." He stared at her.

"I am not pathetic," she said. "I had some bad luck and then I got divorced and stopped doing photography. And that's okay. There's only a tiny fraction of people who can make a living at it anyway. And I'm employed. I have friends. I'm not a cautionary tale."

"Of course not."

She took a breath. "Is that why you wanted me to do your workshop? Because if so, you don't need to do me any favors. I have a job, and I'm stable, and I'm fine."

"That's not why I asked you." The wind blew around them for a moment. "But if you're asking if it bothers me that you don't still shoot, then yes, it bothers me. Because you're talented. And I know your photography is how you processed things."

"No. You don't get to say that to me."

He frowned, reaching one hand towards her arm. "Sarah—"

"You of all people. I would never have been with Danny if you hadn't—"

She couldn't finish, so she turned and walked away, farther and farther across the dark lawn that seemed to shake like the fur of a wild beast in the wind, her figure lit up by boxes of light from the hotel windows. She kept going until there was no more light, her body cold and shaking, past the edge of the lawn and down to the six-foot cliffs that led to the beach.

The tide was low and the air smelled of broken shells. She climbed down the rocks in her jumpsuit and landed with a stumble on the beach, where waves and stones and sky were all she could see. The stars above were pinprick sharp, tears in the eyes of the night sky. It was quiet for a moment, all sound drowned except the hiss of the wind and the waves attacking the rocky sand.

His voice called from behind her, out of her sight. "Sarah? Can I talk to you?"

"No!" she called back up. "I'm fine. Just leave me."

A long moment passed. "I'm going to go finish up shooting the wedding. But I'm here if you need me."

"I don't need you."

"Can we talk later?"

She was silent. After a long moment, she said, "No."

She waited there until she was sure he was gone. There was

nothing to look at now but the waves and the darkness. She pressed one hand against a rock that stood at waist height and waited to see if she could vomit. But no, she was stuck with the lump of pain in her stomach, immobile and permanent.

She couldn't have kids. Danny had wanted kids. He had wanted kids enough to be careless with birth control once he started cheating on her. He may have started cheating on her so that he could be careless with birth control.

Abby, Paul's bride, could get pregnant in her late thirties, which made her very much not like Sarah.

After a few minutes, Sarah managed to pull herself together and climb back up the rocks, walking alone across the vast lawn and back to the party. She needed to make sure that her mother felt taken care of. That was one nice thing about adulthood. There was always something you had to do next, another responsibility to keep you from letting your emotions rise like the wind and push you off a cliff.

The dancing had begun in earnest by the time she got back. For all of her joking with Ren about choreographed dances, it turned out that she hadn't been far off: Laura and Ollie were doing some kind of polished dance that looked choreographed but wasn't. Abby and Paul were wrapped around each other, staring into each other's eyes to a song that was definitely not designed for eye staring. Her mother was watching from a table in the corner, sipping on a white wine.

"Come on, Mom," Sarah said. "Let's dance."

"Oh, I don't know," she replied. "I don't really dance anymore."

"Come on. Get up."

"Oh, no. You go ahead. I'm a little tired."

Sarah wanted to drag her mother up onto the dance floor, but her heart wasn't in it. Instead, she slumped down in a seat next to her. They sat there for a long time, watching the happy couples swaying and laughing.

Ren wasn't dancing either. He was watching her intently from across the room. She frowned and looked away.

"Do you think I gave Paul enough money?" her mother said after a while. "I just want to give the right amount."

Two hours later, Sarah lay in bed near the sleeping figure of her mother, staring at the ceiling. The clock told her that it was just after midnight, and she knew that somewhere in the hotel was Ren, probably sleeping but maybe still awake. Steps away.

She stared at her cell phone for a long moment, wondering if she still had his number. Not that she was going to text him. What would she say? He had wanted to talk and she had said no. So tomorrow morning was the last time she would probably ever see him—if she saw him at all. They were going to go home, and that would be that. That would be the end of their friendship forever.

She got up out of bed, threw on some shoes and a sweatshirt over her pajamas, and put her cell phone in her pocket before tiptoeing into the hallway of the hotel and then down the stairs. The hotel was mostly closed up for the night, though Sarah could hear some staff members still moving around the kitchen, cleaning up. She walked quietly through the empty lobby and out the back door to the porch. She wasn't concerned about being locked out. Newfoundland was extremely casual about the locking of doors. Her home province probably had jewelry stores that didn't bother to lock up at night.

Outside, she found a low, wooden deck chair on the back patio and sat down in it, feeling the painted wood like a soft, cool hand against the back of her neck. She could hear the distant rush of the waves. No traffic. A slender finger of cloud came and went across the moon.

She shivered a little and looked up.

The sky was spectacular: clear and endless and filled with billions of stars stretching out to eternity. Her heart felt as empty as a hole.

Maybe she should have agreed to spend the week with Ren, but she knew what the result would be. She would fall back in love with him. He would tease her, give her a taste of her old life, restore her to optimism, and then leave. He would go back to Nevada and they would text for a while...and then nothing.

She couldn't handle that from him again. She wasn't strong enough.

A dark figure was crossing the lawn coming back from the beach, its outline oddly shaped in the dark. She identified him instantly, carrying a tripod on one shoulder and a camera bag on the other.

She didn't want to startle him, so she stood up and walked to the edge of the porch to wait. She felt it like a touch the moment he saw her.

"Shooting?" she asked just loudly enough to be heard over the wind.

He nodded. He took the few steps up onto the porch and stood near her, his green eyes looking grey in the half-light. "Couldn't sleep?"

She nodded.

"Not much moon for your workshop," she said.

"Anytime you're hoping to get with the Milky Way, you schedule for the new moon. Reduces the glare."

"That makes sense."

He gave a quick smile. "And then you hope for clear skies. This is great right now, but there may be some weather blowing in around Wednesday. I'm hoping the cloud cover will be minimal."

"If there are rainy days, do your clients ask for their money back?"

"Worse. I have to hang out and socialize with them."

She smiled a little.

He took a breath. "I know you've already said no, but can I explain one thing? I didn't invite you because I felt sorry for you. Paul said you'd stopped doing photography, and it bothered me. But I also wanted to know you again. And I know a day or two isn't going to cut it, especially if we're busy shooting the wedding. I wanted to see if we could be friends again." Ren went silent for a moment, as the waves continued their endless cycle of advance and retreat. "I know I messed things up with you. And I knew I couldn't apologize without at least explaining myself. I don't know when I'm going to get another chance."

She considered this, looking out toward the water. "What will you do if you don't find an assistant?"

"I'll figure it out. It'll be harder but I'll make it work." He sighed. "I just really hoped I could talk you into it."

"You haven't contacted me in years." He still texted her on her birthday and she on his. But that was it.

"I know. I thought...after what happened...I thought I had messed up our friendship so much that I needed to apologize in person, and by the time I could make it there to do it, you were involved with someone, and it felt inappropriate to talk about it." Inappropriate? The idea that Ren had feelings for her felt so implausible that Sarah dismissed it out of hand. He couldn't possibly mean that, could he?

"And then you got married," he went on, "and I didn't want to hear about how great your marriage was. Or if it was shitty, I didn't want to hear that either."

"It didn't start out shitty," she said.

"I kept waiting for news that you were having a kid."

"Ha. Irony."

"I wish you had. I wish you'd gotten everything you wanted. I just didn't think I could be friends with you and watch it happen."

"I was friends with you when you were married."

He looked down. "I know, but that was different."

"Why?"

He took a step closer. "Because I hadn't messed everything up yet." He looked at her until she finally met his eyes. "Can you just give me a chance to get to know you again? I miss being your friend."

It was such a simple request that Sarah's heart melted a little. She took a long breath.

"I'll see if I can get off work this week."

He nodded, his eyes sparkling in the darkness. "Thank you. I appreciate it. I know it's a long drive to Gros Morne, but I can probably get you a plane ticket out of St. John's if there's still one available. Last time I looked, the flight was booked, but it's possible that..."

"I can drive out. It's fine," Sarah said.

"No need. I'll be driving anyway," he said. "I have a rental car for the week. So if I can't get you a flight, maybe I could just come with you when you drop off your rental car, and then we can drive out there together."

"I have my mother's car. I have to take her home tomorrow, and then I was going to call a taxi service to get back to St. John's. So if we go together, you will have to follow me all the way to my mother's house and leave from there."

"That's fine. I'll get to see your hometown."

Her mouth crooked at the thought. "Population six hundred? I don't think you'll be impressed. It's pretty low on culture. Nowhere to watch a sad indie film."

"On the other hand, it sounds like the perfect setting for a sad indie film."

"I do have a dead father, so maybe you're right."

He smiled, his eyes full of feeling. He had said that he wanted to be her friend again. And like a fool, she wanted that, too. The rest of it, the nonsense about how sad he was that he'd lost his chance with her...she knew better than to take any of that too seriously. This was Ren.

11
SUNDAY

"SO," Sarah said, keeping her voice carefully casual, "my friend is going to pick me up at our house a few minutes after we get back." They were in Maureen's car on their way back from the wedding. Sarah was driving, and she had noticed that the mileage on the car was barely more than it had been when she had come home for Christmas. Her mother worked at a local grocery store, and Sarah suspected that she did most of her food shopping at work and never went anywhere else except for church on Sundays.

"And she's going to drive you all the way to the airport? That's nice." Her mother had been fretting about whether she should drive Sarah to the airport herself, but Sarah knew that Maureen got nervous whenever she drove more than fifteen minutes from home.

"No." Sarah took a breath, debating for the hundredth time whether it was better to lie about her plans. "He is actually going to take me out west to help with a photography workshop he's running."

"He's the other photographer?" Her mother's eyebrows shot upward. "The handsome one?"

"Yes, he's an old friend from McGill."

"And he knows Paul, too?"

Sarah nodded. "They met in Toronto."

There was a long pause as her mother watched Sarah's expression. "You're not in love with him, are you?"

"No, I am not in love with him," Sarah confirmed.

"Because men that handsome..." Her mother gave her a meaningful look.

"I know, Mom. You've said."

"I just worry."

"I know, Mom. It's fine. He is definitely not interested in me like that."

They had gotten on the road early, so they arrived at her mother's house at a little after nine in the morning and immediately checked on the parakeets, who were remarkably unperturbed after their hours of horrible abandonment.

"I guess they're okay," said Maureen as she changed out the little compartment of water in the birds' cage. "They don't seem too upset."

"The parakeets are fine, Mom. Let me know if there's anything you need me to do before I head out. He should be arriving soon."

"And then you have to leave." The gut punch of guilt was familiar, but it still hurt.

"I was always going to take a flight home this morning. Now I'm doing a few days of work first, that's all."

"I know. I know you have to go," her mother said, her voice cracking with sadness. "You have work."

"Hey," Sarah said softly, "you should move to Toronto. I mean it. This place is too quiet. It's too easy to be sad here."

"Oh, no. I don't want to move to a whole new place where no one knows me."

Sarah looked around their small house. It felt like a memorial more than a home, frozen in the era when Sarah had been a young child with two living parents. Since then, the house had never really changed, never shifted décor. Her mother didn't see the point in buying something just for herself. The one new armchair in the corner had been purchased by Sarah as a Christmas gift, and Maureen had accepted it only with great reluctance.

"If you're happy here, that's fine," Sarah said. "But if you're not..."

Her mother looked around. "I didn't know anyone would be coming over. The house is such a mess," she said, although it wasn't. Maureen didn't get into enough trouble to make messes; there were a few knitting projects on the sofa in front of the TV and a couple of mugs on the counter.

"It'll be fine. The house looks great. Ren won't stay long," Sarah said.

"And then you'll be leaving."

"I'm sorry."

Sarah took her mother's suitcase and brought it to her mother's bedroom, placing it carefully on the bed.

"Do you want me to start your laundry?" she asked. Doing tasks together was a reliable trick for pulling her mother out of these spirals of sadness.

"Oh, I can do it myself, sweetheart."

Ren knocked on the door only a few minutes later. Sarah walked over to let him in. He was wearing one of his especially charming smiles, which Sarah suspected would only make things worse.

"Hello," Ren said, putting out a hand to Maureen when she approached. "I'm Rene Durand, a friend of Sarah's. We didn't get to meet at the wedding."

"Oh, yes, of course." Her mother stared at him for a moment. "You met her at McGill?"

"First semester."

"Well, come inside, it's not very..." She waved a hand vaguely. "Can I make you a cup of tea?"

"Tea would be great," Ren said.

"I only have milk, not cream."

"Milk is perfect. Thanks."

"Well, I wish I had cream, but I didn't know I'd have people over. So I only have milk."

"Milk is great."

Maureen began to walk around the kitchen with the nervous, fluttering energy she always had when guests came over. Sarah led him into the small living room, thinking about how much it looked like a Newfoundland cliché: hand-knitted blankets, fishing lures in a glass case, carved duck decoys. She would have been mortified for Ren to see it during school, when Sarah still hoped to seem cool to people. His childhood home was probably full of books, while the only book in sight here was a dogeared paperback on the coffee table called *Touched by Angels: Real-life Stories of Angel Encounters*.

"My family estate," she said, gesturing towards the solid oak furniture and the ancient rocking armchair.

Ren smiled reassuringly, then walked over to the wall of family photos. The images in the photos were faintly yellowed, peeping out of circular and square cutouts.

"That's your father?"

Her father had been a friendly man with curly brown hair and clothes that reflected his love for the outdoors. In the photo Ren was looking at, Sarah was probably five years old and looked winsomely adorable, her rosy-cheeked face tucked under her father's chin as she crouched in a friend's wooden canoe. Sarah had kept that same face into adulthood, alas: round and cute rather than dramatic and sexy. She had so desperately wanted to be waifish in her teen years.

"That's my dad," Sarah agreed.

Ren continued examining the photos carefully as Maureen spoke from the kitchen. "Her father died!" she called. "That's why she has no brothers and sisters. We were thinking about having another, but I had trouble getting pregnant and then he was killed by a drunk driver."

Sarah's eyes went straight to her mother. "I didn't know you had trouble getting pregnant."

"Oh yes, we wanted children two years apart, but it didn't work out. And then he was gone."

Sarah had never explained her own fertility issues to her mother, not wanting to cause her more anxiety. She had said that she and Danny didn't want kids, because it seemed easier to surprise Maureen with good news rather than constantly tormenting her with bad news. Now she felt the loss of an opportunity to connect.

She watched her mother standing stock still, frozen in place in the kitchen for a moment, before she collected herself and opened the cabinet to get out the mugs. Sarah hadn't seen her mother entirely happy since her father was alive. It was a wonder that Sarah had ever found the courage to fall in love at all, growing up in a house where this was the devastation that followed when you lost someone.

She felt Ren watching her.

"And this?" he asked, pointing to a young toddler doing an awkward somersault.

"You know who that is. That's the groom from this weekend's wedding."

He smiled at the tiny image of Paul. "He's exactly the same."

"He was always hilarious. And very sweet. I'm glad he's acting again, even if it's just improv."

"Me, too." Ren gave her a look, something mischievous in his eyes. "So I know we have to get on the road soon, but I will never forgive myself if I don't ask you a question."

"Oh, no."

"Do you have a childhood bedroom with your stuff still in it?"

She sighed. "Let's get this over with."

She pushed open the door to her bedroom, a small space off the downstairs hallway, and stood back for Ren. He entered with the focus of an anthropologist, standing in the middle of the room to take it all in. Her mother had left a few in-progress crochet and knitting projects on her desk and bed, but the rest was the same: the fantasy novels, the Tim Burton movie poster, the Belle and Sebastian and Elliot Smith CDs.

"Just say it," she said. "Get it out of your system."

"There is no way I can say anything while my brain is storing up every single detail to memory."

"Okay, okay."

"This is so perfectly you. This is the you I first met."

He walked to her bookshelf, looking at the classics from college tucked between rows of science fiction paperbacks.

"Anne McCaffrey *and* Anne Rice." His voice was full of laughter.

"I'm sure you spent high school reading Kafka. You once told me that you refused to read anything written after 1980 because you weren't sure if it would stand the test of time."

Ren gave her a mischievous look. "I was trying to impress you. I read plenty of Terry Pratchett growing up."

"Oh my God, Ren, if you tell me that your entire intellectual snob thing was an act..."

"It wasn't an act," he replied. "I just exaggerated it around girls."

"Now I want to see photos of your childhood bedroom."

"It's been turned into my father's office," he said. "You'll never get the dirt on me or my movie poster of *Magnolia*."

She smiled, finally. "Okay, enough, get out. I need to dig through my drawers to see if I have any clothes that I can use for this trip. I didn't bring the right clothes for a photography workshop when I was packing for a wedding. So you are not allowed to judge me if I spend this week wearing Pearl Jam T-shirts."

"I was going to stop and buy you more clothes, but now I don't want to." He was giving her such an affectionate look that she fell silent. That gaze felt unfair. He had no right to look at her like that, not without apologizing...not without him giving her the apology that she had insisted she didn't want.

"Your tea's ready, Rene," came her mother's voice. "You said milk, right? I hope milk is okay because I don't have any cream."

"Milk is great!" Ren called. The moment was broken. Sarah let out a relieved sigh when he headed back to the kitchen.

Her mother pulled Sarah quickly aside as Ren was carrying Sarah's small duffel bag to the car.

"You're not dating him?" she asked urgently.

"No, Mom."

"He's just...you know, men that handsome...he's not going to stay."

"Wow. Thanks."

"You know I didn't mean it like that."

"I'll call you this week to tell you how it's going, okay?"

Sarah gave her mother a huge hug. She wasn't going to see her again on this trip; Ren had managed to book Sarah a flight out of Deer Lake, near their workshop, straight to Toronto, so she wouldn't be flying through St. John's on her way home. She had the same terrible feeling she always did when she left her mother, like a heavy weight was dropping from the top of her chest to the bottom, breaking everything it hit on the way down.

She hated to go. She loved her mother so much, but she always felt like she could breathe easier when she was far away.

Maureen's eyes filled with tears as they hugged goodbye. It might be six months before they saw each other. Sarah promised to call every Sunday.

Then Sarah climbed into Ren's red SUV rental car and closed the door.

"Ready," Sarah said without making eye contact with him.

She could feel his sympathetic gaze all the same. "Thanks for doing this."

Ren started up the car and gave a last wave to her mother, who was watching their departure through the front window, the white curtains framing her face like two walls crushing in from either side. Sarah managed a last bright smile until they were out of the driveway, and then she felt herself crumbling, her shoulders dropping. *Grieving,* she thought again. She was grieving the times she had come here with a husband in tow. Danny had been such a bright light when he came to visit, so cheerful, making everyone laugh. Her mother had trusted Danny to take care of Sarah. Everyone had trusted him. She sighed, shaking her head to clear the memories.

"What are you thinking about?" Ren asked.

"Nothing important." They headed down the road. "My mother just told me you were too handsome for me to date," she added a moment later.

"What?" He stared at her for a moment as they reached the town's only stop sign.

"She doesn't trust handsome men," Sarah said. "She said if we dated, you would leave me."

"But what does that imply about...I mean...you're..."

Sarah shrugged. "She just worries."

"Your self-doubt makes more sense now," Ren said quietly.

"If you want the real reason for my self-doubt, drive up the road twenty minutes to my high school. For four years, I had exactly three friends and two hundred people who hated me. Someone took the air out of my tires the night I was going to drive my boyfriend to prom."

He stared at her. "Why?"

She shrugged. "Because I was different. And I refused to be normal. I had blue hair for a while. It caused my mother so much stress that I wouldn't just fit in."

He considered this. "Well, for my first couple of years of high school, I was the resident gay guy who wasn't actually gay."

"Why did they think you were gay?" She remembered his comment once about having girls' eyes.

"The usual reasons. I dressed well. I read books. I listened to weird music."

"So you got your revenge by sleeping with every girl you could."

"Not really. I only slept with five girls in high school."

"Ren, that's a lot!"

"Is it?" He frowned.

"I've only slept with five people my whole life."

He glanced at her while she put up her fingers to count. "My high school boyfriend, then Ivan, Liam, Matthew, and Danny."

"Which one was Matthew?"

"When you moved to Las Vegas. I saw him for a couple of years. You and I were still texting, but we didn't talk about personal stuff."

"No, we didn't." He was silent for a moment as they drove down the road. "So what was the high school boyfriend like?"

"You'll love this. He was our school's only goth."

Ren laughed. "Black hair, black clothes?"

"Black eyeliner. Black combat boots. He wrote anti-capitalist song lyrics and planned to change his first name to Crow when he started college. I don't think he went through with it."

"But his actual first name was..."

"Philip. I broke his heart when I broke things off before going to McGill and he wrote angry songs about it. What was your first girlfriend like?" She thought about how strange it was that they'd never talked about this stuff. At university, they'd talked about music and books, but never about their lives.

"First girlfriend or first person I slept with?"

"Either." The answer itself was interesting, Sarah thought.

"I had an in-retrospect deeply problematic relationship with a twenty-one year old when I was sixteen."

Sarah was appalled. "Ren."

"I guess she qualifies as a girlfriend. In retrospect, it wasn't a good idea. I was acting out a lot around then."

"Was that after you saw your mother's article where she regretted having kids?"

Ren shot her a surprised look, as if he hadn't expected her to remember that. "Yeah, partly. And our household was very tense in the years leading up to their split, which I guess I blamed on myself."

"So what happened with the twenty-one year old?"

Ren shifted his eyes away. "So I have a question about Ivan, while we're on this topic."

Sarah nodded, noticing Ren's deflection. "What about him?"

"Why that guy? I hated him so much. He was so into talking about his feelings and his taste in movies was boring David Fincher shit. And then you got right back together with him after you finally broke up. Like two days later."

"Well, first of all, he was the only person who asked me out at McGill."

"There's no way that's true."

"It's true," Sarah said. "I wasn't somebody people were into. You must remember this. I wasn't sexy and elegant like Kristie or a blond fairy princess like Anya."

"You know what's funny," Ren said. "You talk about yourself like you're not attractive, but in the twenty years I've known you, you've almost never been single. I've been single for probably ten of those years, and you've been single for maybe three. And when you were single, you turned it into an amazing photo series. So I don't get this theory you have that you aren't attractive."

"Oh come on. Compared to you, my love life has been staggeringly boring. You were hooking up with two or three women a month."

"One a month, maybe," he replied. "And I should get a little credit for the ones I turned down."

She laughed. "Rene Durand, hereby awarded sainthood for the million women in Montreal he managed not to sleep with."

They drove past another small town made up of little more than a gas station and a fish and bait shop.

"I think you're just better at falling in love than I am," he said after a moment. "It always seemed like you could fall in love with *anyone*. And it took me forever to even *like* most people."

Sarah shrugged. "Not to dig up old issues, but it's not like you asked me out. There was one night when you said we could have sex but you definitely didn't want a relationship, but aside from that..."

The corner of his mouth quirked up. "I thought about asking you out after Kristie broke up with me, but I was sure you would laugh in my face."

Sarah frowned in confusion. "Why would I have laughed at you?"

"Because you hated me back then. Or I thought you did."

"We talked a lot."

"Yeah, but mostly because you were mocking me," he replied. "Your default attitude towards me was that I was an asshole."

"But that didn't mean I didn't like you!"

He smiled. "Oh, okay. Wonder why I didn't pick up on that."

The past seemed very close for a moment. She thought back to all the times when they had been together as part of a larger group, all the times they had wound up next to each other, debating books and movies. "I liked you when you were being normal," she said. "It was like you dropped the cool guy act sometimes and became a really nice person. But then you would start doing this brooding, mysterious, Kerouac quoting thing, and I didn't know how to deal with you."

His mouth twisted into a half-smile as he looked out the window. "I wish I'd..."

"Yeah," Sarah agreed. "I wish we hadn't been so young when we were young."

"If we'd dated, I would have messed it up, though," Ren said. "That's the one thing I'm glad about. I would definitely have done something stupid if we went out, and you would have left. Never spoken to me again. There is no way we would be friends now if I had dated you back then."

"Well, I messed up all my relationships, too. I was too insecure. That was the good thing with Ivan. I didn't have to be insecure around him because he was so clingy. I had to worry about whether I was making him happy, but not about whether I was pretty enough for him."

"You were always pretty enough," he said quietly.

She kept her eyes out the window. None of this had to do with now. "It's funny to talk about all this, all these years later."

He nodded. "All I had to do was kidnap you and lock you in a car for seven hours."

"And pay me ten thousand dollars," she added. "That's my price to talk about the past."

"It's worth it."

Her heart warmed at the words. She didn't want to kiss him anymore, but this felt like friendship, and friendship was good.

"So you started a photography business," she said after a while, when they were heading down the highway. "And now you are some kind of international superstar."

"If only." Ren shook his head. "I don't sell a lot of work. A few pieces a year. Most of my income is from teaching workshops."

"Sure. But how did that all happen? It's really impressive."

He didn't look at her as he began to speak. "Things weren't good for me and Paola when I moved to Las Vegas. I don't remember how much I told you back then, but things were bad pretty much right away. It was the combination of not being able to work much because of visa issues, staying home with Jandro, and living in the same house as Paola's parents. She had a job working for her father, and he offered me a job too, taking photos of real estate, but I said no. I felt like that would make things worse, if Paola and I were working for her father and living with him. He would have had control over every aspect of our lives. But when I turned him down, he decided I was lazy."

Some of this was what Sarah had feared would happen back in Toronto. "So did Paola end up getting her American law degree?"

"She took the bar exam, but she didn't practice. Her father offered her a raise if she agreed to keep working exclusively for him."

"That's..."

"Controlling? Yeah. And meanwhile, I was home with Jandro all day and really isolated. I got a little depressed. Sometimes Paola would get home at night and I would just take off in my car and drive out into the desert an hour or two until everything was quiet. There were some of the most amazing stars I'd ever seen out there. So I started taking my camera. And it was like I got a piece of my soul back." He shot her a look. "It was a learning curve, but I went on a lot of message boards about night photography and met other people who did it. And eventually I got a few of my shots into a gallery in Vegas."

"And all was forgiven with your father-in-law and he started taking you seriously?" Sarah asked lightly.

Ren gave a weary smile. "It's like you've heard this story. He did not take me seriously. And I wanted to move back to Canada, but I had done everything wrong in terms of being able to move away and share custody. We did eventually move out of her parents' house, but her father gifted Paola the house we moved into, so he still had control over us that way."

"Right." She could see it all: the outlines of the whole divorce.

"So when we split, I doubled down on night photography because I could schedule it around spending time with my son, since it was the exact opposite of Paola's work schedule. I started running workshops on weekends. And once I had a few clients who liked shooting with me, they started suggesting places. 'What if we did one at Yellowstone? What about the Grand Canyon?'"

Sarah nodded. That was how her photography career had taken off: recommendations from a few loyal clients.

"By that point, Jandro was in school, so I worked out a schedule where I could be home for three weeks and then go away for a week on a workshop. Sometimes I was assisting friends with running workshops, sometimes I was running my own. But it gave me a life back. It's why I was worried about you when Paul said you stopped shooting after your divorce."

She shrugged. "My *Single Life* series was fun, and my babies series was fun. The problem was that I stopped feeling fun, so I couldn't seem to shoot anything people wanted to buy. People don't want images about loss and grieving. There's no money in grieving."

"Was there one thing that happened that caused the divorce?" Ren asked.

Sarah shuddered, looking out the window. "I don't want to get into it."

Ren nodded and flipped on the radio, searching for stations. The pickings were slim. Newfoundland didn't do radio especially well. It did two things well: it had a lot of trees and it kept going. There was one road across the northern end of the province, a long stretch of the Trans-Canada Highway, and once you were on it, there was not much to see except rolling hills, clusters of small houses, and lots and lots of balsam firs and white spruces, on and on to the horizon, broken by the occasional lake that mirrored the bright blue sky.

"Should I play some music?" she asked as Ren searched the static. "I have an app on my phone. Or I could connect your phone."

"You can play anything as long as it's Pearl Jam."

She picked up her phone and put on a playlist for him. "I've actually been on an eighties kick," she explained. "I'll do the first hour of music and you pick the next."

They listened to Sarah's current favorite mix, filled with songs from The Cure, Echo and the Bunnymen, and The Clash. Somehow, the despair that seemed to bubble just beneath the surface of those songs had suited her this past year.

"I bet your high school boyfriend loved this stuff," Ren said after a while.

"He was more into Marilyn Manson," Sarah said with a grin. "We don't need to talk about it."

"And did you do goth make-up too?"

"Like I said, we don't need to talk about it."

"I wish *that* photo had been on your living room wall."

"They're all burned, and that's all you're going to hear about it."

Ren laughed and Sarah let herself be happy for a moment. He was her friend, in spite of everything. And they were on a road trip.

A Joy Division song came on that they both knew the words to, and they sang along. She had never heard him sing before.

An hour and a half into the journey, they stopped at a larger town to buy a few last items they would need: a sleeping bag for Sarah, some hiking sneakers and practical clothes for her, and a few odds and ends that would help them survive a week of night shoots. Ren paid for everything with his credit card.

"I feel like a teenager with my mom at the mall," she said as they walked out of a store. "I can pay for my own clothes."

"But you're only buying them because I needed your help and didn't warn you ahead of time," he said. "I imagine you prefer slightly more fashionable stuff than this." Then he smiled. "Or at least, twenty-year-old vintage versions of this."

"Do you still wear leather jackets? I haven't seen one on this trip."

"I had the one I wore at McGill until recently. My son just stole it from me."

"I have to meet this kid."

Ren grinned. "He's very funny."

As if on cue, just as they were crossing the small shopping mall parking lot, his phone rang.

"Jandro," he said. "*Qu'est-ce qu'il se passe?*"

Sarah pointed to the driver's seat, offering to drive, and Ren nodded and then handed her the keys and stepped away to talk to his son in French. She watched him rubbing the back of his head while pacing anxiously for a few minutes before he returned to the car with a sigh.

"Everything all right?" she asked, starting the engine.

"Jandro wants to come with me on my workshop to the Galapagos Islands later this summer, but his mother says it will interrupt his tutoring schedule. She's trying to get him ready to do testing so he can apply to private schools for high school next year. He thinks I can talk her into letting him go, but I try not to get between them in fights."

"Makes sense."

"Paola thinks his whole future is on the line, which doesn't help because he has test anxiety. And I want him to do well, but I hate how intense she gets about it." Ren sighed and rubbed his face. "I just think it wouldn't be the end of the world if he comes on that trip with me. But I can't admit that to him without starting a fight with her."

She nodded. "Agreeing on how to raise kids is hard even when you're married," she said. "Anya's always getting into disagreements with Jeremy about Ilona, and they're both pretty easygoing. Paola always seemed..." Sarah stopped herself.

"She wants what she wants," he filled in. "Like a freight train that you can climb aboard or get out of the way. Anyway, I was going to stop over in Toronto on my way home from this workshop, so I'm going to see if I can get her to bring him up and I can spend a weekend there with Jandro instead, so he still gets a fun trip this summer. He could spend a day or two and visit some universities in Toronto with me. Paola wants to inspire him to get excited about college."

"How often do you come to Toronto?" The thought hurt a little. Had he been passing through town often without telling her?

He gave her a quick look. "I usually make it up once a year or so."

She nodded. "Right. Well, it's your turn for music." She tried for a casual smile. "I want to see if you're listening to the same stuff you were listening to in Las Vegas."

"What was I listening to? I don't even remember. I remember we listened to that Lord Huron song."

"It was a lot of male singer-songwriters who were deep in their feelings."

Ren connected his phone to the rental car and put on a playlist. "Here's my current favorites. You can tell me whether my taste has changed." The songs now were by Tom Waits, Leonard Cohen, and Nick Cave.

"Huh," she said as she looked through the list. "Now it's all men who are disappointed with humanity."

Ren gave a little laugh. "Probably accurate. Right after my divorce, I was sad, but I wasn't angry yet."

"When did you get angry?"

He looked at her for a long moment. "So can I explain what happened? That night?"

Sarah hesitated, then shook her head. "No. Not yet. We're getting along right now, and we have to work together this week. I don't want to fight."

He took another long breath and released it. "Okay. Not yet."

Sarah felt like a coward. A long stretch of highway opened ahead of them and Leonard Cohen muttered in their ears about the darkness of modern society.

"So you promised to talk me through the basics of shooting the stars," she said at last.

"Sure," he said. He looked at the road. "You know a lot of this already, but the basic problem with night photography is setting your exposure and shutter speed, right? If you set your exposure correctly for the stars..."

"Then the foreground is too dark," Sarah filled in.

"If you set it for the foreground, the stars look fuzzy and blown out. And if you do a long exposure, let's say you do a three-minute shot with your shutter open so that enough light will hit your sensor to show the foreground, then you get star trails. The stars are constantly moving in the sky, circling around the North Star, right? And sometimes you want star trails. But if you want pinprick stars, you have to do something else. So there are a couple of solutions I use. One is to add light to the foreground, to paint it with flashlights while your shutter is open, so you can keep your exposure short enough so you don't get star trails."

"Light painting. You never use a flash?"

He looked disgusted. "Ugh, never. Flashes have no nuance. They make the scene look flat."

"I like that sometimes," Sarah said.

"You use flash for that throwback 1970s paparazzi thing. Not the same at all," Ren said, and she felt briefly gratified at how well he remembered her work. "On shoots, I prefer painting with flashlights to give objects definition. And the other option is to do a photo composite."

"So you take one shot exposed for the stars and another for the foreground?"

"And combine them in photo editing. Some people go overboard with that, though. There are photographers who will make the moon look giant, or use stars from one location combined with mountains from another. I don't believe in that. To me, it's morally wrong to use the same stars for multiple shots. A photo should record exactly what stars and constellations were in the sky on the night that you took the picture, even if you're taking multiple shots to create the image."

"There's your journalism background," Sarah said. "You think photo editing is unethical."

He smiled at her. "I do realize you built your career on photo editing."

"Believe me, if I could have gotten those babies to climb the ridge of a barn by themselves, I would have done it."

Ren chuckled. "Anyway, every workshop I teach, it's half about teaching folks to get proper exposure, showing them light painting, and half about how to do post-processing to make their photos look good. A lot of Milky Way stuff needs you to push the saturation so you can see the colors."

"So you mostly shoot digital?"

"I prefer to shoot on my Hassy, but a lot of the time on workshops, I shoot digital because—"

"Did you just call your Hasselblad camera your Hassy?"

Ren looked embarrassed. "That's not a—"

"Oh yes, it is. It's like calling a BMW your Beemer. 'Hold on. Gotta pull out my Hassy for this shot.' Still so pretentious."

"No, if I were being pretentious I would explain that my vintage Hasselblad 501cm was picked up at an estate sale and reportedly owned by Frank Sinatra."

"Are you serious? I hate you."

"He loved cameras, Ol' Blue Eyes."

"Why is your life so much cooler than mine?"

Ren frowned. "It's definitely not."

"So are you in Vegas for good, then?"

"It's tricky to say," he replied. "I mentioned Jandro is applying to high schools. So depending on whether he goes away for school next year...that changes things. A year from now, I wouldn't necessarily have to be there."

"But you escape pretty often."

"I get time off for good behavior."

She considered his life for a moment. He had been all over the world. She was excited that she'd been to Paris a couple of times. "And why Newfoundland? Aren't there places in the Rockies where you can shoot? Especially if your clients are from Silicon Valley?"

Ren smiled. "It's all about exclusivity with these guys. The tech guys who sign up for my workshops could create any photo they want in A.I., right? But that's not what they want to do. They want to be able to put a shot up on their wall and say, 'I took that photo up in Newfoundland,' in some park that their friends from Palo Alto have never been to. Or Easter Island. Or Finland. The reason we're doing Gros Morne is because none of the guys who sign up for my workshops have been there yet. So it's pretty, but it's also about taking the photos that nobody else has."

Sarah smiled. "I had no idea I grew up somewhere so exclusive."

"Newfoundland will really be on the map when some tech billionaire decides to buy up land to build his post-apocalyptic compound."

"If that happens, I'm blaming you personally."

Ren considered the road ahead. "Some of the folks in my workshops are great. But it's like any other service job. I have to keep the clients happy."

It was fascinating to see Ren—intellectual Ren, who loved to critique capitalism back in school—talking about the realities of keeping a small business running. Of course he had grown up in the last twenty years, but he had grown into someone who seemed mature and practical.

Though maybe he was not that mature about women. That part of his life remained a mystery to her.

Sarah's cell phone rang and she picked it up. She knew the number. She had left a message for her manager Owen that morning to say that she had to take the week off, expecting to hear from him Monday, but he apparently checked his messages over the weekend, because of course he did.

Owen wouldn't spend his weekends hiking with friends or catching up on old movies; he would wake up and instantly respond to work emails with phone calls, because he was the worst person on earth.

"Sarah," Owen began immediately, "you know you can't just take off any amount of time you want. You have limited vacation time."

"I know that. It's a family emergency." Sarah felt Ren's eyes on her as she spoke.

"This kind of thing is cause for termination, as you should be aware," Owen said.

"I understand. I certainly won't make a habit of it. If you need me to recommend a freelance photographer for the week..."

"The whole point of having an in-house marketing team is that we don't have to hire freelancers." She hated him with a fiery passion at that moment. It wasn't just his smug tone. It was the timing of it: a Sunday at noon, because dressing her down couldn't possibly wait until Monday morning. No, he needed to act fast to drag her away from whatever she was doing and back to her desk by Monday...not because he needed her, because Sarah knew that absolutely nothing critical or time sensitive would be occurring this week, but for the principle of the thing. Just to show that he could force her to obey.

"I know that," she said with forced politeness.

"If we hire freelancers, we don't need you."

"I know."

Owen sighed bitterly. "I'll speak to people, but I don't think this is getting approved."

"Thank you. I understand."

She wondered if she was about to be fired, and as she hung up the phone, she waited for panic to set in.

But it didn't.

Why wasn't she panicking?

She was going to *lose her job*.

She should be freaking out. And she felt...fine.

She stared out the window, letting the strange dissonance of her reaction sink in. She must *really* hate her job. She had never articulated it that way to herself, but if she had liked it even a little bit, she wouldn't be feeling this complete, Zen-like calm about possibly losing it.

Ren glanced over at her. "Trouble at work?"

"It's fine."

"I didn't mean to cause problems for you."

Sarah almost laughed. Ren always seemed to cause problems for her, one way or another. But she didn't feel angry at Ren right then, either.

THE NEXT FEW hours passed in a strange mix of feelings. Sometimes, Sarah felt the uncomplicated boredom of long car trips: none of the trees were very tall nor the houses very large. Her home province rolled past them in its epic loneliness, always beautiful, often poor, the roads practically empty except for occasional trucks passing them a little too aggressively.

Other times, Sarah felt a delirious sense of unreality at sitting next to Ren again, like he couldn't possibly be here, and they couldn't possibly be chatting about movies and the best places he had travelled and the weirdest clients she had dealt with during her *Existential Innocence* series. It felt strange that they could still make each other laugh. They could still talk for forty-five minutes about books they had loved and movies they had seen.

When they sat across from each other at a tiny restaurant for lunch, ordering milk shakes and eating fries, she felt like she was in a strange dream.

Occasionally, she remembered that she was still mad at him. He had hurt her and probably would again. He was too easy to fall for—that was the problem. It wasn't just his looks or intelligence. It was the way he seemed to know her so well, the way he remembered stories she had told him when she was twenty years old.

"That was when you were taking care of Anya's cat," he would say in the middle of her reminiscing about getting locked out of her Montreal apartment. Or: "This was the owner of the Kristman Gallery?" when she talked about an annoying comment at one of her shows. Or: "Ah yes, your Agnes Varda period," when she talked about an unfortunate haircut she got during her third year at McGill. It was irritating every time he did it.

She had sworn off romance for a reason. The whole point of putting your heart out of reach was that it couldn't get broken. It belonged to you again, not to the whims of people who came into and out of your life without warning. Maybe her mother had been right to stay single. Feelings were like a roller coaster ride: they were exciting and terrifying, but they always ended up with you at the bottom of the ride—never at the top, never at the high point. The high points were temporary. The low points were where you landed.

Finally, almost six hours into their trip, a thought came that settled her nerves. Whatever happened with Ren—whether he befriended her, or flirted with her, or remained entirely professional and hurt her that way—he was going back to Nevada at the end of this trip. There was no possibility of anything happening, so she wasn't at risk of getting her hopes up. There was nothing to get her hopes up *for*. She could be present for this trip, with its music and milkshakes and scenery and jokes. She could enjoy it and move on.

THEY ARRIVED at their hotel at sunset and climbed out of Ren's rental car slowly, shaking out stiff legs. Sarah felt like someone had folded her in an envelope and shipped her overseas.

"This place looks fancy," she said in surprise as she took in the three-story shingled hotel nestled into the top of a hill. Somehow, she hadn't expected they'd be staying anywhere especially nice. Most of the province kept things simple, but this was Newfoundland's version of a mountain chalet, curved around a driveway with wings outstretched towards stunning views of a distant bay.

Ren nodded. "Remember what I said about Silicon Valley tech guys? They can rough it, but they prefer not to. We'll do one night of sleeping under the stars at the end of the week, but otherwise there's room service."

When they walked up to the desk, a young woman in a hotel uniform greeted them with a grave expression. "Mr. Durand," she said. "I left a message on your phone. You requested an extra room?"

"Yes," he said, glancing down at his phone in puzzlement. "Sorry. My cell service is terrible here..."

"Unfortunately, we couldn't find one for you. I called around to the other hotels, but this is the busy season and the whole area is pretty booked up. The nearest I could find was a place forty-five minutes down the road. Something should open up by Wednesday."

Ren frowned and glanced at Sarah. "Oh."

"I do want to warn you," continued the young woman, "that our restaurant kitchen is closing soon, so if you haven't eaten, I would recommend doing that first and then we can help you to book a room at a different hotel if you would like one."

"I am so sorry," Ren began, looking at Sarah. "I can take the room down the road."

"Let's eat something," Sarah offered. "Then we can see about the room situation."

They were grown-ups, Sarah thought as they followed a hostess into the hotel's dining room. Everything would be fine, even if they shared a room. They were just friends, sitting down to dinner over candlelight while looking out at one of the most spectacular sunsets she had ever seen.

"So later tonight," Ren said, his eyes intense. Sarah looked down, embarrassed. He continued, "We should go out to do a little test shoot and talk more about camera settings." She relaxed again. What had she thought he was going to ask her? "There will be a classroom lesson for the attendees who are newer to night photography tomorrow, so you can pick up more then. But I'd like to take you out for an hour, and then I can drop you back at the hotel and I'll go scout a few locations."

"Don't you need to sleep at some point?"

He lifted one shoulder and gave his crooked half-smile. "I don't really sleep much during these workshops. I usually stay up until about five or six a.m. helping folks, then I wake up at ten or eleven in the morning. Some people like to keep shooting until dawn."

"That doesn't sound healthy."

"It's only for a week at time, so I can push through. I never needed that much sleep anyway." He looked at her, concerned. "But you don't need to stay up that late. We usually have a group of people who are happy to shoot for a few hours and go home around midnight and then a smaller group who want to push through all night. So we'll figure it out." She watched as he fidgeted with the watch on his wrist.

"It'll be fine, Ren. And the hotel room—let's just see what the situation is. It would be fine to share if we have to. We can get a cot or something."

He gave her a quick smile and then fixed his gaze out the window as the sky turned a heavenly pink. He didn't say anything until the check arrived.

They stopped by the hotel room after dinner to drop off their luggage. There were two beds, Sarah saw right away, which was helpful. All the same, stepping into a hotel room with him brought her back to the last time they'd stepped into a room like this. They had kissed in the doorway, a passionate kiss that she could still replay in her memory, even though part of her would rather erase it. Now he was standing next to her in a similar position and she had to carefully moderate her voice.

"I think we can share," Sarah said lightly, stepping into the room. "It'll be fine."

"Okay, good," he agreed, his eyes on the floor. "And you don't have to come for a lesson tonight if you're too tired."

"No. It'll be helpful. I'll be teaching this to people tomorrow night, right?"

"Right," he said quietly. "Right." He looked up. "Let's go. It's clear skies, at least."

THERE WAS something eerie about driving with Ren at night through the lonely hills of the Gros Morne area. The region itself was lovely: sharp hills rushing down to fjord-like bays, intervals of large empty rock, stretches of pristine fields and forests. They were driving up a hill at night, the road lit only by their headlights and the last sliver of a moon, a haunting song about lost love playing quietly. The world seemed painted in shades of grey and blue.

She looked at him in the half-light, his moody cheekbones and curly dark hair, and thought that he looked like an idealized memory rather than a person. Even being here with him, she could imagine looking back on this later on, wondering if it had actually happened or if she had dreamed it. Ren glanced at her with an intense, serious look before his eyes went back to the road.

When they finally climbed out of the car in a small parking area, Sarah found that they were next to a field of large rocks, scattered like the dropped pebbles of some ancient god. The waving grasses stretched out to either side of them, while hills in the distance were silhouetted against the last touch of twilight before true darkness. Ren grabbed his camera bag and tripod from the back seat as Sarah looked up at the sky. He handed Sarah an extra headlamp to put on her forehead as a flashlight. She put it on before grabbing her gear.

"How did you find this place?"

"Recommendations," Ren said. "I spend a lot of time on local message boards. Not too many professional photographers make it all the way out here, though. It's not like Yosemite, where you can't throw a rock without hitting another photographer. It's one reason I'm excited for this."

They started walking along a wooden plank path into the field together, their feet thudding softly in the stillness. There was the faint, hushed sound of the breeze stirring the grass around them, and the occasional buzz of an insect in her ear, but otherwise the quiet was nearly total. They could hear a distant truck on a road that must be two miles away, and then the truck was gone, and there was nothing but the murmur of the wind touching green things.

She looked up and thought of the theory the ancient Greeks

once had that the stars and moon were singing in a silent harmony. It felt true tonight. Then came the faraway call of an animal, and she froze for a moment. Ren looked back at her.

"Coyote, right?" he asked. "I forgot to check if there were wolves."

"No wolves in Newfoundland," she said. "Sometimes one or two turn up, but it shouldn't be a problem."

"Good. I could easily fight them off, of course, but it would be inconvenient while I'm carrying all this gear."

She smiled at his tone. "You should charge your clients extra if wolves attack. Then it becomes a wildlife photography workshop."

"I'll put that in my contract."

He stopped a hundred meters down the trail and paused, looking around with a considering gaze. "Turn off your headlamp," he said after a moment. "Once we're in place, we should start to let our eyes get adjusted to the dark."

She flipped it off and stood still, waiting for the objects around her to solidify as her eyes adjusted. Ren was busy setting up his tripod and framing a shot. With their flashlights off, the skies seemed so vast and empty that it felt like she was going to fall upwards into the stars and disappear.

"Okay," he said after a moment. "Come have a look at the test shot." Ren had framed a shot on his camera LCD screen that perfectly arranged the arc of the Milky Way over a portion of the path in front of them. It would be a gorgeous shot, the hiking path on the ground seeming to continue upwards into the path in the sky, but the foreground would probably need light added to it. He explained some of the settings he was using, then showed her the app on his phone that anticipated the rising and setting of the moon and stars. Then he stepped even closer to her and slid a flashlight into her palm, his hand warm in the cool night.

"Ready to do some light painting?"

Ren walked her to a place where she could stand just out of frame while he took the photo. Her job was to graze the landscape for a few seconds with the small flashlight to allow him to set an exposure that could capture the bright stars, the grass, and the scattered rocks at once.

"I've got a remote trigger." He held up the button to show her. "I'm going to go over there and paint the path with my flashlight while you hit the rocks and grasses."

Finally, Ren called out and opened his camera shutter with a remote button.

"We have twenty seconds!" he called.

This meant the camera shutter would be open for twenty seconds, an exposure short enough so they shouldn't get star trails. While it was open, Ren and Sarah gently sent their flashlight beams over the portions of the shot that they wanted lit. Ren could run through the shot without the camera 'seeing him' if he was moving fast enough. He did so, tracing the contours of the walkway itself with a soft light.

When the shutter closed, he called Sarah over to look at the results.

The shot was as stunning as she'd anticipated, although some of the grasses and a portion of the path were a little too bright. The grasses had been moving in the breeze, which gave them a hazy, undefined air, like the path was a walkway through some mystical fairyland.

"What if I focused more light on the rocks?" she suggested.

"I think just send the light across the grasses for less time," he offered.

So they tried the shot again. And again. And again.

On a professional level, she enjoyed the process of trying to get the optimal shot. It was a familiar experience: the tiny tweaks that led to different outcomes, the art of storytelling baked into the act of photography.

But on a personal level, she couldn't help but feel like they were two kids running around playing with flashlights in the dark. They were trying different things, experimenting, not quite sure what would work best. Ren tripped once during a shot, and the photo captured the light of his flashlight tumbling to the ground and a dim outline of his body as he sprawled face forward.

"That one's a keeper," she told him.

"I'll put it on my website."

She posed once for him as a silhouetted figure, silent and backlit along the path.

Then they moved the tripod to try a different angle, then walked a little further down the path to find a new shot. At a little after eleven p.m., she answered a question with a yawn.

"It's been a long day," Ren said. "Let's get you back to the hotel."

"I'll have to get used to the late schedule."

"You went to bed early even back in school."

"Unlike you, who insisted that your best ideas came at two in the morning."

"Anything to justify my procrastination." He unlocked her car door first, holding it open for her. "Consider it your professional responsibility to get out of bed late tomorrow. Most of the workshop participants won't arrive until well after lunch."

"If I must sleep in for the good of the workshop, then I will manage to do it somehow."

As they drove back, Ren put music back on and she looked out at the night sky, leaning her head against the glass. Everything seemed to be moving slowly, like she was on a ship crossing the ocean at night. Her heart felt full. It felt like they had never stopped being friends, which was a dangerously intoxicating feeling.

Ren dropped her off at the hotel but didn't come inside, telling her that he'd be back in a couple of hours but needed to check out some of his planned shooting locations. This also meant that she would be able to get ready for bed with total privacy, and she wondered if he'd done that on purpose.

A half hour later, she lay in the dark in one of the beds in the green silk pajamas with printed tigers on them that Anya had given her for Christmas. She loved them, but she had never anticipated anyone seeing them on this trip, and they were exactly the kind of quirky-girl-in-an-indie-film clothing that Ren liked to tease her about.

It felt strange to know that Ren would eventually be in the bed next to hers. He was here. She was with him on an adventure. She felt a little giddy. She and Ren had run around in the dark together, waving flashlights, running through fields. And she was doing photography again. And he was going to be here when she woke up. She had never slept in the same room with him before.

She stirred from sleep when he finally came in. There was a faint light in the sky through the windows, which meant that he had stayed out until almost dawn. For a long moment, she listened as he moved around the room using his headlamp for light, getting ready for bed.

"Ren," she whispered, "if you need to, you can turn on the lights."

"No need."

She heard him settle into bed a few minutes later. He shifted and sighed before his breath became slow and even.

He was right there. She had him, but she wouldn't get to keep him.

12
MONDAY

IN THE MORNING, she woke up to see that Ren was sleeping in the other bed. He looked tired, she thought, which made sense after he had stayed up checking out locations almost until dawn. He looked scruffy, unshaven, his hand pushed against his face. He was not an elven prince this morning; he looked reassuringly real. She let herself watch him for a long moment before she forced herself to get up.

There was a message on her phone from Owen: "I confirmed that you cannot take vacation without more notice. If you do not return to the office today, we will have to let you go."

Sarah leaned against the wall for a moment, considering what to do. She suspected that Owen hadn't had time to ask anyone about firing her. This felt like an executive decision coming from him. She was blowing up her life, and it didn't feel like that big of a problem. Why didn't it feel like a problem? She let out a delirious little laugh. Maybe she would regret this later, but she couldn't bring herself to regret it now.

She showered, got dressed, and then walked outside the hotel onto the wide wooden deck that stretched out from one side of the lobby to overlook the view.

Standing in the breeze with the spectacular vista of a bay and mountains, she dialed Owen's work number. He answered at once.

"Hello, Sarah."

"Hey, Owen. I'm so sorry that I won't be able to make it back. I can provide the names of other photographers—"

"Sarah," he said, "if we bend the rules for you, we have to do that for everyone. I hope you understand that this is not how professional businesses work."

A year ago, she would probably have groveled and agreed to come back. But she couldn't bring herself to do it, not after running around in the dark taking pictures with Ren all night.

"I'm really sorry," she replied. "I'll be back next week, but I can understand if you can't hold my position for me."

"I'm sorry, too."

She said a polite goodbye before she hung up the phone. *What a beautiful view*, she thought. *And also, I'm fired.*

She had a quick breakfast in the hotel restaurant and then returned to her hotel room, where Ren was emerging from the bathroom, his hair wet from a shower, wearing only pants.

"Sorry, I'll put on a shirt," he said, looking embarrassed.

"It's okay," she said. "I think I can handle your bare chest."

He gave a sharp smile, and she realized that wasn't what he'd meant. "Brutal, Sarah," he said. "You're brutal."

"No!" Now she had to scramble to get out of the hole she had stepped into. "I just meant that I'm immune. I'm immune to all men right now."

"Oh," he said, grinning. "So if I did this..." and he struck a mock bodybuilder pose, "you would feel nothing? This isn't sweeping you away?"

He was teasing, but he looked nice. And even worse, he was being charming and self-deprecating. "Okay, okay. Put your shirt on, Durand."

"Sarah Drakenberg checking me out. After all this time."

He grinned as he pulled a shirt on.

WHILE REN HEADED out to meet a workshop participant who had arrived early, Sarah checked her work email to see if she had received any kind of 'you're fired' missive yet, but so far even Owen didn't seem quite that organized, so she headed to the lobby.

Ren was standing next to a tall, handsome man who had the casual confidence and square-jawed good looks of someone selling expensive watches on the back of a men's magazine.

"...not nearly as good as yours," the man was saying. "If I go back to Namibia, I'm definitely doing it with you. Which is a good idea, speaking of. We should plan something in Africa."

This must be one of the workshop participants. She had heard Ren talk about his Silicon Valley clients and had pictured computer nerds in the Bill Gates mold, but this man looked like he owned a yacht but didn't make a big thing about it.

"Kyle," Ren said when he spotted her, "I'd like you to meet Sarah. She's going to be my assistant for this week."

The man threw Sarah an assessing look, his eyebrows raised. "Freya couldn't make it?"

Ren gave her a strange, nervous glance. "No, not this time."

Kyle smirked at the two of them, revealing a dimple above his artfully scruffy jaw. If Sarah had missed any of the implications of the exchange, Kyle's amusement and Ren's embarrassment would have told her enough. Ren had been bringing a female assistant on his photo workshops, most likely a girlfriend, and Sarah was presumed to be the replacement.

"Sarah's an old friend from undergrad and an excellent photographer," Ren added.

Kyle turned at last and shook Sarah's hand. "Of course she is. Nice to meet you. Kyle Allenby."

Sarah felt frozen under his gaze. The effect of these two handsome men next to each other was almost anaesthetizing; she felt like she'd been hit by a brick for a moment. "I um...I was thinking of borrowing the car, picking up a few last odds and ends at the store," she said to Ren after a moment.

"Sure," Ren said. "Actually, can you pick up some food for the workshop? Everyone is supposed to have lunch before they get here, but a few of them always forget or don't have time, so it's helpful to have a few snacks."

"Sure thing. I'll get some options."

Ren smiled and took the car keys and his wallet out. "Thanks. Any expenses," he added as he handed her his credit card. "I appreciate it."

He was looking at her warmly, but Sarah found herself eager to get away from Ren's careful friendliness and Kyle's amused gaze. As she drove Ren's rental car down the mountain, she found herself taking the curves just a little too fast and had to take a deep breath and deliberately slow down.

Of course his ex was named Freya. Ren would never date someone named Kathy or Jen. And she had apparently broken up with him recently.

'Nothing serious in that department,' Ren had said. Not quite true, was it?

How soon afterwards had Ren decided that he needed a female replacement? How soon afterwards had he thought of Sarah, recently divorced and probably desperate to get back into photography? How could he not have told her any of this?

It was all so *Ren*, she thought. No matter how well they were getting along, no matter how much he said he cared for her, Sarah still felt an echo of that hurt from school: that she was the last one picked after he had dated the prettier women first.

Now she was the replacement because his girlfriend had left him or couldn't come and he didn't want to be alone. She should have seen it coming.

She had composed herself by the time she returned. Ren entered their hotel room just as she was sliding some drinks into the mini refrigerator.

"Hey," he said. "Thanks for picking up some snacks. Kyle wants to do a quick location scout with me somewhere further down the coast, in case it rains this week, so I was going to head out with him for an hour or so, take some test shots. Nobody should need anything from me before we meet up in the conference room at three, but if they do, have them call my cell phone."

"Sure thing," Sarah said. "But your cell service isn't reliable, right? You can give people my number, too."

"The service is worse than I hoped," he agreed. He paused, giving her a searching look. "I'm sorry about the shared room. I could probably stay with Kyle if you want. He and I have known each other for a few years, so he wouldn't mind."

"It's fine, Ren," she said, keeping her eyes on her task. "This is fine."

He watched her for a moment like there was more to say, then nodded and left.

Sarah arrived a few minutes before three in the small hotel meeting room that Ren had reserved for their daily workshop classes, ready to do whatever he might need. He clearly had things well in hand, though: a polished presentation was being projected on a screen and there was a demonstration camera set up on a tripod.

He glanced up from his laptop as she entered. "Hey. The way I usually do this is I spend the beginning of the first day giving an overview of the whole schedule, and then I let people who already know how to do night photography take off until dinner, and the new folks stay for the classroom portion, since our first lesson is all basics."

"Perfect," she replied. "I'll learn along with them while nodding like I'm an expert."

Ren smiled, then gave her an oddly strained look, like he was working up to something. "Oh, so by the way," he said with an artificial casualness, "this woman named Freya used to be my assistant, and she came along on a couple of my last workshops."

"Okay," Sarah said in what she hoped was a natural tone of voice. She waited for him to go on.

"So the thing is—"

"Hey everyone! Are we interrupting?" A woman with a round, cheerful face poked her head in the door.

"Not at all, come on in," Ren replied.

The woman was followed by several others, and Ren directed them to help themselves to snacks and drinks and to find seats around the table. As the ten workshop attendees entered and sat down, introducing themselves in turn, Sarah began to mentally categorize them into different groups. Five of them were single men, including Kyle, and several of the men seemed familiar with Ren from previous workshops. Two of them looked older, probably retired—those were Fred and Grisha—and the other three single men, Kyle, Jack, and Cole, were her age or a little younger.

The rest of the group included a middle-aged husband-and-wife pair who were experienced photographers but brand new to night photography, a pair of women in their fifties who had done almost no photography at all (including the cheerful first arrival), and a gorgeous blond woman who immediately walked up to Ren as if they were old friends.

"Sorry I couldn't make Iceland," she said in a light German accent.

"Nice to see you, Elka," Ren said. "I'm glad you could make this one."

"So no Freya?" Elka scanned the room, her eyes landing briefly on Sarah.

"No, not this time," Ren agreed with a frown.

The woman seemed happy with the news as she placed herself near him at the table.

Had Ren slept with this woman? Sarah decided that there had certainly been flirtation, at least on Elka's side. And now Ren appeared to be single again. Perhaps this woman would make her move.

As Ren began his opening talk, Sarah watched him and considered for the first time that Ren's good looks could pose a challenge in workshops like this. If people were interested in him romantically, they could sign up to spend five nights with him under the stars, flirting with him constantly, handing him hotel room keys that were only a few doors away. She noticed that Ren carefully wasn't looking at Elka, but that could mean anything.

Putting aside her reserve of adolescent jealousy, Sarah realized that perhaps having a female assistant could be a strategy for keeping interested clients at arm's length. Maybe it would even be useful for Ren if the participants thought Ren and Sarah were dating, especially if this blond woman was persistent and Ren wasn't interested. After a moment's reflection, she realized she wouldn't mind pretending they were dating, if that would help him. Sarah had been harassed occasionally at work and knew how unpleasant it could be.

"Everyone," Ren began once everyone had introduced themselves, "this is Sarah Drakenberg. She is a brilliant photographer who is going to be assisting me on this week's shoot. She's based in Toronto, but I talked her into helping out with this one."

Sarah smiled. "Happy to be here."

Elka shot Sarah an intense look that confirmed Sarah's suspicions.

Ren began giving the practical logistics of the workshop first: where they would go, what would happen if it got too rainy on Tuesday or Wednesday, when they would probably have their overnight shoot, options for fun activities and shooting locations during the day for those who were interested (and for those who could manage to stay awake.) Ren explained the daily plan: they would meet each day an hour or two after lunch to review photos from the night before and to have a lecture on shooting and processing techniques. The shooting portion of the workshop would begin around sunset and run until midnight (for those who wanted to go to bed 'early') and until sunrise for anyone interested in shooting all night. Kyle gave a knowing smile to Ren.

"Signing up for the dawn crew," Kyle said confidently.

"I expected no less," Ren replied with a smile.

The presentation paused as Ren let everyone leave who already knew the basics of shooting at night. As Sarah had anticipated, most of the men left, including Kyle. That left behind one of the Silicon Valley-type men, Jack, the married couple, the pair of women who might also be a couple, and Elka, who walked up to Ren and smiled.

"I think I know the basics," she said in a low murmur. "But let me know if you want me to stick around."

"You're already an expert," Ren said with a polite smile. "You'll find this boring."

"I doubt that, but I'll see you at dinner," Elka replied. She put a hand on his arm and squeezed it before heading out. Sarah carefully felt nothing about the exchange.

She found that she enjoyed Ren's introductory night photography lesson. It was a useful review for her after their discussion the previous day, but it was also an opportunity to observe Ren in his new incarnation as a teacher. She had known him best when he was young and restless, with a tendency to bounce off the walls and switch topics. To see him being so organized and articulate was new. She also got a general sense of which people were likely to need the most help once they went out shooting. The married couple, Binita and Tanjul Dangol, had a number of targeted questions but seemed to understand photography in general, while the two middle-aged women, Rita and Selassie, needed introductory concepts like focal length and f-stop explained to them. Jack, a corporate executive near Sarah's age, was by turns confused and irritated, like he was annoyed that this wasn't instantly easy for him. He had a very expensive camera but seemed unsure of how to navigate its menus, which meant he would need a lot of personal attention, Sarah suspected. She also suspected that, like many prickly and easily frustrated men, he would prefer the help from Ren and not from her.

She could see how one teacher would not have been enough —not if these people were paying thousands of dollars to learn how to take great photographs of the stars.

"And one huge request," Ren concluded, "I beg of you. No using your camera flash. It never, ever looks good."

"Rarely," Sarah said, and he jokingly glared at her. "It's a tool like any other tool," she added.

"Don't listen to Sarah," he said with a smile. "She's a bad influence."

At the end of the lecture, Sarah helped Ren pack up the gear before they walked into their hotel room together.

As soon as they were alone with the door shut, she turned to him.

"Hey," she said quietly. "Your previous assistant was someone you dated?"

He grimaced. "Yes. I'm sorry I didn't tell you. I wasn't sure it was relevant." They were right in the doorway again, near to each other. Would she have to flash back to that kiss every time they stood like this? Apparently so.

"Well," Sarah began, "if you need me to pretend to date you to make your life easier, just let me know."

He stared at her. "What?"

"I'm not trying to come up with some crazy fake dating scheme," she said in a rush. "I just thought that if someone was hitting on you, and you didn't want them to...you and I are already staying in the same hotel room. It wouldn't be a huge stretch to say we were together."

"A huge stretch?" he repeated, as if unsure of her meaning.

"I just know how hard it can be when a client is interested. If it would help you to pretend we were dating..."

"Oh. Right." He blinked. "You mean Elka?"

"I just thought... You know what, never mind. Maybe you want to hook up with her and I'm misreading the whole situation."

"No." He grimaced. "No. I um...no. I appreciate it, but I don't need you to do that. Elka is...I can handle her. If something comes up, I'll figure it out."

"You got it. No pretending that we're madly in love."

Ren gave her a strange, artificial smile, and Sarah felt oddly hurt by his flat response. It shouldn't feel like a rejection, but it did.

"Anyway..." she began. "We should get to dinner."

"Actually, that reminds me. At dinner, I usually sit at a different table than my assistant so we can answer more questions. It's for practical reasons, as well. A table of twelve always takes forever to get service and finish a meal, and we need to get outside for shooting, so I always make reservations for two tables of six."

"Right." He was telling her that she was not supposed to sit with him, which was fine, of course. "Whatever you need."

"Okay." He looked at her for a long moment and then turned to put away his laptop.

When they entered the dining room, Elka waved to Ren. "Ren! I've saved you a spot." She was already at a table with four people: Jack, the Dangols, and Kyle. Ren gave Sarah a questioning look.

"Go ahead," Sarah said. "I'll see you later."

Ren nodded, then walked to the seat next to Elka. The blond woman shot Sarah a triumphant glance, and Sarah tried to mentally shake off the weirdness of the whole dynamic. She took a seat at the other table next to Rita and Selassie, who were bubbling over with excitement about the shoot. Both women were pretty, brown-skinned, and in their early fifties, but with very different builds: Rita was short, curvy, and freckled, and her black curly hair sparkled with bright red highlights. Selassie was tall and fit, with wide brown eyes and her dark hair tucked into a practical bun. Despite their mismatched heights, they had perfectly matched energies—sociable, voluble, and quick to laugh—and Sarah found herself charmed by them even though she suspected she would spend most of the week helping them figure out their cameras.

The rest of the table consisted of a man in his early fifties named Fred who wore a nice dinner jacket and turned out to be a politician from Ottawa, a blond American in his thirties named Cole who explained that he had sold a tech company the year before and was currently starting a new one, and a retired man named Grisha with close-cropped silver hair who sounded

Russian but explained that he had made his money in crypto and currently lived in Greece.

After they had placed their orders, Fred gave her a thoughtful look.

"So you wouldn't happen to be the Sarah Drakenberg from the 'Babies' series, would you?"

She was frozen in a brief moment of panic. "Yes, that was me."

"We have one of your photos with our daughter Haley," the man added. "Fred Corbeau. I never met you, but you may remember my wife Ella."

She only distantly remembered the name. "Of course. How is Haley doing these days?"

"She's great. She's eight now. She's our youngest and the older ones are jealous of that photo and wish we'd done all three of them. So are you still shooting babies these days?"

Sarah forced a smile. "No, I've been busy with a divorce series," she joked.

"Ah," he said, catching her tone. "And what does that consist of?"

"Lots of burned out trucks in the middle of fields."

He laughed as Grisha raised his eyebrows. "Baby photos? What is this?"

"It was something I did for a few years in Toronto," Sarah explained. She had taken down her website, but she pulled out her phone and Googled her own photo series and handed the phone to Grisha, not looking closely at the images.

"It paid the bills, but it has definitely run its course," she added. For the first time, she had managed to say those words without instantly connecting them to her own life, her own disasters. Grisha gave a quick nod of amusement, then handed the phone to Cole.

Meanwhile, Fred pulled out his phone to find his daughter's photo: Sarah remembered it as soon as she saw it. The baby had been made to look like she was clinging to a log floating down a river as part of a log drive in the Canadian wilderness. Sarah had arranged a real log drive at a historical re-enactment site for the purpose, sending thirty logs down a river to procure that part of the photo, then had taken the closer image of baby Haley leaning over a slightly damp log in her studio. The end result of her photo editing was worth it: the baby looked at once terrified and like a total daredevil, riding a log down the Canadian river rapids.

It was a gimmicky shot, Sarah could acknowledge, but a well-composed and funny one.

"Hilarious!" Rita said when Fred passed around the image. "So Rene saw these and asked you to help him?"

"Oh, no. We've been friends since university," Sarah said.

"The last woman he had as an assistant," Grisha said, "she was beautiful. Like a model. Stunning."

Of course she was, Sarah thought.

"So you and Rene, you two are together, right?" Selassie asked.

Sarah shook her head. "No. We're just very old friends."

"He is so gorgeous," Rita said. "He looks like he should be a movie star."

"He's very talented, too," Sarah offered.

"Well, so are you," Selassie cried. "Now I want a photo of me on a log floating down a river."

"Maybe in my twenties," Rita said. "Now I'd look like one of the logs." The joke bothered Sarah a little, the casual dismissal Rita had made of her own body. It was too close to what Sarah had often felt about herself.

"You know what?" Sarah said. "If you two wear swimsuits under your clothes tonight, then after we get some Milky Way shots, I'll take a portrait of you two. We'll do some kind of mermaid-themed shot on the beach at night."

Selassie applauded. "Oh, we're doing it," she agreed. "That is definitely a plan."

The conversation paused when the food arrived, and Sarah thought again about her casual joke about doing a 'Divorce' series. Even though she had been kidding, as soon as she had spoken the words, she had gotten a vivid image in her head: a cherry-red pickup truck from the 1950s, alone in the middle of a wheat field in fall, ablaze with flames that shot up ten feet tall as it burned alone, no water nearby, no source for the fire, ready to burn down the whole world.

She could shoot it in autumn, she thought. She would just need the truck. Or...she could do that if she were still doing photography. Which she wasn't.

Then another idea followed the first one in her head, like a dam inside her had broken.

What if she created a *My Divorced Life* series that followed up on her *Single Life* series? What if she restaged the same photos, over a decade later...with her in similar poses, only the details would be different: different books on the bed, different pajamas, her face looking weary instead of hopeful, pessimistic instead of gleeful, her make-up smeared instead of perfectly applied, but still somehow...funny?

As soon as she had that thought, she could visualize the show at the Kristman Gallery: the old and new images lined up side by side, her then and her now. Single and divorced. It would sell, she suspected. Or at least it would gain attention, create conversations, be the kind of thing that might get covered by the press.

It could launch her career again.

Why hadn't she thought of it before? It was a clever idea but also an obvious one. So why hadn't she thought to do it?

She hadn't thought of it because she'd spent the last few years feeling hollowed out. By infertility. By Danny's infidelity. By giving up on her baby series and then her career. By the finality of divorce.

There had been no Sarah left to come up with ideas.

She glanced at Ren, who was leaning over to joke with Kyle under Elka's admiring gaze. He didn't belong to her; she knew that. But he had sensed that she needed rescuing. It was frustrating—annoying—that it was working, but it was. Being around him was slowly making her feel like herself again. She wondered if this whole week was an elaborate plot to help her make her way back to photography.

Or maybe it was just convenient for him to have an assistant who was already in Newfoundland.

Either way, she knew—as soon as she thought about the 'My Divorce' series—that she was going to do it. It came to her as clearly as her best ideas always had: all at once, and with a sense of certainty. Her heart thrummed with a desire to get back to work.

When they stopped by their room after dinner to pick up their gear, Ren paused in the doorway. "Hey, we're doing some carpooling tonight because there's not a lot of parking at the beach location. Elka asked me to give her a ride and Kyle offered to take you. I thought Selassie and Rita could follow you and Kyle in their car. They don't seem very confident navigating the area, based on their questions earlier, so I think they should follow someone else."

"And you'd be alone with Elka?" She couldn't help but watch his expression carefully.

"Kyle thinks it will be good for me to deal with Elka one way or the other."

Sarah raised her eyebrows.

Ren caught her eye and huffed out a laugh. "It's fine. Kyle likes to put me in tricky situations to see how I'll react. He's a friend but he likes giving me a hard time. Are you okay driving over with him?"

"Of course," Sarah said. "We can ask other people to come in our car, too."

In the end, though, Sarah ended up driving to the location alone with Kyle in his giant SUV, while the married couple Binita and Tanjul drove behind them with Fred, and Rita and Selassie followed in their rental. The remaining men—Grisha, Cole, and Jack—had agreed to share a vehicle, proudly announcing that they were part of the 'dawn crew' who planned to shoot all night long.

"That's part of the challenge for me with these workshops," Kyle explained as he headed onto the curving two-lane road. "I shoot all night. And sometimes all day, too. It's about mental focus. A couple of years ago I went cold turkey with alcohol, so I learned to set a goal and make it happen."

"Sure," Sarah said politely.

What was it with men like Kyle and the compulsive need to announce their accomplishments? She had known clients like him in her photographer days: handsome, wealthy men who had everything going for them, but still felt the need to tell everyone that they had gone vegan, were training for a marathon, had just gotten their pilot's license. It was like life was a game and they wanted to make sure everyone knew that they were constantly leveling up.

"So you've known Ren for a long time?" Kyle asked, his eyes going between her face and the road.

She nodded. "We met when we were eighteen."

"Eighteen?" Kyle looked shocked; she wondered if Kyle had assumed that the 'very old friends' descriptor Ren had given her was a euphemism for something else. "So has he changed much since then?"

Sarah considered the question. "Yes and no. The same as all of us, I guess. He was always clever and artistic. And kind. But he's grown up, of course."

"So he was immature?" It was an odd question, like Kyle was trying to find ways to score points.

"No more than any of us in undergrad," Sarah said carefully.

"Well," Kyle began pointedly, and his eyes went right to Sarah again, as if gauging her reaction, "Elka was very insistent on getting time alone with him."

"Sure. As long as Ren doesn't mind."

"Right. Exactly. Elka just needs to be told no. If he wants to say no. Ren can be a little..." Kyle gave a wolfish smile. "He's not always clear on what he wants when it comes to women."

This hit Sarah hard, and she wondered if it was directed specifically at her. But if Kyle was playing some kind of a game, testing her feelings, she wasn't interested in participating. "Well, it can be tough when it's a client. I used to do family photography and a couple of husbands flirted with me, and there was definitely a dance involved in getting them to stop."

Kyle glanced at her. "So you said you're a photographer, but I couldn't find your website."

She flushed a little at the idea that he had tried to find her online. Was it an ego thing? Was he trying to assess whether she was worthy of being there? "I took it down when I was dealing with my divorce. I'm going to put it back up again."

He nodded. "Fair enough. I got divorced a couple of years ago. No kids, fortunately."

"None for me either."

"It's so much easier without kids involved, isn't it?" Kyle

gave her a half-smile as he steered the SUV around another curve in the road.

It was an insensitive question, which she knew Kyle would never realize. But on the other hand, maybe he had a point. She had never thought of it that way: that having no kids with Danny had simplified the divorce. It had always seemed to be the reverse. If she'd been able to get pregnant, would there have been so much tension between them? Danny might have cheated regardless, but she doubted it. They would have been too busy with diapers and children's theater and carpools. He wouldn't have spent so much time thinking about what he couldn't have.

"So if you're not dating Ren," Kyle went on, "maybe you'd be willing to have dinner with me some night this week?"

Sarah's eyes flew to Kyle. She had not sensed him building up to that. "Oh. Maybe at some point," she replied lightly.

"Maybe?" He smiled. "Maybe is my least favorite word."

Sarah had no patience for overconfidence; she never had. She kept a light tone as she replied, "Well, that makes this harder for you, then, not for me."

He laughed out loud. "No wonder Ren likes you. You're very direct."

"Brutally honest, Ren called me."

"I could see that." Kyle's smile had more warmth, now, and a little less calculation. "I can respect it."

She considered Kyle for a moment. Ren had mentioned that Kyle had flown in on his own plane, which was why he'd arrived so much earlier than the others. He was a millionaire who looked like a movie star, and she probably ought to at least consider the offer.

But he couldn't actually be serious about her. Selassie and Rita were too old for him, Binita was married, and Elka had set her sights on a different target. Sarah was probably the only choice aside from the hotel staff if he wanted female companionship. It wasn't flattering, even if she had been remotely interested.

"Just be sure to tell me," Kyle said, "if you're secretly in love with Ren or something."

Sarah smiled. "No."

"Good," Kyle said. "Because I think Elka is going to get him into bed. I've been on about ten of his workshops, and I don't think I've ever seen him successfully fend off a very beautiful woman except when he was with Freya. And she started as a workshop attendee."

Sarah's heart sank a little...not that it should, because she didn't care one way or the other. "Honestly," she said, "it's none of my business."

The location for the night's shoot was different from the place she had scouted with Ren the night before—they would not be returning to that rocky field quite yet. Tonight, they were at a trailhead that led to some cliffs looking out over the ocean, with a narrow trail down to the beach. It was a pretty spot, glowing like a creamsicle in the last light of sunset.

Ren approached their car from where he had just arrived with Elka, and Sarah tried and failed to interpret the atmosphere between them.

"Can you look after Rita and Selassie tonight?" Ren said. "Binita and Tanjul have a lot of specific questions, and Jack asked if I could talk him through things again. But Selassie and Rita seem like they'll need help with just using their cameras if you're up for it. They asked me if they needed a tripod tonight," he added, rolling his eyes.

Night photography was pretty much impossible without a tripod because the camera shutter stayed open for so long that handheld work always looked blurry. That was rule number one, which meant that the women would need a lot of guidance.

"Of course," Sarah replied.

Fortunately, Rita and Selassie seemed very content to be handed off to Sarah for the evening. They all put on headlamps and followed Ren and the rest of the group along the rocky trail about a kilometer down to a portion of the beach that Ren had selected as the location for the shoot. The sun was just disappearing into the sea.

"So Ren," Kyle said in his take-charge voice, "you and I talked about going south, right?"

"Yes, we did," Ren agreed. He addressed the group. "We can divide up the group, half north, half south. Everyone should stay on the beach, but you can spread out. High tide is in four hours so we may need to move to higher ground then. Make sure you tell me or Sarah and whoever drove you here if you decide to turn in early or leave in a different car. No photographer left behind, eh?"

The group scattered over about a kilometer of beach, but all roughly within sight of each other, pointing their cameras at the cliffs and the stars and the sea. Sarah helped the two women put together their gear in the fading light of magic hour.

The evening continued pleasantly enough as Sarah reviewed the basics with the women. Selassie and Rita weren't a couple, Sarah discovered; they were two best friends who had started taking a yearly trip together three years ago, when Rita's children were moving out of the house to go to college. Now they made a habit of doing something cool together each summer.

"This was Selassie's year to pick," Rita said. "My year was scuba diving."

"The first year, we worked on a ranch," Selassie called. "And my ass was sore for weeks."

The nice thing about the women was that they weren't too picky about the content of their shots. In fact, they seemed to be thrilled with all the photos they took: first some photos of the Milky Way and the sliver of moon (which would be a new moon the following night), then photos of the ocean in long exposure. If you left your shutter open long enough, the water started to look like it was pouring over the rocks like a veil, a technique that Sarah could teach them easily. They took photos of a cliff-face while Sarah helped them graze it with the gentle touch of a flashlight. They took photos of the moon reflected in a tiny tide pool. The women needed everything explained to them three times, but they were having a great time laughing and complimenting each other's work.

"Did you think about my mermaid idea?" Sarah asked at last.

"We brought swimsuits!" Selassie said. "But we didn't put them on. Come on, Rita. Let's get changed."

"It's cold!" Rita said with a sigh. Sarah found them an area protected by rocks to change into their swimsuits. When they emerged, though, only Selassie had changed.

"She's going to do it first," Rita explained. Sarah inwardly sighed but then walked Selassie over to a large boulder about four feet tall that was close to them on the beach. Sarah helped Selassie find a comfortable position on the boulder while she sent Rita to collect some seashells and seaweed to decorate the area around her. In the background, the Milky Way arched up as the moon began to set behind the cliffs. Selassie laughed as she shivered in her swimsuit in the darkness but then draped herself dramatically backwards. Sarah encouraged her to shake her dark hair loose so that it covered part of her face, and Selassie spent a moment combing it out with her fingers. Then Sarah set up Rita to give some fill light from one side with a soft, battery-powered handheld light, while Sarah pulled out her flash, set up the tripod, and took a shot with a quick flash of light.

Just as she was leaning over to check out the result, she heard Ren's horrified voice from fifty meters away.

"Did someone just use a *flash* in my workshop?"

"It was me!" Sarah called. "It's going to look amazing! Wait and see!"

"You're killing me, Drakenberg!" he called back.

Sarah and Rita rushed over to check out the shot. It looked rather fabulous, Sarah could acknowledge: Selassie was arching over a rock with seaweed draped around her like some legendary sea siren, the sparkling trail of the Milky Way curving above her to the heavens. It just needed a few adjustments.

So Rita and Sarah took the shot again. And again. And again.

By one a.m., the women both announced that they were exhausted.

"Long day flying in from Toronto," Rita said. They lived in the city only thirty minutes from Sarah, it turned out.

"I just hope we can find our way back to the hotel," Selassie said. "She almost made three wrong turns coming here and we were following someone."

"I can lead you back to the hotel in Ren's car," Sarah said.

"No, we got it!" Rita insisted. "We have GPS."

"The GPS kept getting confused because of all the water," Selassie said.

"I'm coming with you," Sarah said firmly.

When Sarah walked up to Ren, she noticed that Elka was only a few steps away from him, setting up a shot that would give her an opportunity to seek his advice.

"Hey, I'm going to borrow your car to guide Rita and Selassie back to the hotel and then come back," Sarah said.

"No need, you should go with them, stay at the hotel and turn in," Ren said. Sarah couldn't help but notice that Elka looked pleased at this. "Most of the other folks are pretty self-sufficient and it's a long drive back. I don't want you to have to come back just to drop off the car."

"We can give her a ride! We don't mind!" Rita called out.

"Take the ride," Ren said. "You've had a long day. I've got this covered."

"But what about your rule about someone getting injured?" Sarah asked.

"You're there if I need you," Ren said.

Sarah nodded, warmed a little by his words. She was exhausted. And if Ren was going to end up in Elka's bed, there was no help for it. Sarah stopped by where Kyle was taking pictures and told him she was leaving in a different car.

"No problem," Kyle said. "I told you I'm a dusk to dawn guy. It's my triathlon training. I don't expect everyone to keep up."

The ride back was a long, winding stretch of blue darkness with Sarah navigating in the passenger seat to make sure that they found their way to the hotel. Rita was driving, while Selassie had set up her phone to send music to the car stereo, playing a gorgeous set of old soul singers like Ann Peebles and Sam Cooke, mixed with some nineties R&B. By the time they were at the hotel, Sarah felt bone-tired and a little maudlin.

"Tomorrow, you're hanging out with us!" Selassie called. "And we're going to talk Rita into doing a swimsuit shot of her."

"It's a plan!" Sarah replied enthusiastically.

It felt strangely lonely to step into her hotel room and look at Ren's empty bed, knowing that he might not return at all. That was always the problem with Ren; he was too easy to miss.

13
TUESDAY

WHEN SHE WOKE in the morning, though, Ren was asleep in the bed next to hers. The sight made her happy, which she knew was a warning sign. Nothing could happen with him, she reminded herself. After this week, she might not see him again for years. She got up, showered, and then went to the breakfast buffet in the hotel restaurant. After eating a quick meal with Binita, who had also turned in somewhat early the night before, Sarah selected some fruit and a croissant for Ren and returned to their room, leaving the food by his bed for whenever he woke up.

She sat on her bed and opened the laptop she'd brought with her, then began collecting reference images for the *My Divorce* photo series she was thinking of. She also put her website back online, because Kyle's smug insistence that she wasn't a real photographer rankled.

Ren finally stirred at a little after eleven in the morning. He sat up and looked at the food next to him, then gave her a sleepy, affectionate smile that she couldn't look at for more than a moment.

"How did it go with the dawn crew?" she asked.

"We got some good stuff. Is this for me?"

"Of course. The coffee and tea should still be available in the lobby but they were taking the rest of the food away."

"Thank you." He slid up and looked at her. "How was your evening?"

"It was fun," she said. "It was good I went back with them. Their sense of direction would have put them somewhere in the Atlantic."

"Thanks for helping with those two," he said. "I got a lot of questions from some of the more experienced folks, so you being able to help the novices was tremendous."

"We got some good stuff, I think."

"With a flash?" he asked, grinning now. "I have one rule, Sarah. One rule."

"Wait and see. You'll love it."

Ren sat the rest of the way up in bed and watched her for a moment. "Kyle told me he invited you to have dinner with him. Is that okay?"

She waved a hand. "I think I gave him a vague enough answer that I should be able to dodge that," she said, her eyes back on her laptop.

"Do you want to dodge it?" He was watching her closely, like he was trying to read her thoughts.

"He's not my type."

"Millionaires with private planes aren't your type." Ren's mouth crooked up at one corner.

Sarah dropped her voice in an imitation of Kyle: "'I push through until dawn. It's my triathlon training.' He's probably one of those guys who asks you how many books you've read this year just so he can point out that he's read more."

"It's just interesting," Ren said.

"What's interesting?"

"You told me that you weren't dating right now, and you

didn't say that about him. You didn't say, 'I'm not dating right now.'"

Right. Sarah had forgotten about her 'no dating' policy. "Well, the difference is that I couldn't have anything real with him, so it didn't matter."

He looked at her curiously, and something inside her twinged with nerves; there was something in Ren's expression that she couldn't put a name to. She looked away when her phone buzzed.

"It's Rita," Sarah said. "They wanted me to go on a boat tour with them today."

Ren was still watching her. "Sarah—"

"I'll go meet them in the lobby."

She fled the room.

WHEN SHE ARRIVED in the lobby, she was pleased to find that Selassie and Rita had talked Binita into coming on their boat tour as well.

"I don't need as much sleep as my husband does. It is from being a surgeon. I learned to cope with no sleep, but Tanjul is a lawyer so he is soft," Binita explained with the deadpan humor that Sarah was realizing was her trademark.

They drove down the hill to one of the docks on the bay, getting in line for a small cruise boat that held about thirty tourists. Soon they were aboard, cruising around past small houses, out into the Atlantic, and then back again.

The day was lovely and cool, a perfect, breezy summer afternoon, aside from...

"Clouds," Binita observed.

There were fingers of clouds reaching across the sky—nothing serious in terms of spoiling the weather—but clouds would be a problem when photographers were trying to get pristine shots of the Milky Way.

"Can't Ren do something about those?" Rita joked. "I'm going to be demanding my money back."

"I'll see what we can arrange," Sarah promised. "We'll make some phone calls."

She stood alone on the deck for a while, thinking about how she was fired and how she ought to be more worried, and then let the thought drift away with the wind. She hadn't gone on a trip like this in a very long time.

THE WHOLE GROUP met after lunch to review everyone's photos from the night before. Kyle's shots—on his ten-thousand dollar camera—were compelling but without a lot of heart, Sarah thought, like he wanted to get in as much of the space and the sky as possible, using wide lenses to exaggerate the vastness. Jack seemed frustrated with his output, though none of it looked especially bad: he had gotten one shot of the Milky Way arcing down towards a rocky outcropping that was quite beautiful. Seemingly boring Silicon-Valley Cole had a surprisingly clever eye for lovely foreground elements like plants and flowers against his backdrops of stars and sky. His were among her favorites. That was one of the magical things about visual art, Sarah had always thought. You couldn't always match people's work to their external personality. Sometimes people showed hidden depths.

Then they reached Sarah's shot of Selassie, posed like a sea siren on the boulder, and the room burst out in a mixture of amusement and delight.

"That is fantastic," Ren said decisively.

On the big conference room screen, the photo was even better. Selassie was arching backwards on the rock, one leg kicked up, and from her toes the whole Milky Way seemed to rise like a magical mist. Around her on the rocks were a tangle of seaweed and scattered seashells. She was lit from the side with Sarah's pop flash, emphasizing her long torso, but Rita had also given her side light from the flashlight to give her more depth. She looked like a queen of the stars, Sarah thought.

"That goes above your fireplace!" Binita said.

"I want one of those for me," Tanjul announced. "But I will have both arms up like the Milky Way is shooting from my hands."

"I want one, too," Cole said, grinning.

Ren gave Sarah a look filled with pretend horror. "What have you done to my workshop? This is a night sky workshop! We don't shoot *people*!"

Sarah laughed. "How about this? I will do one portrait of everyone by the end of the week. I want to get one of Rita rising naked from the sea."

Rita laughed, but Grisha practically snorted, which irritated Sarah; he seemed like one of those men who didn't believe women should bother trying to be sexy once they had passed the geriatric age of thirty.

Ren gave a weary sigh. "Fine," he said. "Breaking my heart with flash photography. This is the problem with bringing someone along to help who has actual artistic opinions."

The most fun part of the afternoon was that Ren kept asking for her feedback about the various shots everyone had taken. He often deferred to her on questions of composition, even though his own eye was excellent. She got to talk about photography and debate with him for over an hour. She had forgotten how much she missed it.

"Given the weather coming in, let's meet a little earlier than sunset tonight," Ren suggested as they finished the discussion. "We'll put off some of the classroom stuff until Wednesday when it will probably be rainy. Tonight, I think everyone should eat dinner at five, and we'll go out to a fjord and get some sunset shots looking west. It's going to turn cloudy by nine and rainy by midnight, so we might as well take advantage of it and use the clouds to get some nice color."

WHEN THE GROUP broke apart for dinner, Elka waved her over.

"Can I talk to you?" Elka's voice was low and serious.

"Yes, of course." Sarah couldn't fathom a possible topic of conversation between them, but she nodded politely.

"Outside, maybe? I'd like it to be private."

Sarah followed Elka out onto the hotel's large deck with its view of the distant, sparkling bay. The trees dropped away a few feet below them, so they could see an expanse of tumbling hills and pristine forests.

"Sorry to bother you," Elka began. "I had a question about Rene."

Of course she did. "Yes?"

"Are you and Rene..."

Sarah shook her head. "No. We're just friends."

"Good, yes. Because the truth is," Elka said, "that I think I have fallen in love with him."

Sarah grimaced. She really didn't want to be having this conversation.

Elka continued. "He and I...we met on one of his workshops. Two years ago. And when I meet talented, handsome men, they are usually so arrogant. But Rene is so patient and kind. I haven't been able to get him out of my head. Please don't tell him this."

"I promise," Sarah replied flatly. Ren did have that effect on people. She knew that from personal experience.

"And I think there is something between us," Elka said. "I mean, I hope there is."

"Honestly, Elka," she began, "you should talk to Ren about this. Just remember that he's at work."

Elka frowned. "Of course. I'm not going to harass him." She looked a little offended at the suggestion. "I just wondered if you could tell me, as a woman, whether you think he is over Freya yet." The words felt like a kick in the gut.

"It's not something we've discussed," Sarah said truthfully.

"So you and Rene aren't close?"

Sarah wanted to argue the point, but it seemed easier to concede it. "I suppose not about that kind of thing."

"Okay. The way he talked, I thought you knew him well."

Sarah shrugged. "We mostly talk about photography."

"Okay, good," Elka replied. "I see. I misunderstood. I was trying not to be worried about you and him, because I know you're not his type, but I thought you were friends because you were sharing a room."

Not his type? Was Elka being malicious? She didn't seem to be, which made it worse.

Elka must have caught something in Sarah's expression, because she hurried on. "I don't mean that as an insult, it's just, you know. He is always with someone who is dark-haired, twenty-five. I'm worried I am too old for him." Elka didn't look older than thirty.

Sarah had nothing to say to that. "Well, I should get back and check in with him about tonight," Sarah said, pointing vaguely toward her hotel room.

Elka looked confused. "Isn't he out with Kyle right now?" Sarah tried not to react to the fact that Elka knew more about Ren's whereabouts than she did.

"Right. I meant texting him."

"Right." Elka gave her a little smile, and Sarah turned and walked away, feeling sick to her stomach.

She didn't want to, but she spent the next few minutes back in her empty hotel room searching on Google for Rene Durand and Freya anybody, until she found an Instagram photo posted by a workshop participant from a year or so ago. Ren was grinning, his arm slung around the shoulders of a beautiful woman tagged as Freya Arnadottir; she had an elfin face and heart-shaped lips, her hair pouring over her shoulders in dark waves. The two of them were standing in front of a spectacular glacial lake, dressed for hiking, a camera slung across Ren's shoulders. Ren looked so cheerful and relaxed that Sarah couldn't help but feel glad that he had been this happy once.

But then something had gone wrong, and Ren was here with her instead.

That night at dinner, she found herself once again at a table that didn't include Ren or Elka. This time it included Kyle, Jack, Cole, and the Dangols.

"I noticed you put your website back up," Kyle said, which meant that he was definitely checking up on her.

"You taunted me into it," Sarah agreed.

"Why did you take it down? The photos from your *Single Life* series were amazing."

She shrugged. "I needed a break from the 'Babies' series after the divorce," she said. "Probably because I realized I wasn't having any babies. And a lot of my commissions were for that." It was strange to talk about it so normally.

"Ah." Kyle sat back, looking thoughtful. "I'm sorry for teasing you about it, then."

She smiled. "How could I be an artist without a tragic backstory?"

"You know, I live in Ancaster these days," he said after a

moment. "Right outside Toronto. I travel a lot for work, but that's my home base. If you ever want to meet there."

That was not far from where Sarah lived. It seemed like a nice gesture, him trying to show that he lived near her.

"Maybe," she agreed with a smile.

"My least favorite word again."

Sarah laughed. She couldn't help but be charmed by his persistence, even if she couldn't take him seriously. She noticed Ren watching them from across the room.

"So tell me about your work, Kyle," Sarah said. "It seems to give you a lot of opportunity to photograph pretty places."

Kyle shrugged. "I'm semi-retired. My company mostly runs itself at this point. We're building data hubs for A.I., so that's obviously had a good couple of years."

"What kind of data hubs?" asked Cole, and the two men launched into a discussion about hardware architecture that Sarah couldn't follow and didn't particularly want to. She glanced over at Ren's table, where she saw Elka leaning towards him again.

"So Tanjul and Binita," Sarah said, "let's talk about what kind of portrait we could do for both of you."

AFTER DINNER, they headed out with the workshop participants to the rocky field where Sarah and Ren had shot during the first night. The area was truly stunning at sunset, glowing orange and peach, like the fields and sky were vibrating at the same frequency. Clouds might be terrible for Milky Way shots, but they made the sunset look particularly impressive, a radiant ballroom of swirling movement. She helped Rita and Selassie get some settings for their shots, and then approached Cole as the clouds turned to a carmine red.

"Have a minute for a portrait?" she asked. Sarah wanted to

get a shot with him with the wildflowers in the foreground. It was a little nod to Cole's own photos with their carefully selected foreground objects.

"I've got my camera doing a time lapse," he said, "so I have fifteen minutes."

She smiled. "Perfect. I'm going to go low angle to get the flowers and the sky."

She posed Cole against a waving wall of wildflowers in the last glow of flaming light. He opted to face away from her, looking at the scenery, as a single shaft of red struck out from the clouds behind him. Sarah posed him in silhouette, his camera in his hands, a photographer at work. When she showed it to him, he nodded once.

"I like it," he said.

"Do you want one with your face?"

He considered for a moment. "This captures me better. At work." He smiled and returned to his camera.

Selassie came by to ask for help with settings that would help make the trees look less silhouetted, and Sarah showed her how to do a bracketed series of photos at different exposures that she could combine in photo editing software later.

Ren approached, his jacket flapping in the wind as the sky turned grey-blue. He tilted his head towards where the clouds were blowing in ominously from the east.

"I think we have about ten minutes. You take the car back. I'm sticking around with Kyle for a bit."

As he said the words, a warning drop of rain hit her cheek. "It's going to pour."

"We have ponchos," he said. "We've done it before."

"Knowing Kyle, he probably prefers it this way," she said. "More of a challenge."

"I'll tell the others. You should move fast," Ren said, as another gust smacked their faces with more droplets.

Sarah collected everyone to return back to the hotel, but Elka again insisted on staying behind. As they hurriedly packed their gear in their cars, Fred suggested a side trip to swing by a local pub on the way back.

"If we're not shooting, we should be getting to know each other," he insisted, ever the politician.

Sarah was pleased to discover that the pub that Fred had found nearby was a grungy little place with dartboards on the wall. It reminded her of the local watering hole in her hometown: unassuming but lively. They took over a corner table and ordered beers.

"I think Elka has her eye on Ren," Cole observed as the drinks arrived.

Jack shrugged with his usual cynicism. "Yeah, I know guys like Ren. They don't settle down. It's why he gets along with Kyle. If a man is good looking enough, he doesn't need relationships. He gets female companionship whenever he wants."

"And sometimes when he doesn't want it," Binita said sagely.

Selassie shook her head. "The way he looks at you, though, Sarah... I think he's in love with you."

"No." Sarah replied in a carefully gauged tone of dry amusement. "He's just grateful I showed up last minute to help out."

Grisha leaned back. "He liked that other one a lot. Freya."

"How many of these have you been on?" Rita asked Grisha, and the conversation continued around her.

Sarah took a remote sense of satisfaction from the fact that people were talking about Ren's love life so casually; it meant that none of them suspected how much it hurt her to hear about it. It meant that she had everyone fooled. She pressed her head back against the wooden booth, her eyes on the row of lights that hung from the ceiling. The light fixtures had the familiar glossy green lampshades that she always associated with cheap beer and bored waitresses, each one sending a jaundiced circle of light onto the table below. The thought came to her that she was good at hiding her feelings because she'd been dealing with her mother for her entire life. She had mastered the 'everything's fine, don't worry about me' performance early, probably when she started university and needed to reassure her mother almost daily by phone. She could do it so well that people could stab her in the heart and she wouldn't flinch.

"So," she said lightly, "what is everyone doing during the rainy day tomorrow? I think Ren wanted to fit some extra classroom time in, but we can work around your schedule if anyone has plans."

SARAH WAS STILL awake and working on her laptop when Ren made it back to their hotel room a couple of hours later. She slid up in bed, flipping on the light. She could see that the shoulders of his coat were dark.

"You got soaked," Sarah said, her voice husky. She closed her computer.

"A little," Ren said. "We had to call it a night."

"I worried Kyle would insist on 'pushing through.'"

"Oh, he tried," Ren said wearily. It still felt strangely intimate to be sharing a room like this with him, watching him peel off his coat and slide off his shoes.

"Get anything good?" she asked.

He took his digital camera out of his bag and walked over to her bed to hand it to her before he continued unpacking gear. She flipped through some images. It looked like he, Kyle, and Elka had driven to a lighthouse and shot it in the fog, capturing the long beams of light disappearing into the fingering mists of rainfall.

"Damn it, Ren. These are gorgeous."

He nodded. "Lighthouses are great in fog."

"Which I guess is the whole point of lighthouses."

He smiled as he sat down on her bed next to her, taking the camera and advancing it back a few more shots.

"See that violet there?" he told her. "On the horizon? That was when it cleared up for a few minutes. I think we'd be getting an aurora if it was clear. The Northern Lights are more common in winter, but subtle versions can happen in summer, too. These clouds are frustrating."

She nodded, and he gave her a soft look that was hard to read.

"Your curls are out," he said after a moment.

"It's the humidity," she said.

He nodded. "They're cute paired with those pajamas."

She stared at him. His hair was damp from the rain. She had an impulse to drag him into bed with her. Not a helpful thought. She watched him take a slow breath and release it. Did he want to kiss her, too? Was that what was happening? Her breath grew shallow as his gaze searched her face.

"I need to ask you something," he said quietly. "It's one reason I invited you on this trip."

She couldn't breathe at all.

"I used to date this woman named Freya. She lived in Europe but she would fly out to come help with my workshops. I recently broke up with her, and I was wondering if you might be interested in the position. As my assistant. I run about seven of these workshops a year, and I could pay you about ten thousand dollars each. Some would be less, some more, depending on the length. I would cover airfare and hotel as well, of course. I'm not saying it would earn you a great living, but if you wanted to go back to full-time photography, it would give you a chance to do it. And I think this week has gone really great so far."

Her heart ached. Some stupid, childish part of her had wanted him to tell her he loved her, desired her, even if it wasn't in the same, all-consuming way that he had once loved Freya or his wife.

But it was just as well that he hadn't. Her head had been drifting into the clouds, and now she felt like she was firmly back in the real world.

"That's a really kind offer," she said, looking away from him so he couldn't read her expression. "Can I think about it?"

"Of course." He got up off the bed. "Absolutely. There's no pressure at all. I was hoping maybe this could be a trial run to see if you liked it."

"I do like it," Sarah said. "I have to think whether I can commit to that."

"Sure. Take your time."

She watched as he walked around the room, slipping his camera batteries back into a bank of chargers set up by the wall, putting an SD card into a reader attached to his laptop, then heading into the bathroom to shower.

When he was out of sight, she lay back and considered what he was offering her. If she became his assistant, she wouldn't get rich, but it was enough money that she could quit her job. It would give her the time to do the *My Divorce* series she was thinking about. It would give her a creative life back. And the only cost would be that she would pine for Ren, just a little, for a few weeks a year.

Who was she kidding? She would pine for Ren all the time.

She took a long deep breath and slid deeper into the covers.

She thought of Selassie's words: *The way he looks at you... I think he's in love with you.*

He must look at everyone like that.

14
WEDNESDAY

THE HOTEL WAS SURROUNDED by a wall of grey mist when Sarah woke in the morning; she couldn't even see down to the bay that stretched out a few hundred feet below them.

Ren was already gone. (Did he ever sleep?) There were a croissant and some fruit waiting for her on a plate. She glanced at the clock; she had a few more minutes to get breakfast in the hotel restaurant, which meant that Ren had brought this just in case she didn't wake up in time.

She was being wooed...wooed to be his assistant.

She sat up and rubbed her face, then saw that he had left a note: *Kyle wanted to grab some shots of beach at sunrise in the rain. Rest up. See you this afternoon.*

She felt a brief flash of annoyance at Kyle for treating the week like some kind of macho no-sleep marathon with Ren, who couldn't easily say no.

When she was up and dressed, she grabbed a quick cup of coffee in the lobby, where Tanjul and Binita were looking out at the view, and then returned to her hotel room and opened her work email. Still no official email saying she was terminated.

Was she? Or had Owen just been throwing a fit as part of his 'management philosophy?'

The ambiguity gave her a moment to think. She could start answering work emails, responding to questions about the weeks ahead, communicating in her usual way with the corporate communications team, and she might be able to smooth things over. Or she could take a leap and land somewhere entirely different.

She paused to look up Ren's next three workshops on his website: the Galapagos Islands in August; Antelope Canyon in Arizona in October; Lapland, Finland in mid-December to shoot the Northern Lights.

She could go to the most beautiful places in the world with Ren and help people learn photography. Or she could go back to her safe corporate job and deal with Owen's emails about how she hadn't taken appropriately detailed minutes for a meeting that only involved the two of them.

She was going to say yes to Ren, wasn't she?

She was going to get her life back and her heart broken. She was going to say yes because it was better to feel alive and hurt than to feel safe and dead inside. She refused to be like her mother, chained by fear. She was going to say yes to Ren and his goddamned job offer. Ren, who was so funny and helpful and supportive and so not interested in kissing her.

When Ren appeared in their hotel room later that afternoon, he gave her that same affectionate smile.

"Hey, sorry about taking off again," he said.

"Don't apologize to me. You're the one involved in a sleep deprivation experiment with a millionaire."

"He means well," Ren said, though she wondered. "He's just one of those guys who likes a challenge."

"There are extra sandwiches in the refrigerator. Take one of those and then rest for a few minutes before we have to go set up the classroom."

He nodded. "I will. Thanks." As she gathered the equipment they would need to set up the workshop, she heard his voice behind her, quieter. "Thank you, Sarah."

"Of course."

THE WORKSHOP PLAN was for the attendees to spend most of the rainy afternoon in the classroom, reviewing photos from their shoots and talking about techniques. There was hope they might have a decent chance at catching a subtle aurora on either Thursday or Friday, and the possibility meant getting everyone ready.

That afternoon, Ren talked to them about locations, camera settings, and possible foreground/background options. He explained that he had locked down the plan to charter a boat to a spot on a lake where they would stay all night...and with luck, a bit of an aurora might appear.

Once again, Elka called Ren over to her table at dinner and Sarah accepted it. If she said yes to his job offer, she would get many more workshops to hang out with Ren. She would get many more days of watching women pursue him.

She excused herself from her table as soon as the meal was finished, and Kyle followed her out.

"Hey," he said. "Want to have a nightcap? It's pouring out there, and I picked up some wine."

"I'm sorry. I'm really tired," she said automatically.

Back in the room, she told herself that maybe she should hook up with Kyle; it would certainly distract her from the mess of feelings that Ren provoked. But she didn't work that way; she never had. She got into pajamas and flipped on the television.

On screen was an old episode of *Buffy the Vampire Slayer* that she had watched obsessively in her teens, so she tucked up under the covers, listening to the steady drum of the rain outside.

A few minutes later, Ren surprised her by walking in the door. She waited for him to say that he was stopping by on his way to somewhere else or heading out with Kyle for more shooting.

"I'm wiped out," he said. "This is my night to catch up on sleep."

"I can turn this off."

"No need," he said. "I'll sleep right through it."

She tried to ignore him when he emerged from the bathroom in the t-shirt and pajama bottoms that constituted his sleep wear. It felt like they were having a little slumber party. If she accepted the job offer, would they share rooms in the future? Or was this a one-time thing? She supposed that if he wanted to hook up with pretty women, having his own space was better. Or maybe he would assume she preferred it. They were grown-ups, after all. But this had been nice. She would miss this, she realized, if this was the last time they ever did it.

"*Buffy*? I remember this episode," he said as he leaned back in bed, watching an attractive young teenager tearfully discussed her doomed love for an undead vampire.

"You're kidding. You've seen this?"

Ren shrugged. "I watched a few episodes with Ellen."

Sarah recalled Ren's brief fling with uptight Ellen, whom Ren had dated for a few weeks in the middle of Sarah's early days with Ivan. Ellen and Ren had held intense debates about moral philosophy and feminist theory during their brief three-week relationship; Sarah felt surprised that they were also watching teen television in Ellen's room afterwards.

"Was that your strategy for getting women into bed at McGill?" she asked. "Agreeing to watch their shows?"

"You think I needed a strategy?" he asked with a grin.

"You definitely had a strategy. Anya told me that you insisted that hooking up with you was a way of exploring her sexuality."

"And I stand by that," he replied with a laugh. He leaned back on his bed and watched the show for a while, and she realized she was unconsciously waiting for him to fall asleep or to get out his phone or laptop. Danny had done that all the time when Sarah was watching a show he didn't enjoy, but Ren stayed focused.

"I have so many questions," he said at last when there was a commercial break.

"Go ahead. I've seen the whole series." She pressed mute to silence an enthusiastic advertisement for laundry detergent.

"So first of all," he began, "he is two hundred years old, and he wants to date a high schooler?"

"He's tortured. Dead inside. Until he spots the one girl who makes him feel something."

"But why high school? If I was picking someone to break me out of my cage of loneliness, it wouldn't be someone who still had acne medication on their nightstand."

"She's as powerful as he is and can kill him with a thought, which given his guilt complex, he probably likes."

"So let's leave him out of it. I get that he's handsome, but why does she want a man who is at such a different point in life?"

Sarah sighed. "Okay, so this is embarrassing, but can I tell you about losing my virginity?"

Ren's eyebrows shot up. "Sure. This was with Phil the Goth or Ivan the Terrible?"

"Philip. So...he and I decided to sleep together senior year, but we didn't know what we were doing. So it took a few times before it stopped hurting."

Ren grimaced and nodded.

"And after that, sex became something I kind of tolerated. I didn't hate it, but I didn't really... And it wasn't Phil's fault. I didn't know how to speak up for myself or explain what I wanted. I was worried about hurting his feelings by admitting that I wasn't..." She waved a hand.

"You weren't having an orgasm."

She nodded. "So I tried gentle hints. And he got frustrated because I didn't know what to tell him to do, and he didn't know what he was doing wrong, so I gave up and pretended I was. And this went on for months."

"This is a tragic story."

"But the thing is, when I watched this show at seventeen, the fantasy wasn't that I wanted a much older man. It was that I wanted a teenage boy who knew what he was doing. It would have been nice to lose my virginity to someone who didn't need everything explained to him."

Ren considered this with a frown. "There's a lot I don't recommend about losing my virginity to a woman five years older than me, but I did learn what I was doing."

"What happened there?" Sarah asked. "You changed the subject when I asked about it earlier."

"I know." He considered her, and she turned off the television, which made him smile briefly. But he looked away when he started talking. "I was going through a tough time when I was a teenager... I told you I thought my mother didn't love me. Which wasn't true but it's how I felt. And my father was pretty distant. So I guess I was looking for approval. And when I was sixteen, I met this cool twenty-one-year-old student who worked in a used clothing store. I chatted with her a few times, and she seemed really impressed that I'd seen some Godard films. So she invited me to her place to watch a movie, and when I showed up, she sat next to me and put her hand on my leg, and I remember thinking, 'She can't possibly be doing this. She's too old. There's no way that this is actually happening.' And by the time I realized that it was, I didn't have the words to tell her that I wasn't sure I wanted to do it. I ended up going along with it because she expected me to. And then she told me to come back the next week, and I started sneaking out to see her every weekend."

Sarah considered him. His expression was carefully blank. "How long did it go on for?"

"A few months. And she knew how young I was. I think she liked that she could set all the terms, tell me what to do, and I would do whatever she told me to."

"Ren. That's not good."

"No. I kept telling myself how cool it was that I was having a fling with an older woman. But I think it messed me up in the long term. Anyway, my point is that I'm not judging you for not being able to tell your boyfriend what you wanted in high school because I didn't have the words either. If I'd taken time to think about what I wanted, I probably would have waited and lost my virginity with someone I cared about."

She wondered if his preternaturally beautiful looks had made him a particular target. "Do you think that's why you hooked up with so many girls at university?" Sarah asked. "To get revenge on women?"

He frowned. "No. I don't think so. I never disliked women. It was more that I wanted to get back a sense of control. When Giselle ended things, she did it by just announcing one day that she'd found a boyfriend and didn't want to see me anymore, and I was destroyed for months. Not because I was so in love with her, but because it felt like she had picked me up like a piece of paper, crumpled me up, and tossed me in the trash when she was done with me. So when I started seeing women, I always wanted to be the one who started and ended things. I would offer women this casual fling. And if they said yes, then we could see each other, and then one day I would deliberately annoy them so that they would break up with me. I would say the wrong thing and offend them, because then I could pick exactly when things ended, and nobody would ever surprise me and dump me."

"What kinds of things did you say?" She thought of Anya and Kristie and Ellen—how all of them had given up on Ren.

"Nothing personal or anything. It was pretty ridiculous, actually. I would tell them that I didn't date for longer than three weeks because that's the point when emotional attachments start to form, which is total nonsense. Then I would give them this speech about how I didn't believe love was real, that it was a biochemical response, and that sex was the world's only self-administered intravenous drug, and they would eventually roll their eyes and tell me I needed therapy. Which I would always agree was probably true. And then I would ask them if it was okay if I kept exploring, but that I was available for casual sex, and they were usually glad to be rid of me."

Sarah glanced at the dark television screen. "I can see why you aren't a fan of huge age gap relationships on television shows."

"And I can see why you are. Your story about losing your virginity offends me just from a craftsmanship perspective."

"Craftmanship?" Sarah laughed. "Satisfying women in bed is like crochet?"

"Or woodworking or knitting? Absolutely. It requires patience, attention to detail, and occasionally the right tools."

Sarah laughed. "I was too embarrassed to tell anyone about me and Phil. I haven't even told Anya that story."

"I didn't tell anyone about Giselle. You and Paola are the only people who know about her, aside from my therapist. It took a long time to admit that I was a victim in that situation."

She watched him for a moment. He gave her a quick, rueful smile and then looked down again.

"Can I give you a hug?" she asked.

He looked confused. "Why?"

"Because I can't go back and push that woman into traffic, so this is what I can do instead."

Ren was silent for a moment. "You know when you talked about how you didn't want pity? I don't either."

"Okay. I'm sorry."

After a long moment, he shifted on the bed and she realized he was making room for her. She stepped over to Ren's bed and sat next to him, putting her arms around him. After a moment, she let him go and they just sat there, legs pressed against each other, saying nothing.

"I wish we'd talked more about real things back in school," Ren said quietly.

"I made it hard. I was always making fun of you."

"I didn't mind that."

Sarah sat there with him for a long, quiet moment. She didn't know what any of this meant, but it felt natural to be with him. It had always felt natural, even back at university, on the rare occasion that they were sitting on a sofa next to each other or pressed against each other in a bar. It was one reason that things were always so confusing.

After a moment, Ren spoke again. "When Paola and I were getting a divorce, she said..." He stopped speaking entirely, like he'd hit a wall.

"What?"

"She said that I was probably emotionally stunted at sixteen because of what had happened. That I was emotionally still a teenager."

Sarah felt appalled. "That's not true at all."

"It's probably true on some level."

She looked up at him. "No. You're grown up about a lot of things. I know you're a good parent. And you're organized. You look out for people. Even in school, you made sure people were okay when they were drunk, or cold, or needed help coming up with ideas for a paper. Maybe Paola's the only woman you ever loved, but I don't think she was seeing you clearly when she said that."

He shook his head. "Paola's not the only woman I ever loved."

"I thought you said you only loved one person."

"I didn't say it was her."

Sarah felt herself holding her breath. She waited for him to tell her who it was. The thought that it was Sarah herself drifted across her mind like a passing cloud, but she knew better than that. Surely if that were true, he would have asked to date her at some point. Surely he wouldn't have let her go.

She spoke after a moment, her head leaning a little against his shoulder. "I'm afraid to become your assistant because I don't want my whole life to revolve around you. If we had a fight or something, I don't want to lose my friend and my job and my financial stability."

"I understand that," Ren said quietly.

"But we could try it. For a while. Because I really hate my job right now."

"I know you do," he said. There was a touch of humor in the words. He had been able to see it. The first time she had talked about her job, he had known how miserable she was.

"And I don't think I'm going to stop wanting to be your friend," she said softly. "I haven't yet. Even when you've hurt me, I still missed you."

She felt his chest rise and fall slowly.

"I'm sorry I hurt you," he said quietly into her hair. "I am so sorry."

She nodded, resting against him. He made no move to slip away from her, and she decided to stay there until he did.

They sat there together for a long time until her eyes slowly closed and his breathing became a warm, steady rhythm against her hair.

When she woke, the lights were still on. She was lying down in Ren's bed on top of the covers, and she could feel him asleep next to her. Their bodies weren't pressed together but they were near enough that one of his hands rested on her hip.

She rolled slowly in place to face him. She knew she should get up, turn off the lights, set an alarm, and go to her own bed. Instead, she watched him. If she took this job, she wouldn't need to say goodbye. There would be many more days with Ren: they would spend a week together every month or two. And she knew he wouldn't fire her or pick fights with her. He would respect her ideas and pay her properly. And she would love him, like she always had. And she would bear that for as long as she could.

She stirred to pull away, and he opened his eyes and looked at her. She waited for him to remove his hand from her hip, but he didn't. He smiled at her tenderly, and she couldn't help it. She smiled back, knowing he didn't feel the same for her as she did for him.

Then she moved a couple of inches closer, putting her face so near his that she could feel the warmth of his breath. She saw something in his eyes, a hesitation. She didn't move, waiting for him to pull away. He always did. He was going to tell her that this was a bad idea. She closed her eyes and waited.

Instead, he came closer to her by another inch, so close that their noses touched, his breath uneven. She opened her eyes and he was still there, looking at her with a soft expression, their breathing exactly in sync. She kissed him lightly, touching her lips to his, just because she wanted to.

He kissed her back. It was slow and sweet, and then his hand was up against her cheek, warm and gentle. He kissed her again, and a warning hovered on the edge of her consciousness, but it didn't matter. She wasn't going to listen to it.

After a moment, he slid up on one elbow so that he was above her, and he kept kissing her tenderly, one hand sliding into her hair, his fingers disassembling her curls. Her whole body felt warm and alive, but at the same time there seemed to be no pressure to do anything but this, no pressure to intensify things, just a slow, sleepy kissing that felt as gentle as a dream. Then he drifted his lips across her cheek, down the edge of her jaw, and started kissing her neck, and she melted completely. Her whole body felt like it was drifting away except her hand that was caressing the back of his neck, her fingers running through his dark curls, her other hand gently sliding up his arm. He shivered from the touch and pulled back to look at her, his lovely eyes dark, one of his hands gently curling around her waist.

"Sarah," he said with such sweetness it made her heart break.

Meeting his eyes was too much to bear, so she closed hers tightly and pulled him close enough to kiss again. His whole body began to line up against hers as he softly tilted her head back to kiss her more deeply. He was so good at this. Ridiculously good. But more than that, he was being so careful and slow that she felt like crying. She took a quick breath as he touched her breast with one hand and he stilled, his lips still resting against hers.

This was the moment when he always told her no, and she didn't want him to do it again. She wanted to wrap a leg around him and roll on top of him and not let go. But instead, she waited, her breath slow but her heart racing.

She opened her eyes, and there was that look again: the one that seemed so affectionate, so confusing. "We should go to sleep, right?" he offered gently.

She hesitated and then nodded once. "Okay."

She watched him roll away from her and look at the ceiling.

What had just happened? Her brain felt like a traffic jam of hopes and worries. Maybe he'd been kissing her because he was too polite to reject her. Maybe this was his form of letting her down easy. Maybe he didn't want this, didn't want to ruin their friendship, and he had gone along with it, just for long enough not to be insulting. Just long enough to give himself a polite way out. And meanwhile, her whole body was still vibrating from what had just happened. Her heart was beating too fast. She felt lightheaded.

Another moment passed before he spoke, his voice full of sincerity. "I want you to know that I'm always going to be here for you no matter what."

"I know," she said. She looked at him for a moment, then forced herself to get up and get ready for bed. She wasn't sure if that was the kindest thing anyone had ever said to her or a definitive rejection. Maybe both.

When she woke the next morning, he was already gone.

15
THURSDAY

BY THE TIME the group met for class on Thursday afternoon, the sky had mostly cleared and the workshop participants were buzzing with excitement about their planned night under the stars. When Sarah entered the conference room, Ren and Kyle were busy comparing various phone apps predicting the night's weather.

"KP index is high. It won't be the full Northern Lights," Ren explained to the group when he looked up, "but there may be some extra green and violet in your shots. You'll see it if you use a longer exposure."

The plan was to have an early dinner after class, and afterwards, Ren had chartered a boat to take them deep into Western Brook Pond, one of the most spectacular fjord formations in Newfoundland. They would get dropped off an hour before sunset and would be picked up the next morning, shortly after dawn. They weren't allowed to cook anything or bring food into the park because of fire and wildlife risk, but they were allowed to bring sleeping bags so that if anyone got tired or cold, they would have a way to keep warm or nap for a few hours. Sarah knew from experience how much effort must have gone into convincing Newfoundlanders to do something like this: a chartered boat tour to a pristine location that operated outside the usual tourist boat schedule. It must have cost Ren a few thousand dollars and a lot of personal charm to set this up, Sarah suspected; this was the kind of exclusive access that helped Ren keep his photography workshops in high demand.

It felt strange to sit watching Ren answering people's questions and giving advice about gear, knowing that they had kissed and were going to say absolutely nothing about it. They discussed everyone's sunset photos and Kyle and Elka's lighthouse shots. Then Ren gave tips for how to bring out the color in the Milky Way in photo editing software, and Sarah got to see more of Ren's images from his trips to Iceland, Norway, and Alaska. There were never people in the shots, and Sarah couldn't help but wonder how many women had come on those trips, how many women had come before Freya.

That night at dinner, Ren smiled at her and pointed to a chair next to him. "Join my table tonight?"

"Don't we need to split up to answer questions?" she asked.

"They've gotten all their questions answered by this point," Ren said with a grin. He was acting charming, which alarmed her a little.

Elka walked in, took in the seating arrangement, and went to the other table, where she launched into an intense conversation with Kyle. Ren kept giving Sarah warm glances and making light jokes over the course of the meal, but it was impossible for her to tell whether he was trying to be reassuring after rejecting her or acting flirtatious after their kiss.

She sighed quietly to herself. It had come to pass exactly as she had feared: she had feelings for Ren again, and she didn't know what he wanted. *This* was why she had been worried. This was what always happened around him.

Binita and Tanjul were at their table, and Sarah caught

Binita looking between Ren and Sarah knowingly. She felt tempted to ask her for life advice. *What should I do? What does it mean? Does he like me?* Binita had three children, two of them at university and one in high school, and she seemed to know how life worked. Sarah's own mother would have just advised Sarah to assume the worst.

Sarah was tired of assuming the worst.

Whatever else Danny had cost her, she realized that she didn't want his behavior to make her so cynical that she gave up on love entirely. It hit her for the first time that by swearing off relationships, she had given Danny too much power. She had let him ruin her chances of finding anyone else.

He didn't deserve that. He didn't deserve anything else from her, and certainly not more of her time...certainly not all of her possible future relationships for the rest of her life.

Looking back, she realized she had never really yelled at Danny for what he'd done. She had simply gone quiet. No wonder the idea of a 'Divorce' photo series had started with a mental image of setting something on fire. Sarah was furious... and not even at Danny. She was furious with herself for how much time she had spent on him.

Ren caught her eye as she stared at the table and leaned over to speak softly. "You okay?"

"I'm okay."

"You look like you want to kill someone."

"Not you," she said. "Not this time, anyway."

He smiled that sweet smile, and she realized that she was angry at him, too. Not with the same intensity, but she was tired of being confused by him. They were going to have to talk. And she was going to have to set some boundaries.

The evening boat ride to their shooting location was bumpy, breezy, and one of the most spectacular visual experiences of Sarah's entire life. The simple name of Western Brook Pond belied how stunning the setting was; the pond had been formed as a fjord and was now a narrow strip of water surrounded by cascading cliffs that framed a winding stretch of sky. The last few pink clouds trailed above as the sun set somewhere on the unseen horizon. It was pure wilderness on all sides: no houses, just endless stretches of trees and cliffs, occasionally interrupted by narrow waterfalls tumbling down from above.

Deep in the fjord, the captain cut the boat engine near the shore and they drifted the last few feet to an inconspicuous wooden dock. The captain roped in the boat, and they climbed onto the wobbly planks of the dock one-by-one, then walked the few feet out onto the rocks where they gathered as a group, taking in the surroundings.

"No fires," the boat captain repeated in a loud voice. "Not even a cigarette. Keep your flashlights on, don't try to climb the cliffs, and don't wander off."

"We'll stay close to shore," Ren promised.

The captain nodded once and then handed Ren a walkie talkie to reach him in case of injury. "Have a good night. Don't do something stupid. See you at dawn."

When the charter boat hummed away, it was just the twelve of them with cameras and tripods at the end of the world, the sky festooned with twisting scarves of color.

"Let's start by setting up a sleeping area as a base camp," Ren said. "Then you can walk anywhere within about ten or fifteen minutes to find your shot. Just stay in pairs in case anyone twists an ankle. Don't go too high up the hill because there are cliffs and rockslides. The ground is all shale around here and very unstable to walk on. My advice is to focus on shots around the water. And keep your headlamps on and go very slowly as soon as it gets dark."

Their spot in the wilderness had been carefully selected: there was a small path upwards that was used by some of the wildlife management team, and nearby was a low flat area under some trees where the rocky ground was softened by needles and grasses. It was an ideal spot to spread out sleeping bags and stage their gear. Ren started by assembling a soft, hazy battery-powered lamp in the middle of the sleeping area so everyone would be able to find it once it grew dark.

Sarah tossed out her own sleeping bag on the fir needles. It was a simple bag that she had picked up a few days earlier with Ren on their drive to the west coast. She watched as Ren set up his own sleeping bag next to hers; his bag was thick and expensive and looked designed to handle the arctic tundra.

"I'll probably be up all night," he said as he unrolled it. "But I'll put this here just in case." It was right next to hers, which maddeningly seemed to imply everything or nothing.

She turned to help Rita and Selassie arrange their gear and sleeping bags.

"Ready for your portrait?" Sarah asked Rita. "Is tonight the night?"

"Let's just skip mine," Rita said. "I'm not wearing make-up."

Sarah and Selassie met each other's eyes. "I'll find you later," Sarah replied.

She wandered along the edge of the water through the pale pink sunset, picking through the shale and climbing over bits of tossed driftwood until she noticed Fred, who had just finished taking a shot of the water as it mirrored the sky in the last light of sunset.

"What about staying in pairs?" she teased.

"Sorry!" he called back. "I'll behave once it gets dark."

"How about your portrait now?" she asked him. "I was thinking we could use the reflections on the water as a background before we lose light."

"The boulder?" he asked, pointing to a large rock that rested at the edge of the water like it had rolled down from high above and then decided to take a rest a few feet shy of the shoreline.

"Perfect."

"Shall I climb on top?" he asked when they arrived.

"We won't get good reflections that way. What if you lean against it?" she suggested, and he did, resting his back against the boulder and giving her a little smirk that brought to mind what he might have been like twenty or thirty years ago, before he'd chosen a career full of public scrutiny. Here was Fred, with his staid fashion sense and political background, posing like a rock star on an album cover.

Sarah stepped closer until she was capturing him from the waist up with the dramatic view sweeping away to one side of him, the water glowing pink and the cliffs rising in the distance. Even the breeze settled down for an instant, giving her a moment when the reflection of the cliffs on the far side of the water was clear. His face was a little too dark in the half-light, so she threw a little soft fill light on him with a battery-powered light. The rest she could fix it in the developing process.

She took the shot and then showed it to him.

"Amazing," he said. "First my daughter's portrait, now mine. My wife is going to be jealous."

Sarah smiled. "She can give me a call next time you're in Toronto." She realized that she meant it.

An idea for Grisha's portrait came as she watched him talking to Kyle about the position of the stars.

"Hold on," she said. "Grisha. Point to Polaris again."

Grisha gave her a quick, dry smile, then turned and pointed to the star with one finger, and she took a quick picture of him in the last light of 'blue hour,' pointing towards the North Star so that it was right at the tip of his finger. Then she let him walk away and left her camera there on its tripod, pointing it at Polaris, for a thirty-minute-long exposure. Later, she could combine the shots so that it looked like the star trails were circling around the point of Grisha's finger.

The Milky Way sharpened into clarity as darkness fell, and Sarah went to find Tanjul and Binita. They had chatted with her about doing a portrait that included both of them, and it was time to put it into action. It was a trick shot, one that Sarah would create as a photo montage stitched together from multiple shots, but it would make Tanjul look like he was raising a hand at one end of the Milky Way and Binita look like she was reaching out to touch the other end. Both of them stood by the water, raising one arm towards the arc in the sky, and Sarah put her camera on her tripod and created a panorama of shots of the water and sky that she could stitch together later. She used a soft light on the two of them so their faces were visible. The final version would be a photo with the Milky Way arcing between them as they raised hands on either end of it: a cosmic connection between two souls.

Jack was nearby as she finished the shot. Sarah called to him.

"It's time, Jack," she said. "Your portrait."

He sighed. The whole week he had been so pessimistic that she had begun to feel for him. Nobody could learn photography in a week, but he had perhaps forgotten how hard it was to learn something new. All he saw was his own limits.

"Come on," she said. "We're going to light paint you so you look like a dangerous bad boy."

Jack barked out a laugh and glanced down at his fleece vest. "Not likely."

"Get him to take his shirt off!" Selassie called. "I did!"

"No," Jack said with a frown.

He eventually agreed to lean against one of the small conifer trees next to the water. Sarah grazed him and the tree with side light to set him off from the dark background, the stars reflecting on the water behind him. She thought it made him look mysterious and cool.

He walked forward to look at the photo on Sarah's camera screen.

"See?" Sarah said, thinking of all the times she had reassured nervous actors that they looked good in her headshot days. "You look a dark prince from a fairy tale."

He considered the image for a long moment. "Yeah, okay," he said at last, and turned to walk away. But he was smiling a little.

"It's time, Rita," Sarah said at last, approaching the two friends.

"Can't we just do my head? I don't want my whole body. Maybe if I was wearing something nicer."

Sarah sighed, but she agreed. She took a shot of Rita's face with her chin tilted up, the stars behind her.

"You look great, babe!" Selassie called out, holding up a soft fill light. "You look..."

Her words were cut off by the sharp sound of rock sliding against rock; Sarah turned to see Selassie on the ground clutching her leg.

"That was stupid," Selassie said weakly. "I don't even know what happened..."

By the light of their headlamps, Sarah looked over the woman's ankle. She didn't seem badly hurt enough to need serious medical attention—but she was injured enough so that Rita had to support her as they made their slow, careful path back to their sleeping bags. Sarah ran ahead to find Binita, who agreed to examine Selassie's ankle.

"You will not die," Binita pronounced. "That is my professional opinion. No long hikes, though."

"If you insist," Selassie joked, though her voice was strained enough that it was clear she was in pain.

Binita borrowed some of Ren's first aid tape to wrap the ankle while Selassie continued to insist that there was no need to call the boat back. Instead, the two friends turned in for the night, chatting quietly with each other in the darkness.

Grisha turned in soon after them, saying that he had to get back on an early schedule before his return flight to Europe on Saturday. He had some kind of jetlag plan mapped out that involved him waking up at four in the morning for the dawn shoot. Then Jack returned to the sleeping area, asking to be woken at dawn as well. Fred, Binita, and Tanjul turned in as the night cooled off at close to two a.m.

Sarah, for the first time, wasn't tired yet. She felt restless, knowing the workshop was almost over, knowing there was a major conversation she ought to have and no Ren around to have it with her. Her heart felt like the needle of a compass, searching for him, but he was nowhere nearby, from what she could tell. He must have gone off with Kyle on some mission...farther along the water or up on some forbidden ledge of the cliffs above. That seemed likely from Kyle: the desire to push against any limits they'd been given for safety reasons.

Sitting alone, waiting for Ren to return, she saw the faintest light of an aurora near the remote horizon, green in hue. It looked a bit like light pollution, too subtle for her to wake people up for, but it might show up on longer exposure shots.

She stepped a little closer to the water and set up her tripod for a ten-minute shot filled with star trails, catching the cliffs in the distance. As she sat in silence, she heard people speaking behind her, but as she was about to get up and greet them, she realized it was Elka and Ren having an intense discussion. Her camera was in the middle of the shot so that she couldn't easily move away to give them privacy, so she hunched low and hoped she would not be noticed.

"No," he said. "I don't regret it. That's not that I'm saying. But Elka—"

"I'm in love with you, Ren."

Regret what? So he had slept with her, it seemed? Sarah was frozen.

She saw the faint outline of Ren as he sighed. Then he gave Elka a warm, affectionate look and leaned over to say something in her ear.

A warm, affectionate look. Like he had given her when she threw herself at him.

Sarah watched, immobile, as Elka regarded Ren for a long moment before turning to walk away.

When her shot was donc, Sarah quietly moved to a rock by the water's edge, hoping that neither Elka nor Ren would spot her and put together that she might have overheard them. Her face felt flushed in the cool air. Her long exposure shot of the star trails had caught the faint aurora, making the sky look touched with both violet and green.

When she heard slow, careful footsteps picking their way across the rocks behind her, she knew without turning that it was him.

"Hey," he said quietly. "Are you in the middle of a shot?"

"Just finished."

"Can I see?"

She showed him. He nodded. "Nice capture."

"You can just call it a shot."

Ren smiled as he sat down next to her and looked out at the water and the sky. A breeze came fluttering across the water and raced up Sarah's arms. She shivered. He peeled off his fleece jacket and held it out to her.

"Take it."

"No," she said.

"You can give it back when you go to bed."

"I don't need it."

"Please put on the jacket, Sarah."

She shook her head, not looking at him. She could feel him watching her. He took a long, slow breath.

"So I wanted to ask you a favor," Ren said quietly. "You know how you offered to pretend to date me?"

Her eyes finally went to his, trying to read his expression. "Yes?"

"I wanted to ask the reverse. Elka just expressed feelings for me, so I was thinking it might be kinder to her if we don't admit that anything is going on between us during the workshop. Just for another day or so."

"Is there something going on between us?" she asked pointedly.

He frowned at her for a moment, then spoke slowly. "Do you want there to be?"

She took a breath. "I..." It was a long moment before she could answer. "I want to work with you."

Something drained from his face. "Okay," he said.

She shook her head. She tried to find her courage, whatever was left of it. "It's just," she went on, "you just went through a break-up, right? And everyone has been talking about Freya and how great she was. And I don't...I can't be that. For you. A replacement. I can't be the person you date after the woman you were in love with."

Ren stared at her for a moment, then huffed out a laugh. "Sarah, you infuriate me sometimes."

A corresponding anger rose in her chest. "I infuriate *you*."

"Have I said anything about missing Freya?"

"No, but—"

"Freya and I had a nice time. But she was twenty-five. She

listened to trap music. She was never going to move somewhere to be closer to me. And I was sure as hell not moving away from my son to be with her."

"Did you sleep with Elka?"

"No. We kissed once. Two years ago. And I decided it was a bad idea and stopped things. Why does that even...where is this coming from?"

Sarah shook her head. She was not going to let him wave away her fears. "You know, you were the one who stopped things when we kissed. Both times. Last night and back in Las Vegas. So you can't blame me for not being sure whether you're interested when every time we kiss, you tell me that we need to stop."

He spoke very quietly. "I stopped things because I didn't want to offer you a job and then turn around and start sleeping with you. I wanted you to know that you could take your time to decide things, because you're too important to rush things with. But you seem determined not to trust me no matter what I do."

"I've spent the whole week listening to everyone telling me how gorgeous your ex-girlfriend was."

"So?"

"So am I just a replacement for—"

"I broke things off with Freya the day I found out you were getting a divorce."

Sarah stared at him for a moment. There was no way that could be true. Why would he say something that was obviously untrue? "That's...you haven't spoken to me in years. You never called me when you came to Toronto."

"To say what? That I was in love with you? You got married too fast for me to get the chance."

She was silent again. It was so quiet that she felt like her heartbeat must be audible to the whole world.

He spoke gently. "If I had shown up at Paul's wedding and

told you I'd been secretly in love with you for years, would you have believed me?"

She shook her head slowly. "No."

"Right, exactly. I know you better than that." He drew closer, then very cautiously took her hand. "I know you, Sarah. So I have been trying everything I can to earn your trust back. And to show you that there could be a way for us to be together. To show you that I want to make this work, and maybe in another year, if Jandro goes away to school, I could move to Toronto to be with you."

The words were coming too fast for her to make sense of them. "You could move to Toronto?"

"Assuming he goes away to high school. But worst-case scenario, in five years he's in college. But if you won't even trust me to even—I just don't understand what you want from me. You seem to assume the absolute worst of me, all the time."

"Danny left me." The words poured from her faster than she could stop them. "He got a twenty-four-year-old pregnant and left me for her."

Ren's expression changed. For once, she didn't mind that he was looking at her with pity.

"We were having fertility issues," she said quietly, "both of us, not just me, but I think he figured he was fertile enough to get someone younger pregnant. I think he deliberately was careless with birth control when he cheated on me, because then he would not only have an excuse to end things but he'd get the baby he wanted in the process."

Ren's voice was low and hard. "What an absolute fool."

"So if I'm worried about not being a twenty-five year old, it's because I was left for one. And I *had* gotten more confident. I *liked* the way I looked. And then my body failed me and he left."

"No, he failed you. He was the one who failed. You always

date these guys who are never worthy of you. Why didn't you wait for me?"

She stared at him. "Wait for you?"

"After Paul and Trish's wedding, I told you I was going to figure things out, I went to therapy, and then six weeks later you were bringing a new boyfriend home. Why didn't you give me a chance to explain things? Or call me and yell at me before you moved on?"

"Because it hurt too much!" she said, her voice breaking. "Because you always picked me last. Even in Las Vegas, you slept with some stranger the day I arrived and then wouldn't sleep with me."

"Because I loved you!"

She shook her head. "No, you don't get to just..." She thought about her mother and father—the way her mother had fallen apart completely when she lost the man she loved. Maybe Sarah had tried to avoid being with men she was madly in love with because she never wanted to break like that. "You don't get to say that to me."

"I know." He was quiet for a moment. "I should have told you back then how I felt. I should have told you years ago." He sighed. "I told you that I grew up convinced my mother didn't love me. It wasn't true, but it felt true. So when I met Paola, she had this... this low-level contempt for me, and I thought, 'Great. She's smart, like my mother. She's capable and independent. If I can get this woman to love me, that proves I'm worth loving.' But Paola never respected me, because I wasn't like her father. And I was never going to be this dominant, take-charge businessman. So our whole marriage, I was trying to prove that I was worthy of being loved, and she was trying to turn me into someone worth loving." He paused, waiting until she met his eyes. The night was wide and quiet around them.

"By the time I got divorced," he said, "I realized that Paola and I had never really loved each other. Because she never saw any of the good things about me. So when I reconnected with you, and you told me that you saw those things, and that you loved me, I panicked. Because I wasn't ready. I went to therapy to figure out what happened. And one of the things I did in therapy was finally talk to my mother. She told me she had spent my teen years stressed about her marriage. None of it was about me. I'd carried all that self-hatred for nothing."

"And maybe because of what that older woman did to you."

"Maybe because of that," he agreed.

"And now?" she asked, so quietly that she could barely hear her own voice.

"Now I just want to be with you," he said, sounding almost resigned. "It's why I created this whole workshop in Newfoundland. It's why I offered you a job. And I know I can't ask you to wait for me. I can't even guarantee Jandro will end up going away to school, and if he doesn't, it might be five years before I can move closer to you. I just want to try. I want to see what would happen if we try. And if you just want the assistant job and don't want to be involved with me, that's fine. That will always be fine. But don't turn me down because you don't think I'm serious about you. Because you're it for me."

She felt as immobile as one of the rocks. His face was barely visible in the dark, but she could tell that he was nervous, gazing at her. He truly didn't know what she would say.

"You can yell at me now," he said after a moment. "If you want."

"I love you," she said, her voice breaking. "I've always loved you. It's terrifying."

He moved closer to her and took both her hands, squeezing them tightly. "I know."

It was still hard to believe that anything between them could be real, but she wanted to hope. She wanted to have faith that something good could happen to her.

His gaze shifted to look above her head. "Look up," he whispered.

She turned to see that the skies were now lit around them with a glow of violet and green, like a ghostly echo of a different world.

"Aurora," he said.

Her heart felt full from the beauty around them, a silent harmony of stars and light. She took a long breath and squeezed his hand. "I guess we should wake everyone," she whispered.

"Not yet." Ren put one arm over her shoulder and stayed there, looking at the glowing light, the world spread out in front of them in endless beauty. They were silent together for a long moment, his arm warm around her shoulder.

"Ren!" It was Kyle's voice calling from somewhere further along the shore. "Look up, man!"

"I see it!" Ren called.

"I'll wake the others to see if they want to get a shot," Kyle called. "Hey, everybody! Look up."

They heard Kyle scrambling through the brush somewhere behind them. Ren and Sarah looked at each other, and then he pulled her against him, kissing her fiercely for just a moment.

"You said no kissing."

"I did." He took a deep breath. "I'm hoping Kyle is distracting Elka right now. But it is probably best if we don't tell anyone about this for the next day or two."

"I've spent twenty years pretending not to be in love with you," she said. "I can handle another few hours."

He pressed his forehead to hers. "I love you so much."

"Hold on," she said. She lifted her cell phone camera to take a photo, posing the two of them against the night sky. "Before we go back, we need a photo of us together with that sky."

"No," he said with an affectionate tone. "Not like that. If you take a picture of us with a flash and no tripod, so help me, I will never forgive you." She laughed as he found his camera to set up the shot.

16
FRIDAY

SEVERAL PEOPLE WOKE up to shoot the green and lavender haze that made up the summer version of the Northern Lights, and the rest woke only three hours later to capture the first pink light of dawn on the still water. By the time the boat arrived to pick them up, everyone was sleepy, hungry, and dirty from a night of shooting and curling up in sleeping bags in the woods. Only Kyle looked fully refreshed.

"Didn't sleep once," he announced as he followed the other workshop participants aboard the boat. "It's all about focus."

"Kyle," Selassie said from where she was carefully resting her sore ankle on a cushion, "someone is going to murder you one of these days, and I'm not going to stop them."

Ren announced that they would meet for a final photo review at five, then dinner at a local pub before a last night of shooting at a different beach.

Then he and Sarah drove back to the hotel together through the crisp early morning, stumbled back into their hotel room together, and put down their gear.

"I know I should download my photos," Sarah said. "But I think I'm showering and then falling asleep."

"Me, too," Ren agreed. "But first..."

He stepped her backwards until she was against the wall and kissed her until she felt breathless.

"I've wanted to do that all week," he said.

"Me, too. Every time I entered the room with you, I thought of that time in Las Vegas."

"Me, too. That was the best kiss of my life."

She ran her hands through his hair and he pushed her against the wall again, one hand on her waist, the other gently cradling her neck. It was so good that she almost didn't remember that she was exhausted and tired. And dirty. And probably had sticks in her hair.

He ended the kiss gently before leaning over and whispering in her ear, "You can shower. I'll put your camera batteries in the charger and get your card reader set up." It might have been the sexiest thing a man had ever said to her.

When she got out of the shower a few minutes later, wearing her tiger pajamas, Ren had already set everything up for her and had started downloading his own images, too.

"My turn," he said, standing up.

She crawled into bed. "I may not be awake when you get out," she said. "But you can sleep in my bed if you want."

He smiled and opened his mouth to speak, then just nodded once.

She was half-asleep when he finally crawled under the covers next to her and held her against him. He was wearing a thin t-shirt and pajama pants, and her whole back felt warm when it was pressed against him. He smelled like soap and like Ren, familiar and perfect. She turned over, wanting to kiss him forever, her body stirring, but all she managed was to kiss his neck once and snuggle into him before she fell asleep.

. . .

She woke to mid-afternoon sunlight, wrapped around him, one leg twisted over his thigh. It should have been impossible to sleep like this, but she had slept deeply and without dreams.

When she stirred, he opened his eyes and smiled.

"What time is it?" he said quietly.

She looked over her shoulder at the clock on the nightstand.

"A little after two in the afternoon."

"I can work with that," he said.

"Is there something you have planned?"

He leaned over and slipped one hand gently along her neck and down to her collarbone. "I need to have a closer look at these tiger pajamas, first of all."

He slid his hand down her waist, caressing her gently with one hand so that she shivered.

"I remember all your outfits," he continued as he glided one hand along her ribcage. "The velvet coat. The red lace dress. The green corduroy skirt. The nonsensical t-shirt about demonic marshmallows."

"That was my sexiest t-shirt."

"I agree."

As his hands slid over her, she thought of his comparison of sex and woodworking. It wasn't that he had perfect moves, exactly. It was that his hands were exploring her, paying attention to every reaction, every place that made her melt against his touch. She was afraid to look at how startlingly beautiful his eyes were. She closed her eyes against his steady gaze.

On impulse, Sarah rolled them over so that she was looking down at him. She knew what she didn't want, after hearing Ren's stories. She didn't want him feeling like he had to prove anything, like he had to act the part of an expert lover.

"I want to touch you first," she said.

He nodded, looking vulnerable. "Okay."

"And I want to tell you," she said softly, "that you are lovable." And she kissed his cheeks. "And patient." She kissed him again. "And you have very strong opinions that I love to hear even when I disagree." She kissed him on the neck. "And even though you've sometimes hurt me, I have never doubted that you were a good person."

He caught one of her wrists with his hand. "What are you doing?"

"Telling you how I feel."

He took a breath. She'd found the thing that scared him. Being a skilled lover—he was good at that. He wasn't good at being loved.

She kissed him softly. "And you are supportive of my work and of everybody who shows you their photography. And you're a good father." She kissed him again. "And I don't mind waiting a year for you to move closer to me. And if that doesn't work out, I don't mind finding a way to move to Las Vegas to be with you."

He blinked up at her, then reached for her and pulled her down into a kiss.

"Sarah," he whispered. There was wonder in his voice, surprise, and joy of arriving here at last. "I'm so scared I'll mess this up somehow."

"What part?"

"Everything. Dating you. Going to bed with you."

"It's okay," she said. "Someone once told me that sex can be very healing."

He laughed against her hair. "I can't believe I tried that line and thought it would work."

"You mean it's not true?"

He grinned as he rolled on top of her, taking her wrists and placing them above her head, looking down at her, making her meet his gaze.

"Stay like this for a moment," he whispered. "I have very specific things that I've wanted to do for a very long time."

He kissed down her neck, across her shoulders, and then he paused to take her pajamas off slowly and carefully, taking his time, until she was completely naked and he was looking down at her, taking her in. He leaned forward and kissed her breasts and let out a low groan that surprised her, like he had been waiting forever to touch her. Her hands scrambled for the bottom of his t-shirt like she was a teenager, trying to figure out how to get him undressed, and he pulled it off in one swift motion and returned to kissing her, another hand sliding between her legs.

She could feel him still smiling against her skin as she arched her back. "Stop smirking," she whispered. "You know you're good at this."

He leaned into her ear and whispered, "I have to make up for your high school years."

"Ivan was pretty bad, too," she whispered back.

He stilled for just a second. "I fucking knew it," he replied. "I knew it about that guy." And then his skilled hands were touching her and her whole body arched back.

"We should have been doing this the whole time," she said.

He nodded.

"Maybe not when you were married," she added.

"If I'd known how to be with you, I wouldn't have gotten married."

His hands didn't stop touching her until her breath was shallow and her fingers were clutching his shoulders. He watched as her breath grew faster, picking up on every sound she made, every movement. She came in a sudden, sharp crest that echoed out like waves on a pond.

When she came back to herself, he was smiling down at her. "You made a mistake back then too, you know," he said. "You should have let me make love to you that night. You would never have gotten back together with Ivan if you had."

"You're very confident."

"I'm very confident about belonging with you."

When he was at last inside her, he pressed his face into her shoulder and kissed her there, looking close to tears. Beyond the physical sensations, her heart felt so ecstatic just to be with him, to know that they had time, that this wasn't a one night stand, that this was a beginning rather than a goodbye. He kept murmuring romantic things into her ear that seemed so deliriously perfect that she struggled to believe he meant them. Ren was opening his heart at last, and she held his face in hers and kissed him again and again. She felt the moment that his control slipped, the moment he drove forward until his body shuddered and he collapsed against her.

"That," she said into his ear, "was a very long time coming."

He laughed silently.

Afterwards, they lay in each other's arms and she felt pleased to see that he looked as dazzled as she felt, his eyes on the ceiling, one arm carefully tucked around her as if to make sure she couldn't slip away. One of his hands grazed her breast like he was fascinated with it. She had never thought of him as being into women shaped like her; he had always seemed interested in the French gamine types, slender as reeds.

"You never dated anyone who looked like me," she said after a moment.

"Why would I have wanted someone who looked like Sarah but wasn't Sarah?"

"I thought you only liked me for my brains."

He smiled. "If you're worried that I wasn't objectifying you, I used to have a whole list of things that I wanted to do to you if you ever broke up with Ivan. Even before I realized I had feelings for you."

She rolled over to look at him. "When did you know you had feelings for me?"

"It took a few months. It was around the time Ivan forgot your birthday."

"You gave me that homemade card." Ren had made her a birthday card out of folded watercolor paper with a quote on the front that he had hand-written in ink-pen: *Being afraid is the worst sin*, which he admitted he had paraphrased from Godard's *Breathless*. Inside he had written: *Happy 20th to someone who deserves to never be afraid. Ren.* She still had it somewhere, tucked in a box of precious things from her university years.

"I was so furious at him for forgetting your birthday and so furious at you for letting him get away with it. So I was complaining to Joel about it." Joel had been Ren's roommate at McGill; he was a friendly, easygoing athlete who always seemed like a mismatch for Ren's intellectual snobbery but who had lived with him for their entire time at school.

"And after I'd been going on and on about it for a while, Joel said to me, 'So you like this girl.' And I said, 'No, not at all. I'm just annoyed on her behalf.' And he said, 'You've been annoyed on her behalf for a week.' And I thought, *Oh, no.*"

Sarah smiled. "I had no idea."

"Half of me thought you did," he said. "Kristie knew. I would have asked you out, but I was terrified you'd reject me, and I wasn't sure I believed in dating in the first place. And I also had this fear that if you wanted to date me, it would only be because you thought I was a jerk and you were attracted to jerks."

"I didn't want to go out with jerks," Sarah said. "It wasn't like a philosophy or something. I was in love with Ivan before I figured out that he wasn't very nice to me. But by then I felt like I had to stay because I could heal him if I loved him enough."

"And then you picked Liam, who was so smug. We went

out for drinks once and he didn't ask anyone else a single question, just talked about himself in a monologue, like the rest of us had signed up for his podcast. I didn't understand why you couldn't see it. But now that I've met your mother, it makes more sense."

She nodded against his shoulder. "She's very self-doubting, and she transfers it onto me. I don't blame her, though. We have similar personalities, but I fight it harder than she does. She lost her optimism when my father died. I don't think she ever got it back."

"She's wrong, you know," he said quietly. "I would marry you. I know it's too early to bring it up, but I absolutely would."

Sarah leaned into his arm and said nothing, too afraid of ruining the moment to speak.

"So what will you do when you get back to Toronto?" he asked. "Are you in trouble at your job?"

"I got fired."

"What?" He sat up straighter.

"It's okay. My boss was a nightmare. I'll be okay."

He frowned. "Sarah..."

"No, it's good," she insisted. "Because I need time for my own work. I have an idea for a new photo series."

"You do? Can I hear about it?"

When she told him about her *My Divorce* series, his eyes lit up.

"That photo of you in a bathtub," he said, "will you redo that one? Because that one is burned in my brain forever."

THEIR LAST CLASSROOM meeting had a casual, joking atmosphere; everyone was a little giddy from lack of sleep and more closely bonded after their night in the woods. Sarah and Ren reviewed everyone's photos from the night before and discussed post processing techniques for making them look even better.

"I want to see all Sarah's portraits," Cole said.

"I still haven't gotten Kyle and Elka," Sarah said. "They wandered too far away. So I'll get them tonight and then I'll email everyone the full set."

Sarah noticed Rita looking down. She wondered if Rita was regretting her choice just to shoot her face—not because it wasn't a pretty shot, but because of the rationale behind it. Dismissing yourself was the kind of thing that could feel right in the moment and haunt you later.

"We can retake some, too, if anyone didn't like theirs," Sarah said lightly. "Maybe some people might want to bring a swimsuit." She smiled at Rita.

THEY WENT OUT for dinner at the local pub, joking over beers and not worrying too much about whether they were losing time to shoot. The plan was to go out and do a final night of shooting along a beach to the north. Several people planned to turn in early because they were flying out the next day.

Sarah watched Elka watching Ren during dinner. She looked so unhappy that Sarah felt for her. She had hoped Elka might find sympathy in the arms of Kyle, but it didn't seem to have happened. Kyle, meanwhile, was looking at Sarah with a strange, curious expression. She wondered if he could sense something had shifted between her and Ren, or whether Ren had said something to him.

"Ideas for your portrait, Kyle?"

He shrugged. "We'll find a location," he said. "We'll know it when we see it."

Dark had fallen by the time they arrived at their last shooting destination, a pebbly beach that stretched beneath rocky, striated cliffs. Sarah spotted a rock outcropping that rose up from the tide pools in strange, architectural towers.

"Kyle," she called. "That spot is you."

She posed him in a way that she knew would make him look bold and heroic, since that was Kyle's whole thing, and borrowed Fred and Tanjul to help paint him and the rocky outcropping with flashlights. Kyle examined the photo and had thoughts, so they took three more versions before he was happy.

When the photo was done, she paused to whisper to Ren. "Kyle prefers the version where he is looking away moodily into the distance in profile, and he suggested I make it black and white."

"My favorite," Ren said, his voice thick with laughter.

Sarah went to find Elka, who was not shooting anywhere near Ren anymore. The blond woman had wandered down the beach and was carefully dusting some rocks in the shallow water with side light; in the background of her shot, the Milky Way swept down towards the shore. Sarah had a moment of worry: what if Elka had seen her and Ren together that night and viewed it as a betrayal? But she pressed ahead.

"Do you have a minute for a portrait?" Sarah asked.

Elka turned to her and sighed, nodding. "I used to be a model," she said. "So it's not as exciting for me. But you can take one."

"By the water, maybe?" Sarah said, and they looked at the waves. Elka pointed to a spot where a wide, flat rock formed a little platform, and Sarah carefully checked it for wet spots before having Elka sit down.

"Ren turned me down," Elka said quietly.

"I'm sorry," Sarah replied.

"I used to be able to get any man I wanted. I have to make peace with getting older."

"How old are you?" Sarah said.

Elka sighed. "Thirty-three." Sarah didn't laugh, but it was a near thing. She reminded herself how sophisticated she had felt at twenty-one and how burned out she thought she was at twenty-six. At forty, she felt the reverse: a constant surprise that she had nothing figured out yet.

"It's okay," Sarah said. "If you are feeling sad, then we will get a sad shot."

Elka positioned herself on the rock and wrapped her arms around her knees. Sarah framed her so that the water was behind her and set up soft lights to give her definition from both sides.

"Look up," Sarah suggested. She took Elka's portrait. The woman's lovely, sharply-boned face looked sad but hopeful. Sarah showed her the photo and Elka smiled.

"Yes," she said. "Alone in the world."

"Alone with the stars," Sarah said.

Elka nodded. "Will you give me a copy? This one I like."

Sarah walked along the beach to where Selassie was shooting a tidal pool while Rita held a light source for her. She watched them, feeling proud of how confident they had become in the few days that they'd been shooting. They no longer needed her help at all.

"Sarah!" Selassie called. "Don't you think Rita needs a photo of her in the tide pool like a mermaid, too?"

"I already had my portrait taken. You just want me to freeze off my sensitive parts," Rita replied.

"You know, Rita," Sarah said, "you can do what you like. But I just had to listen to Elka talking about how she was no longer attractive at the ancient age of thirty-three, so if you want my opinion, I say you get in there naked and we do it right."

"Yes!" her friend cried.

"It's dark!" Rita said. "How am I crawling around there in the dark? And what if one of the men comes over?"

"It's portrait photography," Sarah said. "They can handle it."

Rita stood there for a long moment, considering. "All right, fine," she said, peeling off her jacket. "But no putting this on any of the group emails, okay?"

"I promise."

Once Rita had stripped down entirely, Selassie and Sarah each took one of her hands and carefully helped her to wade into the pool of water in the middle of the rock.

"You're going to keep your head and shoulders out of the water," Sarah said, "and we are going to wait until the water is still and get a shot of you with the stars reflected on top of the water."

"You are going to get a photo of me freezing my tits off," Rita said with a shiver.

"Worth it!" Selassie replied, readying a flashlight to add some fill light. A pop flash wouldn't work, Sarah knew. It would create too much glare on the water.

"Twenty seconds until I die of hypothermia," Rita told them.

"Then we'll get the shot in ten seconds."

Rita leaned into the water, supporting herself on her elbows as she faced the camera. Behind her, the Milky Way sent the light of a billion stars towards them as a sparkling backdrop. Rita held still for long enough that the water settled for a moment, and Sarah took the shot.

"Wait," Rita said. She flipped over so that her whole body was just emerging from the water, dripping and cold. She paused like that, looking up at the sky, and Sarah took the picture again.

"That's it," Selassie said. "That's the one, gorgeous."

"Good Lord!" came Jack's voice as he walked past carrying his camera and tripod.

"It's for art!" Selassie called back.

The sky had one last gift for them that night: a small meteor shower that sent a handful of falling stars, one every minute or two, dropping like jewels across the sky to the north. Sarah caught one in a thirty-second exposure, sweeping downward like a promise.

One by one the participants headed back to the hotel to sleep before their flights the next day. Kyle, of course, announced that he was pushing through. Sarah returned to the hotel room in the back of Rita's car at two in the morning. Ren returned at dawn.

17
SATURDAY

SHE WOKE up in the morning to an alarm with Ren's hand lightly resting against her cheek. He stirred when she tried to get up and pulled her back into the warmth of his arms, and they had slow, sleepy sex before she finally got out of bed in time for breakfast.

Ren opted to sleep in for the last hour before he had to pack and check out.

"We are telling everyone in Toronto that they need to get their picture taken by you," Selassie announced as she and Rita stopped by Sarah's breakfast table. "Once that photo goes on my wall, you are getting calls from all my book club friends."

"I hope so," Sarah said.

"You should join our book club," Rita agreed. "We have a very strict policy where every month we go back and forth between something literary and intelligent and something fun and trashy."

"That sounds amazing, actually. Send me an invitation." Sarah felt touched that they actually considered her a friend. She needed more of those.

The Dangols came by after Rita and Selassie left and gave her a quick thank you.

"We will see you at another one of these workshops," Tanjul said.

"Yes. We are coming back. Once Tanjul recovers from the lack of sleep. He is getting old. I am still young, but he can't handle this very often."

Tanjul smiled as if this was a well-worn joke between them.

She saw Kyle stepping out of his room with his gear as she was returning to her room to pack. "Flying out soon," he said. "At this point, my bedtime is 11 a.m., so it's easier for me to just stay awake until I get home."

"Please take a nap if you need one. I don't want you landing in the middle of the Atlantic."

"My mind is zeroed in on the now," he said decisively. "It helps that I've gone entirely off caffeine. I don't have that crutch anymore and it sharpens my thinking."

"Maybe I'll try that sometime," she said, thinking that it sounded dreadful.

"Maybe," he said with a smile, "is my least favorite word." He gave her a pointed look. "And maybe you, me, and Ren should get dinner sometime," he added, "since apparently neither of you bothered to tell me that he's in love with you."

She looked down, embarrassed. "I didn't know he was."

Kyle nodded. "He's so lucky with women," he said. "I hate that son of a bitch sometimes. But he's probably my best friend, so..." Kyle shrugged, smiled quickly and then turned and left. She watched him go, wondering what it would be like to be that successful and still need to turn everything into a competition... whether maybe that was what made him so successful.

She returned to the hotel room to pack up next to Ren, who was up but looking groggy; they would be on the same flight together to Toronto.

"Jandro is meeting me in Toronto," he told her. "He and Paola are flying up today and will meet me at the airport. So I would love to spend time with you while I'm there, but I'm going to be taking the boy to visit some universities and whatever else he wants to do."

"It's okay," she said. "We'll see each other for the next workshop."

"Galapagos is going to be incredible. But I do have to warn you that Kyle is coming."

"Oh God." She laughed. "Think he'll go to bed at midnight this time?"

"Not a chance. I love the guy," Ren said. "I just wish I had a tranquilizer gun for him."

Before they left the hotel room, she kissed him one more time, just because she could.

SHE WAS SEATED FAR from him on the plane because of her last-minute flight change. It was just as well, Sarah realized. He fell fast asleep as soon as he was in his seat. Their time together was ending. And she wouldn't see Ren for weeks.

But he loved her.

He *loved* her.

Ren, of all people.

WHEN THEY GOT off the plane in Toronto, Sarah saw that Paola and a teenaged Jandro were already standing to one side of the luggage area waiting for Ren. It was not the circumstance in which Sarah would have wished to run into Paola again: Sarah was tired and disheveled from lack of sleep and was hauling an awkward amount of gear and a sleeping bag. She waved at Ren and then prepared to walk away, leaving him to greet his ex-wife and son. Then she heard Paola's voice.

"Sarah, right?"

"Hi Paola," she said with a hint of embarrassment. She walked over. "Ren asked me to help out with this one."

"I'm sure," Paola said pointedly.

Ren walked up and kissed Paola on the cheek. "Hey," he said. "Thanks for bringing me the boy."

"I'm going to leave him with you while I visit some friends," Paola said crisply. "My flight home leaves tomorrow morning and I'm staying with Eugenia. Jandro has homework to do for his tutor, so make sure he gets that done in the middle of having fun."

Sarah took a moment to take in Alejandro. He was an awkward thirteen, his face dotted with acne, tangled dark hair in his eyes. He might grow up to be as gorgeous as his parents, but now he just looked wary and hunched as he stared at the floor.

"This is my friend Sarah," Ren said to Jandro.

Jandro looked up at her, and Sarah decided not to announce that she'd met him as a baby; that tended to make kids uncomfortable.

"Hey," Sarah said. "I'm a friend of your dad's from university."

"That's one of the goals for this trip, remember," Paola said to Jandro. "You're going to visit some schools. And hopefully that will inspire you to put a little more care into your schoolwork."

Jandro shrugged and looked down. "Okay."

"I'll let you two talk," Sarah said. "Nice to see you, Paola."

"No, you stay. I have to get going. Call me if anything comes up." She gave Jandro a kiss on the cheek and walked briskly away, rolling her wheeled luggage with the authority of someone who knew exactly where she was going.

"She's been like that nonstop," Jandro groaned.

"She just wants you to stop procrastinating," Ren said gently.

"Unlike your dad who stayed up for thirty hours to finish all his papers," Sarah said with a grin.

Jandro stared at her. "He did what?"

"Sorry," Sarah said. "I'm not helping. Have fun in Toronto. Nice to meet you, Jandro."

Ren gave her an affectionate glance. "I'll call you soon."

"Take care." She smiled and left him there with his son.

18
SUNDAY

SARAH CRASHED EARLY when she got home on Saturday, still catching up from lost sleep.

This meant she woke before dawn on Sunday. She immediately logged onto her computer and checked her email. There was an email confirming that Ren had sent her the money he had promised for the workshop. Then there was an email from the human resources manager at her job, sent late on Friday, informing her that Owen had not gone through the proper channels to fire her and asking her to come in for a meeting on Monday. It sounded like Owen was in a bit of trouble, which delighted Sarah. She didn't want the job anymore, but she might get some severance pay out of this, so she decided to go and see what happened.

She spent a couple of hours doing photo editing on her software, assembling the composite images of Grisha and the Dangols, and working on the color processing for the remaining shots. When she was satisfied with her portraits, she sent them to the group via email (leaving out the shot of a beautiful, naked Rita under the stars, which she only sent to Rita).

An hour later, in the late morning, she received an email

from Ren. It had no text; it was just the photo he had shot of the two of them at Western Brook Pond: Sarah and Ren with the fjord and the stars and the pink and green haze in the sky behind them. They looked ridiculously happy.

There was also an email from Kristie inviting her to a party, which made her realize she hadn't told her friends what had happened this week. She hadn't even mentioned the workshop, afraid they would try to talk her out of it. Now she was excited to share the news. It occurred to her, as she considered an appropriate text to Kristie and Anya, that both of them had already slept with Ren. And now she had to tell them that Ren was in love with her. Maybe that was better explained in person.

She started making a list of props she would need for her 'My Divorce' series. She felt consumed with the old, familiar urgency, the sense of not wanting to do anything except this one task, not wanting to think about anything but her photography. She had a new series to shoot!

A little after lunch, there was a knock on the door as she was sorting through her refrigerator figuring out what food was still edible after her unexpected week away from home. When she opened the door, to her surprise, Ren and Jandro were standing there, both looking equally abashed. She knew Ren had her home address from the employment paperwork that she had filled out for him, but she had never expected him to come see her.

"Sorry to pop in," Ren began. "I was showing Jandro around The University of Toronto campus near here and he asked for more stories of dumb things that I did as a student, and I wasn't coming up with good ones. He suggested we try to drag you out with us for coffee."

Jandro shrugged, looking at her with a half-smile through his hair, and Sarah grinned. It made sense that this particular kid might need to hear that his parents weren't perfect.

"So I have your permission?" Sarah asked Ren. "To tell him stories?"

Ren gave a reluctant smile and turned to Jandro. "Don't tell your mother about this, okay? She'll think it's going to hurt your motivation."

The boy rolled his eyes in the full half-circle of adolescent ennui. "I'm not going to lose my motivation. I just want to hear about embarrassing stuff that he did."

Sarah smiled. "You mean like the time he was giving us a lecture about how pain and comedy could not co-exist in serious art and then walked backwards into a lamppost?" Jandro laughed. "Or the time he said he'd never seen any Hollywood movies and then slipped up and quoted *A Knight's Tale*?"

Ren looked at her, his eyes filled with warmth. "Go easy on me."

"Let me get my coat," she said. "Because Jandro, you are in luck. I know every single embarrassing thing about your father."

19
ONE YEAR LATER

"SO TALK me through this one more time," Ren said. "Your new series..."

Sarah was lying on the bed in their new apartment as Ren unpacked items to put in the closet. She had moved her things into their two-bedroom townhouse a couple of weeks ago, but Ren had arrived in Toronto only that morning, and his furniture would not arrive for another day. In the meantime, he was hanging a small set of clothes in his closet, one black sweater or charcoal shirt after another.

"It's just an idea right now," she said.

Her show at the Kristman Gallery, 'My Divorce,' had been a modest hit in January, and a possible follow up concept had come to her a few days before Ren's arrival.

"It'll be called *Witches*. Or *Crones*, maybe. And it will all be shot at night, and it will be women in their fifties and older, in beautiful natural locations, like trees or beaches or cliffs, and they will be totally nude, with the moon and the stars and their hair wild. But not full New Agey nude. They will look like normal women. Maybe they should keep on their usual accessories, like watches and wedding bands and stuff. Maybe sneakers, too."

"Naked women except for sneakers, under the moonlight," Ren repeated.

"Because sneakers are practical," Sarah said. "And older women are practical people."

He nodded. "I think you should shoot it."

"But you like it?"

"Of course I like it, but you're not making it for me."

He finished hanging up another sweater, light grey this time, and walked over to lie down on the bed next to her. They lay still for a moment, staring upwards, and Sarah thought about how strange it felt that they were now living together. They would be doing all the domestic things together now: laundry, sharing a bathroom, arguing about television shows. It was true that they had spent several weeks together in the last year, but those had always involved hotel rooms at the far ends of the world: the Galapagos Islands, Finland, Zambia, Death Valley.

This was different. This was going to be grocery shopping on Saturday mornings and bringing him to Kristie's parties and discussing what photos to put on their empty walls. This was setting up a combined kitchen and a shared office that would double as Jandro's bedroom. Jandro himself would be coming to stay with them soon for the entire month of July; he was heading off to a boarding school in New Hampshire that fall, and Ren planned to visit him there once a month or so.

Sarah had initially been worried that Jandro might resent her in her new role as Ren's girlfriend, but so far, things had been unexpectedly easy. The boy had come with them to help out on the Antelope Canyon workshop, and Sarah and Jandro had teamed up to make fun of Ren whenever he wasn't in front of clients.

That was apparently all it took to win Jandro's loyalty. She hadn't expected a perfect relationship with a teenager, but she found that her very lack of expectations was exactly why he seemed relaxed around her. She just let him be grouchy, pessimistic, and slyly funny, and she never stood in the way when he wanted time alone with his dad. In return, he rewarded her with a gratifying level of tolerance and even a hug at the end of the trip.

The relationship with Ren still amazed her sometimes, mostly because of how easy it all felt once they got started. Ren had never been the kind of person who sought out conflict, and his broad pronouncements about art and culture still entertained her, even when she mostly disagreed. What was strange was how relaxed they were around each other, in the end...how much it felt like they could have just been doing this the whole time. Except that they hadn't, and maybe couldn't have. Maybe it had taken this long for them to be ready.

Now she rolled on her side to look at him in bed. His eyes were beautiful, but they were soft, now, too. "You're here," she said quietly.

He nodded, his expression full of love. "I'm here."

"Why is this so easy?"

He looked away from her and laughed once. "Sarah," he said at last, "the one thing you have never been for me is easy."

She took him in her arms and kissed him, knowing that they had time now. She felt drunk on it, the endless, ordinary amount of time that stretched ahead of them.

It was like a path that went on forever, across hills and over mountains and up into the sky.

ALSO BY RACHEL CAREY

Arts and Lovers

Yes, And...

Jack and Jill

Long Exposure

ABOUT THE AUTHOR

Rachel Carey writes satirical plays, serious screenplays, and lighthearted books about characters falling into love or trouble. She grew up moving around between rural Vermont, suburban Massachusetts, and New York City, and currently lives in the Garden State.

www.ingramcontent.com/pod-product-compliance
Lightning Source LLC
LaVergne TN
LVHW091255150826
845673LV00006B/1430

* 9 7 9 8 9 0 0 4 3 1 2 2 2 *